Dear Nichy

Merry christmas 1988

Your mom will enjoy this too.

Love Mally

The Hex Witch
of Seldom

Nancy Springer
THE HEX WITCH
of SELDOM

BAEN BOOKS

A Baen Books Original
Distributed by Simon and Schuster
Simon & Schuster Building
Rockefeller Center
1230 Avenue of the Americas
New York, N.Y. 10020

Cover art by Gary Ruddell

1 3 5 7 9 10 8 6 4 2

ISBN: 0-671-65389-X

Library of Congress Cataloging-in-Publication Data

Springer, Nancy.
    The hex witch of seldom.

    I. Title.
PS3569.P685H49   1988   813'.54   87-25484
ISBN 0-671-65389-X

To Joel, who brought me home.

PART 1

The Dangerous Stranger

"They branded him," the old woman said. "They shouldn't have done that."

She was talking to her cane, her walking stick, and the stick nodded agreement. A carved snake, unpainted but finely detailed as to scale and eye, spiraled up the hazelwood shaft then curled its head around a smoky-hued, sphere-shaped handle of glass or perhaps quartz. It was the snake's head that nodded as the old woman talked. Its wood-yellow eyes seemed to glint, but the globe that topped the staff remained opaque.

"Course they didn't know what they was doing," the old woman added. "But that don't change the facts." She was sitting in a hickory rocker time had turned mouse-colored, in front of a cast-iron cookstove set up off the floor on claw-footed legs. She rocked,

3

taking care to follow the grain of the braided rug under the rockers, and she held the cane in her hands. It was evening, and she liked a good conversation in the evenings, sitting in front of the stove when the night was chilly, on the porch when it was fine.

"He'll be bitter now," the cane said. Its voice was very low, yet curiously flat and not at all vibrant. "More than ever."

"Of course he will," said the old woman promptly. "You don't just take a man like that and tie him down and brand him and stick him in a pen without him remembering. And him as moody as he was to start with. And after all that's happened to him already."

"It'll be hard to bring him back now," the cane remarked. This was only one of the many things it discussed with the old woman. The cane cared about it only tangentially. She cared perhaps a bit more.

"Near to impossible," she agreed. "I can help him find his way here, if that's what he wants, if he'd trouble himself to escape. But that's about all." The thought made her wrinkle her brow. She wore her gray hair back from her face, in two long braids wound around her head; the hair was as long as it had been when she was a courting girl. "Near to impossible," she repeated more softly. "I thought he'd be tired of his foolishness by now. A few weeks in that corral, I thought, and he'd have had enough. He don't take kindly to being penned up. But it seems he ain't never going to give in. As a man he went through too much trouble even for one of us. No, likely there's only one thing that could bring him back now."

"Your touch," the cane said.

She shook her old head. "No. I wish it was so, but no. Not since they done that to him. I ain't as strong as him when his will is set."

"What, then?"

"It ain't likely to happen."

The wooden snake on the walking stick stirred impatiently. "Just tell me what."

She said. "A woman's love. A man like that can only be tamed by a woman's love."

The snake made a brief, sneezing noise of scorn through its minute nostrils. "Women are what made him hide himself away," it said.

"I know it." Her eyes clouded like the staff's globe. "And it ain't never going to be no different for him. Part of what he is . . . Well." She blinked and straightened in her rocker, and her eyes no longer looked old. "Least we can do is get him out of that pen."

"You plan to go after him?" the walking stick asked in its smoothest tones, knowing she had no such intention. It took a lot to get her out of the house. She gave her staff a quelling look but did not answer. Her gaze clouded again, and she stared over the serpent's carved head and far away.

"Yandro," she murmured after a while. "They might help. Let me see if I can get through to that muleheaded Grant Yandro tonight, while he's sleeping."

"You'd do better to talk to the son," her walking stick told her. "The ghost."

"The poet. Yes, I mean to talk to both." The old woman gazed off into distance, and her eyes seemed to mist and darken like mountains at nightfall, and the staff held still in her left hand, not speaking. Her right hand had lifted, bent and swollen with arthritis, but steady—and in the air it traced the mystic circle and six-lobed design her people called *hexefus*—the witch's sign.

Chapter One

"You're soon sixteen years old," said Grandpap. "You're almost a woman growed."

Bobbi looked back at him across the width of the cabin without replying. She did not feel like a woman grown. She had never dated, and did not much want to; there was something strange about her, and she knew it. Maybe it was the dim light of the 25-watt bulb overhead deceiving her, but she seemed to see something moving behind her grandfather: just a whisper, a hint, of a form that was Grandpap and yet not Grandpap, like heat haze in the air. She had seen it before and it did not scare her any more except to shiver her spine a tad, but for sure she wasn't going to say anything about it, not to anyone, and especially not to Grandpap. Nearly all her life she had lived with her grandfather, Grant Yandro, and she knew him. Pap was not unkind, but he had no patience for nonsense.

"What you want for your birthday?" he asked her. He was scraping supper's leftover brown beans into a plastic bowl for his hounds. The half-seen form behind him, form of—what? Something hard and jagged, like the gray rocks outcropping from the Pennsylvania mountain sides, but—she could not see it any longer. It faded and disappeared.

"I don't know," Bobbi said. She hadn't thought about her birthday.

Pap straightened and looked at her, his lean, clean-shaven jaw thrust forward as always. An old man with white hair and the body of somebody half his age—she knew he was every bit as tough as he liked to look. A man didn't try to farm these hills without getting tough as the stones. The first settlers had been *Deutsch*, Germans, known ever after in these parts as the "Dumb Dutch" for leaving the rich Susquehanna valley lowlands for these thin-soiled, acidy slopes. But they had stolidly persisted in clearing the land and building their big, womanly, wide-hipped, great-lofted barns. They lived here still, slow-moving egg-shaped people, and amid land going back to bramble and cedars the barns still stood, the hex signs fading on their peaks.

The Yandros had come later, and they were not "Dutch," but a mix of Scotch-Irish and Welsh and something else. Yandros were dark and wiry, hard-muscled and hard-minded, Bobbi had been taught. The neighbors could keep their superstitions and their stories of witchcraft. Grant Yandro would not have hex signs on his barn.

"You do those dishes," he said to his granddaughter, "and I'll get you something right now." He went out into the cluttered yard. The baying of the hounds greeted him.

Bobbi opened the draft of the woodstove a bit to rouse the fire—not for warmth, not now that spring was coming on, but to heat washing water. The water from the wooden cistern overhead ran cold through the kitchen tap. She half-filled the dishpan, added hot water from the kettle on the stove lid, then did the dishes. It was her turn anyway, as Pap knew well enough. He was always fair. Sometimes harsh, but always fair. She wondered what he could be bringing her.

The hounds had quieted. Bobbi heard Pap's holler echoing back from the wooded slope behind the house. He was calling in the horses to be fed.

It took them a while to come in from their pasture, as usual. Without looking out the window she could see them coming down the hillside step by slow, hesitant step. Horses always came to a calling human that way, as if they were suspicious of the person's motives. In her mind's eye she saw Grandpap impatiently waiting, grumbling to himself, and she smiled.

She was done with the dishes by the time Pap came back from the barn, carrying a dusty wooden box on one shoulder. He eased it down and got himself a dipperful of well water from the covered bucket by the sink, and she knew better than to ask him about the box before he was done drinking, though she eyed it curiously. Homemade, by the looks of it. Reminded her of the pine coffin Pap had once made for a child who had died, lost up on the mountain, a migrant's child. She had never seen this box, and she had thought she knew just about everything in the barn. This box had been well hidden up on the rafters somewhere.

"It's some of your father's things," Grandpap told her. "I figure it's time you had them."

Bobbi gave him one startled glance, then kneeled and worked at the clasp. It was corroded shut. She had to bang at it. And when she got the box open at last and saw all the yellowing papers, she got up and carried the heavy box into her cubbyhole of a room, under her studying light, which was bright enough to read by. Outside, night was falling, darker than the fir trees. She sat on her bed, her knees nearly against the beaverboard wall, and lifted the first ragged sheet in shaky fingers. That was Saturday night, a young springtime night when a girl her age should have been thinking of love, maybe going out with Travis Dodd, who lived up the mountainside from her. But Bobbi Yandro was thinking about Travis even less than ever, and for the dark hours she was as good as gone from Canadawa Mountain.

The yellowed papers did not take her too far away at first. Newspaper clippings. Graduating class of Silver Valley Area High School, and Wright Yandro's name on the list. Wright Yandro inducted into army. Wright Yandro weds Chantilly Lou Buige in Louisiana. She was the girl he had met on base in Georgia, and she had taken him home to marry him, but then he had brought her to his own home to live before he shipped out. Wright Yandro sent to Vietnam.

Bobbi gazed down into the stark newsprint face, hard-jawed under the military hat, as if it could tell her something she badly needed to know. It did not.

The strong-boned face so much like her own, the grave gray smudges that were its eyes, might as well have belonged to a stranger. Bobbi had never met her father. Shortly after she was born he had died in Nam. There was a newspaper clipping for that, too. Local Man Killed In Combat.

And a single clipping of a different sort. A poem, signed Wright Yandro, published in the Silver City *Clarion*, Canadawa County, PA.

"The old gods live in hidden forms.
In the autumn nights the wild geese fly,
A cat roams under the bloated moon,
The gypsies ride the highways still,
Somewhere the horses run wild.
The cunning mustangs defy you on the
    mountains.

You have heard the dragon roar in the dark.
You have heard the hounds of hell in the sky.
The old gods chant to the crescent moon;
The mustangs toss their heads and shout,
The mustangs yet run wild on the western
    plains.

Bobbi raised her eyes and stared as if her sight could blaze through the cabin walls, leaving wood smoldering. She felt, she *knew*—what? The words made little sense to her. She doubted that they had made much sense to the editor of the *Clarion*, either. He had probably printed them only to fill a hole in the local news page. They were probably pretty bad poetry.

But—this strangeness of hers, this feeling of being alone inside, this—this affliction of seeing things: all her life since she had been aware of it she had thought it was because her mother had gone crazy. Chantilly Lou Buige Yandro had been taken away to the psychiatric ward one day when Bobbi was three. After that Bobbi's mother had been shuttled like a lost soul from hospital to doctor to hospital, never really coming back, until her parents in Louisiana had placed her in a good private institution the other side of Pittsburgh. Chantilly was not dangerous, but her delusions did not let her cope with life in the real world, the doctors explained.

And the first time Bobbi had seen something that she knew wasn't really there, she had been scared half crazy that she would go all the way crazy, like her mother. The next day she had started to bleed between her legs, and even that hadn't scared her as much. She had told Pap about the bleeding, and he had explained it to her as best he could. But she had never told anyone about the things she saw. She was a Yandro, and Yandros didn't talk rot.

She had not known her father wrote poetry. Nobody had ever told her. Now she held his poem in her hand, and it was as if he had written it just for her, as if he spoke to her across the distance of years and death, reaching out to her through this bit of paper that smelled of dust, withering and crumbling and dry as the bones, his bones, lying six feet under the ground down in Silver Valley Cemetery. She could have wept without knowing why.

Carefully she laid the frail yellow clipping aside and turned to the other things in the box.

There were notebooks. Opening the first one, Bobbi felt a shock, a prickling sense of *deja vu*. It took her a moment to understand why. Wright Yandro's handwriting, the figure-eight g's, the airily looping tails of the y's, the fly-away capitals—like hers. Could have been hers. A strong, wild scrawl, even messier than Bobbi's, but very much like. She might be the only one in the world who could read it.

Until sometime long past midnight, sometime in the silent heart of night, when cats roam and distant dragons roar in the dreams of the uneasy, Bobbi pored over the notebooks. In them she read thoughts, struggling bits of poetry, the scribbled and much-scratched-out beginnings of stories. One such fragment she read again and again, until she could nearly have recited it, though it filled her with questions left unanswered.

"The staff bore a sword inside it," (Wright Yandro had written, years before, maybe when he was no older than she) "and scrying in the shining surface of the sword blade I could see the long history and the hard destiny of the staff. Its name meant 'the wise one.' It had been made of a wand of hazel cut from the living tree at sunrise, for all puissant things draw their strength from the sun. I saw the druid cutting it from the tree with a knife baptized in blood. I saw the staffmaster shaping it. I saw the priest chanting over it during the course of the shaping, to make it a force of good as well as of magic. The staff had a soul and a fate. It remembered the staffs of Moses and Aaron; it could bring up springs of water out of arid land, striking hard at the stony earth with its tip of

steel. It scorned the sceptres of rulers, the swagger
sticks of sergeants, the policeman's baton. It honored
the caduceus, and would not strike an innocent person, no matter what hand wielded it. It knew the
forces of evil, and knew that its own scruples would
bring about its undoing, and hated and feared the
death-wands made of cypress and yew. It had vision-
ary power; it foresaw the manner of its death, and
mine.

"I had a choice. I could take up the staff and
sword, and the staff would speak to me of things
beyond knowing, and lead me into dangers fit to
make me a hero or a spirit. Or I could sheathe the
sword once again in the staff, and place the staff back
in the ground where I had found it, and go away, and
be happy with my woman."

There the story broke off. Bobbi wondered: was
her father speaking of himself, really? Was it possible
he had really found such a staff? Or was he speaking
of an inner self he showed to no one? Or was he
telling someone else's story through his scrawling
ball-point pen?

Bobbi got up and found the old, cloth-covered
Webster's dictionary, and looked up "scrying." Seeing
visions, it meant, in a shiny surface, a mirror or a
crystal ball. Then she came back and read again and
again the words her father had written, and listened
to the way they made her dream.

She read on. She read of girls Wright Yandro had
loved and girls who had scorned him. She read of his
feeling alone, different, odd, hidden. Those feelings
she understood, but often he wrote of things she did
not understand.

"He goes by many names. I call him Shane.

"He is the outlaw the people love, the hero dressed in black.

"He is the desperado who robs banks during the dust-bowl years and gives the money to the dirt farmers. He is the lone gypsy wandering in his wagon across the W.W. II wastelands, who steals from Allies and Nazis alike and crosses borders by night, bringing Jews out of occupied land. He is the riverboat gambler who gets into a fight one night and kills a man, and gives his winnings to an orphanage. He is the master jewel thief who falls in love with a sad-eyed whore and dresses her in diamonds. He is the bandit who is the blood brother of a lawman and goes gunning to avenge his death. He is the gun for hire who gives away his heart to a wisp of a girl and gets himself killed.

"He is the scoundrel, the daredevil, 'Wanted' by the law, loved by those ground under the heel of the law. He is not quite real. Yet he is more real than life. Cold of eye and dark of garb, he joins the Hidden Circle with the others. He is vulnerable, more so than most, because he is great of heart. He is dangerous, more so than most, because he is vulnerable. His enemy is the trickster, who has no heart at all. And the trickster is a gypsy as well, and a thief, and a gambler. But the people, who know, do not love the trickster.

"They love and protect the dangerous stranger. He goes by many names. I call him Shane."

It was as good a name as any. Bobbi shrugged and read on. Her father wrote only once of the staff, only once of scrying, only once of the stranger named Shane. But again and again he wrote of horses, of the mustangs running on the western plains.

When at last she could not stay awake any longer, she lay back on the bed, still in her shirt and jeans, and went to sleep without even undoing her braid and brushing her dun-colored hair. Images formed behind her closed eyelids, and a snatch of poetry, her dead father's poetry, hovered in her mind.

"Horses, galloping horses,
Bay and gray and blood-black horses,
Bright and shadowy, canter by,
Pass before my inward eye.
They are the horses of a dream.
They are not what they seem."

She dreamed that a druid chanted the words to her as she slept. Then she dreamed that her father sat on the edge of the bed and spoke to her, and instructed her.

"You never told me my father was a poet," she said to her grandfather the next morning.

Grant Yandro looked at her over breakfast scrapple, hearing the blame in her voice. But he said only, "News to me."

"He had that poem published in the *Clarion!*"

The old man's granite-colored eyes opened slightly in a remembering look. He said, "I'd forgot."

He was more likely to remember when each of his boys had shot his first deer, Bobbi knew, or trained his first colt, than to remember a poem sent in to the newspaper. He wasn't likely to understand about a poem. But if he'd ever read his dead son's notebooks, he would have known Wright was a poet. She said, "You never read his papers you just gave me."

Grant Yandro said, "He always kept that stuff private." And then Bobbi understood that even after Wright's death his father had respected that privacy. But somehow it was all right for Bobbi, his daughter, to read Wright's secret books. Once she was old enough. Nearly a woman grown. Grandpap hadn't known Wright was a poet, but he knew some things well enough, Bobbi saw, and she let go of blame and gazed at him in a sort of wonder, ready to comprehend what the form was that she sometimes saw behind the man—but this time she did not see it.

Memories of a dream whispered in her mind. Her father had told her what he wanted her to do, and her daytime mind saw no reason not to obey him.

"Grandpap," she said, "I know now what I want for my birthday."

He nodded as if promising the gift before it had been spoken. Grandpap Yandro, king of the mountain.

She said, "I want a mustang. Is there a shipment coming in soon?"

He said, "I'll find out," and though he did not smile she could tell by the mellowing of his face that he was pleased she had asked for a horse. Yandros were part gypsy, way back, he claimed. Always messing with horses. He had kept horses all his life, even when Mam had argued with him about it at night, even when he had to take a job off the farm, working on the county roads to feed his family. He had taught Bobbi to ride before she could read, just as he had taught all his children to ride, in a big Western saddle. English-style riding was for aristocrats, and Yandros scorned aristocrats. Western riding, trail riding on the mountains, was for common people, country people, Yandros. So it seemed right and natural to Grant Yandro that his granddaughter had asked for a mustang. Once or twice before he had brought one home himself from the government center at Lewisberry, a few hours away.

Grandpap said, "I'll get one for myself, too."

He was pleased, but he would not be nearly so pleased, Bobbi knew, if he had known her reasons. If he had known even half of the strange things happening in her mind.

Chapter Two

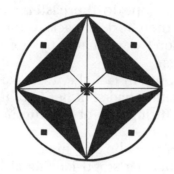

The Regional Wild Horse and Burro Distribution Center smelled of mud and manure. Behind six-foot steel-pipe fences the mustangs milled, some huddling together, some kicking at each other, all of them bolting away from any human who came near; only three days before, most of them had been running wild on the sagelands of Wyoming, Nevada, Oregon. Their bellies round and their ribs staring from worms and poor winter forage, their manes and tails matted with mud and burs, the rags of their winter fur hanging from their bloated bellies like gypsy tatters, they did not look much like the shining wild horses of Wright Yandro's poetry and Bobbi's dreams. She saw one with a clubfoot, several with overgrown, misshapen hooves, a few with terrible scars from barbed wire. And though they were of many colors, the mud coating made them all look dull brown. Like prisoners, puny and defeated beneath a gray and drizzling sky, they stood with their overlarge heads down and the long identification codes showing stark white, freeze-branded, on their necks.

"Now," Grandpap said, "look for one that has long legs and a nice slope to the pasterns. A lot of them are narrow in the chest or back in the knee or cow-hocked. You don't want that. Look for one with good hooves and legs."

She nodded, but in fact she was looking for the one that her dead father had sent her here to find. Though she wasn't admitting it, not even to herself. Dreams were just dreams—

In the fourth pen she saw him.

The black mustang stood looking at her with quiet blue eyes, his brand an angry white beneath the wild tangle of his mane, and behind him, yet part of him, Bobbi saw the—what? A form, not at all like the form her grandfather sometimes wore like a garment of air, but still—there. Form of what, she couldn't tell, and everything seemed strange, and Grandpap was talking at her.

"You don't want that one. He's wall-eyed."

Next to impossible, those blue eyes in a black horse. A wall-eyed horse was usually washed out in color or else had a white face. Yet there they were, blue as swamp flags. Although the half-seen—whatever it was, essence of something black mustang yet not wild horse at all—although the watery form beyond the form had vanished, Bobbi's spine still tingled because of the strangeness of the black mustang's eyes: not their unlikely color but the way they looked at her. A horse's gaze is blank, shallow. Bobbi had known enough horses to be sure. Yet this blue-eyed horse stood watching her with a thinking look: unafraid, aloof, reckoning, like a gambler judging the deal of the cards.

Bobbi suddenly found that the palms of her hands were sweaty. She rubbed them on her faded jeans.

"Come on," urged her grandfather. Grandpap had patience when he needed it, when training horses, but he seldom bothered with it the rest of the time. He saw that swarms of people surrounded the corrals. The good horses would soon be spoken for, and if Bobbi hadn't found anything she wanted in this pen of young studs, she should have a look at the fillies and mares.

Bobbi pointed at the blue-eyed stallion. "I'll settle on him," she said. At her movement, all the nearby mustangs spooked, swirling away with a drum-riff of hooves, the whites of their rolling eyes flashing. The black stud did not spook. He stood his ground, legs spread and planted like those of a gunfighter, head high, unmoving even when other horses careened against him. "Number 6022," Bobbi added, reading the number on the tag hung around his neck by a cord and dangling under his chin, for it was hard to tell which horse she meant in the confusion.

Grant Yandro snorted in disgust. "Cripes, girl, what you want with a wall-eyed horse?"

Hiding the strange thing about her that she was accustomed to hiding, she said, "They're not white like most walleyes. They're blue. And I've always wanted a black horse." True, pure blacks were rare. And it was only partly a lie, that Bobbi wanted one. She had often dreamed of proud horses of many kinds and colors.

"You're as bad as a kid. Don't just look for color!"

Longtime training made Bobbi hesitate to go against her grandfather. She kicked at the dirt with the toe of one old work boot, and the end of her braid found its way around to her face, where her hand pressed it against her cheek. But her eyes never left the black mustang. Her thoughts were crazy, yet—looking at the other horses she had smelled only dirt, and looking at the black she seemed to catch the scent of big sky, as if he had brought it with him all the way from Wyoming. The horse stood apart from the rest of the mustangs. (A loner, Bobbi thought, like me. No running with the herd for him.) He was still watching her with his oddly sensate blue gaze, and she didn't know what sort of legs and shoulders and back and head he had, and didn't care. Her dreams were caught by his eyes.

She raised her hand and signaled the wrangler, careful not to look at her grandfather, feeling rather than seeing his hard stare as the wrangler came over to her.

"Number 6022," she told the man.

A tall, transplanted cowboy in a plastic hat, he hesitated, looking at her. He had been reared to protect children and womenfolk. "You don't want him, sis," he blurted out. "He's been here three months. Don't nobody want him."

"Why not?"

The wrangler grew flustered, looked away from her. "Something wrong with him."

"That's for us to judge," Grant Yandro stated with granite in his voice. He would not put up with impertinence from children, horses, or outsiders, and no outsider had better try to tell Bobbi want to do. He was the only one who could disapprove of her.

The wrangler shrugged, closed the safety barriers and stepped into the corral to bring in #6022.

The black stood his ground, as no wild horse should, even though every other horse in the pen stampeded to the end. At a cautious distance the wrangler circled behind #6022 and tried to move him forward, rattling a plastic bag tied to the end of a long longe whip. This was enough to send the broncs at the end of the corral into a panic, but it did not affect the black. He lashed his tail angrily and stood where he was. The wrangler edged forward and tapped his rump with the tip of the whip—

With fighting-cock speed the black whirled and struck at the wrangler with his forefeet. The deadly hooves came nowhere near the man. Clearly, to Bobbi's eyes at least, the feint was meant as a warning. The black horse stood facing the human, neck arched and head up but nothing friendly about the cant of his ears. Then slowly, with deliberate pride, the horse turned and walked through the gate where the man had been trying to drive him.

"That's no proper horse," Pap muttered. Hearing something unaccustomed in his voice, Bobbi risked a glance at his face. The tough old man looked taken aback. Close to seventy years Grant Yandro had been around horses, and he had never known one to act with such thinking defiance.

Surely, as if to say that he knew his way and would not be driven, the stallion traversed the aisleway to the haltering chute. He walked through the narrow approach, stepped into the boxlike end, the trap, and waited for a man to hurry up and slam the sliding door closed behind his hindquarters. All the men who worked at the wild horse facility had gathered around, sending somber looks to one another.

"You want us to halter him now, miss?" the wrangler asked Bobbi.

"Let me talk to him first, see if I can make friends with him." This was the thing she was expected to say.

She stood in the safety room next to the chute, looking through a foot-square opening at the horse's head. Here a person could touch a wild horse's face and it would not be able to kick or get away. It would be forced to tolerate a wheedling voice, a hand rubbing mane and forehead. But Bobbi did not do any of those things to the black.

The blue eyes fixed on her were full of bitter hatred.

Not fear. She knew fear in horses. There was no fear in this one, not even a memory of fear. But there was a bold, angry hatred of what was being done to him, and what had been done. He had been run to near-exhaustion, harried into a trap by airplanes and helicopters. He had been tied down and violated by vetting. At the proud crest of his neck, the white hieroglyphics of the government brand showed starkly against the black hide. Did freeze-branding hurt? Bobbi wasn't sure, but she guessed it could not have been pleasant. Horses are adaptable, forgiving, but this one had not forgotten and would not forgive. She saw the hatred of a proud, a mindfully proud creature brought low.

But more . . . Dimly she saw the form behind the form. Let herself see it for one prickling moment, let herself know that this mustang's hatred was for what had been done to him—before he was a mustang . . .

"What are you?" Bobbi whispered to the black horse. "Who are you?"

There might have been a sort of answer, she thought, in a moment. But Pap strode over to give her his own answer.

"That horse is loco," he stated.

Bobbi shook her head. She saw no madness in the mustang's actions or his eyes, unless madness is being something you're not supposed to. And by that definition she was crazy, too. As loco as her loco mother in the home for the mentally ill. She felt a shiver of fear at the thought and pushed it away, and pushed away what she had been seeing along with it.

"Send him back out," her grandfather ordered, glaring at the black horse. "Get another one."

"No," Bobbi said. "I'll go with this one."

It had been a long time since she had said no to him. Grant Yandro stood in stunned silence for a moment before his brows drew together and he roared.

"For crying out loud, girl! I thought you had more sense! That horse has got a screw loose for sure. It ain't got no respect for humans, and it ain't never going to give you nothing but trouble. You seen the way it went at that fellow! You want to get yourself killed?"

"He won't hurt me," Bobbi said. The words sounded like a child's backtalk, even to her ears, but she didn't mean them that way. They were true. She could see the pride in the black horse, a dignity that would not let the proud, strong one harm women or children or anything less strong. It was a pride that belonged to another time, so much so that she could not for a moment remember the name of it.

Honor. That was the name.

And her own hidden honor would not let her lay a hand on the black mustang's head to prove her point. She would never do that until she was invited.

"What makes you think he won't hurt you?" Grandpap demanded.

"I just know."

"Bobbi Lee—"

"This is the horse I want. It's my choice."

She felt sure of her ground. Pap had promised her the horse of her choice, and Pap was fair. But his fairness would not prevent him from making her life miserable in little ways because he considered that she had chosen the wrong horse.

The wrangler came over. "Halter him for you, miss?" he wanted to know.

"It's her funeral," Grant growled.

Bobbi spoke carefully. She wanted the man to understand. "I want the horse. But there's no need to halter him. He'll go in whatever holding pen you want on his own. When it's time, he'll go on the trailer the same way."

The man was dumbfounded, then covered it by laughing and appearing to try not to laugh. Grant Yandro was furious. His granddaughter was talking nonsense, mortifying him in front of horsemen. He swore, and for the first time in years he laid hands on Bobbi.

"Jesus Christ, girl!" He grabbed her by the arm, hard, sending her toward the door. "You talk as crazy as your screwball mother!"

She jerked her arm away from him, surprising herself. She had not known she was so strong. Perhaps because she was very angry, as always when Pap talked about her mother that way—but there was no time for anger. There was the horse to be thought of.

"I don't want any halter on him," she repeated to the wrangler.

"If you want this horse, I got to put a halter on him," the man told her. "Rules, miss. Sorry." He spoke as if to a child or an idiot.

The odd thing was, she did not want the horse, not really. Everything about the black scared her. She did not want a horse around that made her see things. She did not need a proud problem with hating eyes. But—what might happen to the blue-eyed black if somebody else got it? Somebody who was not crazy enough to understand?

She went out of the safety room, her grandfather's hand hard on her arm again. She stood and listened to the loud, angry sounds, Grandpap's ranting, the crashing of hooves and heavy shoulders against wood as the black mustang fought the indignity being placed on his head. When the men slipped the door at last, he came leaping out like something berserk. He kicked, sending some careless people too close to the safety barrier jumping sharply back. He pounded into the holding pen. On his head was a red nylon halter, and a yellow nylon lead rope trailed for several feet behind him. The clownish things were wrong on him, Bobbi knew it. Her heart stung. She felt an echo, a ghost, of his hatred.

An hour later, after Grant Yandro had chosen a mustang for himself, signed the papers for both horses and paid the money, he got into his pickup and backed the stock trailer up to the loading chute. His own mustang, a rawboned sorrel stud, went on in the usual way; driven into the chute, frantic with fear. No wild horse will go into a confined space without resisting. All its survival instincts are against it. But mustangs are even more afraid of the humans behind them than they are of the trap.

The men had loaded what they considered would be the easier horse first, while the black watched and Bobbi watched the black. In those weird blue eyes she saw nothing of a horse's instincts. Instead, she saw scorn.

The black mustang's turn came. Three men on foot approached to drive the horse into the chute.

The black horse charged.

The wranglers scrambled for the entry. One of them croaked out a scream. To their way of thinking, a nightmare was happening. Only a vicious horse, a killer horse, will attack. But as Bobbi perceived it, a defiant justice was taking place. The black horse had hurt no one, but merely turned the whip of fear against the men. Through the tall wooden barrier she watched quietly, knowing what would happen.

The black stud walked deliberately into the loading chute and through it onto the trailer.

When Bobbi got there, her grandfather had closed the trailer door. He gave her a peculiar look and did not speak to her as he got into the truck cab to drive. The sorrel was kicking at the inside of the trailer. The black stood quietly.

During the entire three-and-a-half-hour drive home, Pap and Bobbi said hardly a word.

Grant Yandro eased the trailer up the long, rutted lane leading back through the dark fir woods to the stony-hard mountainside farm, pressed small by forest, where the Yandros lived.

Bobbi got out and opened the gate of the six-foot pipe corral where the mustangs would have to go, built on the small, tilted patch of ground where the old bank barn had once stood, outside the metal barn Grandpap had put up a few years back. Grandpap backed the trailer flush up to the corral gate. Four placid horses, grazing in the steep, electric-fenced pasture, raised their heads in mild interest and watched the mustangs unload.

The black came out first, calmly, walking to the center of the corral and looking around at hills like sleeping dinosaurs, the cabin squatting in the shadows, the dark firs and gray sugar maples with their blood-red tinge of springtime bud. The sorrel had to be urged to follow. It had lamed itself with kicking at the unyielding metal of the trailer; it stumbled out and floundered to the fence, looking for escape, its long lead trailing. Mustangs wore halters and lead ropes constantly until they were trained.

Pap and Bobbi watched the mustangs a moment, then closed the corral and the trailer and went wordlessly about their chores.

It was a silent, unpleasant evening. On toward dark, when her grandfather had settled sourly in front of the old black-and-white TV, Bobbi slipped out of the cabin. Half-log, half-stone, it had been there since sometime before the Civil War. Bits of old tools and junk lay all around it. Bobbi dodged around a rusting compressor and down the cluttered slope to the corral to see her horse—if the black stud could truly be said to be hers.

The sorrel scrambled for the far side of the corral when it heard her coming, but the black stood within arm's reach of the gate, and he stood his ground. The clown-bright nylon halter and lead rope on him glowed like fungi in the dusk.

"I'll take those off you, if you like," Bobbi offered from the other side of the gate.

The black tossed his head in proud negation. He

was not ready to accept an offer of help from her or anyone else, this stud. Bobbi felt certain that he had understood every word she said, an absurd, insane certainty, eerie enough to chill her with creeping fear and lower her voice to a hoarse whisper.

"What are you?"

Once again she looked to the horse's strange eyes for the answer.

They glowed like blue fire. Within a moment they glazed so bright that to Bobbi they no longer seemed blue, but strobe-white, engulfing her with their flaring light—she could see nothing. Yet, she could see everything. She saw—things so real, in that white-hot light, it was as if she could reach out and touch them. She saw a dragon with gray hair on its nearly-human head. She saw a gypsy wagon drawn by a mule. She saw an old woman with a walking stick alive and moving in her hand. She saw a young beauty with her white breasts showing above the low bodice of her long, full-skirted dress. She saw a young man with broad, black-shirted shoulders and a black hat; his back was turned. Then she must have closed her eyes. The white blaze burned too hot and fierce. When she opened her eyes again, she stood in a dark, springtime night with the peepers chiming in it somewhere, and she was clinging to the cold pipes of the corral. The strange horse still stood nearby, a black shape in the darkness of the night.

Chapter Three

Bobbi awoke the next morning to the thud of hooves. Outside her window she saw the black mustang circling his corral at a hard gallop, with his head held high and the yellow lead rope flying. Without waiting to wash she dressed and went out.

The sorrel stood stiff-legged in the middle of the corral, snatching wisps of the hay that Grant had tossed there and spooking between bites, afraid. The black continued to run without glancing at either the sorrel or the girl who stood at the fence. He ran with speed and control and, Bobbi intuited, purpose. Like a tough-minded prisoner, the black was exercising himself to stay strong.

Bobbi watched. Since the strange blue eyes were not looking at her, for the first time she saw the black as a horse, saw him the way her Grandpap did, and

with a small shock of surprise she realized he was no
bigger than most mustangs. She had perceived him
from the start as tall, but he was smaller than the
sorrel. It was partly the way he moved, she decided,
that had made her think he was big. When he walked,
she saw a swordfighter walking to a duel; when he
ran, she saw a Green Beret charging. He had presence enough for any half-dozen horses or men.

He was not put together like any horse she had
ever seen. No wonder her grandfather disapproved.
His shoulders were large enough for a larger horse,
then tapered to a slim barrel and hindquarters. His
hooves were small, beautiful to look at but really too
small to carry the weight of those heavy shoulders,
that neck—his neck was a true stallion's neck, proudly
arched. His head was lean, straight, chiseled, slightly
Roman of profile under the red halter. Some Barb
blood in him, the horsewoman in Bobbi thought,
while in a hidden way she knew it was not Barb
blood at all, or any sort of horse breeding, that made
the black mustang look the way he did, move in the
lithe, alert way he always did, and turn on her with
coldly blazing blue eyes.

He ran by her, just inside the fence, almost within
her arm's reach, without glancing at her. She waited
until he was well past, then said, not loudly, "Shane."

The horse plunged his hocks to the dirt, slid to
a stop on his hindquarters, whirled and faced her, all
as fast as a striking snake. His head swung low,
canted toward her, and the blaze of his blue eyes
seemed to burn through her. Dangerous, very dangerous, he was, and Bobbi sensed it surely. Wright
Yandro had written the truth. But oddly, Bobbi did
not feel afraid. Shane was dangerous, but not to her.

She said quietly, "It's your name, isn't it?"

Nothing in the eyes answered her. She had to trust her own sureness. The black forelock fell as a strong man's unruly hair falls over his forehead, ready to be pushed back by the hand of the woman who dared. . . . She had read her father's notebooks again before going to bed, and dreamed of the black horse in her sleep, and awakened to the drumming of his hooves with the name in her mind.

"I know it is, and I will call you by it," she said.

Now that the black had stopped running, the sorrel bolted to the far side of the corral from Bobbi. Shane gave it a scornful look, then walked to the strewn hay and began methodically to eat. Bobbi leaned her arms on a fence rail and watched. Not because she wanted to touch him—or so she told herself, for Bobbi scorned to feel desire for boys or men—but because she wanted to be a friend to him, Bobbi said, "If you would care to come here, I'll take that stupid halter off."

Without raising his head from the hay, Shane narrowed his eyes and gave her a chilling look.

"Well, just remember I offered," Bobbi complained. She laid her chin down on her folded arms and watched the black stud eat while the sorrel cowered against the opposite fence. After a while she said, very softly, so softly that probably Shane didn't hear, "I'd like to groom that mud and fur off you, too, and make you shine. Maybe being dirty is what's making you so sour. Seems to me you would have been a dandy. Gold rings, silk cravats—"

"Who you talking to?"

Bobbi jumped, then sighed with exasperation. Travis Dodd, the neighbor boy from up the mountain, had

come up beside her without her hearing him. She
hated that. She hated the way his eyelids jumped.
She hoped he hadn't heard too much. If he had, he
didn't show it; nervous as always, he blundered on
without waiting for an answer.

"Them the mustangs? Which one's yours?"

"Black," Bobbi replied curtly.

"Oh." Travis stared intently at the horse. Travis
had hair the off-color of homemade soap and a twitchy
grin, and he didn't know a thing about horses. "He's
nice, I guess," he said lamely of the black.

Bobbi wished he would go away and let her alone
with the horse that was no horse and with her crazy
thoughts. She didn't understand why Travis hung
around her the way he did, when she wasn't inter-
ested in boys the way most girls her age were. They
all seemed so—so futile, compared to her dreams.
How could she ever love any pimply boy the way she
loved the images in her own mind?

Moreover, she was not the sort of girl boys were
supposed to hang around. Something in her rebelled
against making herself attractive, or what other people called attractive. She didn't bother with makeup,
and she got her clothes off the boys' rack at the
Goodwill store. Her excuse was that Pap didn't have
much money, but in fact it was all part of her Yandro
orneriness. Yandros were independent, Grandpap said,
and didn't care about fashion or what people thought,
and Bobbi was a Yandro.

"Ain't you coming to school today?" Travis pes-
tered. "Don't you think one unexcused absence is
enough for this week?"

"Crud," Bobbi muttered. She had forgotten all
about school. The day felt like weekend to her since

she had taken off school to go to the mustang place, but it was just Friday.

"Get your stuff," said Travis. "I'll wait."

He would walk with her down the long lane to the school bus stop, he meant. Bobbi found his attentions annoying and faintly embarrassing. She went back into the cabin and, after brushing her teeth, slipped out the back door and walked to the bus stop through the woods to avoid Travis with his puke-blond hair and shy, staring eyes.

She was glad to avoid Pap too. Her grandfather had gone off somewhere, and she did not see him at all that morning.

When she got home in the late afternoon, Grandpap was in the corral with the mustangs. By the look of his reddened face, for once he had lost his patience while working with a horse.

"Bobbi!" he roared as soon as she came in view up the lane. "This black devil has got to go!"

Bobbi dropped her books and came running, but grew angry as she ran. "He's my horse," she said as she pounded up to the fence. "You don't have to mess with him."

"I'm just trying to get to my own horse!"

The sorrel stood huddled against the fence, completely lathered with sweat, as frightened of the black stud as he was of the humans. The black faced Grandpap at a small distance, alert and ready to move in any direction, but unheated. His ears were pricked forward. He was enjoying himself. All afternoon, every time Grant Yandro had tried to approach his own mustang to get hold of the lead rope that trailed on the ground, the black had cut between, spooking the sorrel horse and endangering the man.

Pap told Bobbi, "Get in here. I'll keep the black son of a bitch busy. You get hold of the sorrel's lead."

From longtime habit of obedience to her grandfather, Bobbi opened the gate and slipped into the corral. Then she stopped where she was. Often she had seen Grandpap working with the horses, patient, consistent, unyielding, firm; seldom kind, but always fair and firm. He shaped the behavior of the horses, taking his time but always pushing, pressing, little by little, the way forest pressed on the farm. Bobbi knew that he had trained her the same way, and she loved him, but she did not like being shaped.

She looked at the black. Blue eyes met hers, and she saw in them what she expected to see: an outlaw's defiance of the oppressor for her grandfather, and a grudging sense of honor for her.

"I'll put my horse in a stall for you," she told her grandfather.

"And how you expect to do that?" retorted Pap, not in query but in scorn. Mustangs were afraid of enclosed spaces. They had to be halter-trained before they could be taken into a stall.

"Just open the door. He'll go in by himself."

This should have been good news to Grant Yandro, but he was in no mood to hear his granddaughter say that all he had to do was open a stall door and ask the black mustang to go in. He had spent an exasperating afternoon. He had tried for an hour to get hold of the black stud's lead rope, so he could tie it to a rail and get it out of the way. The black had comprehended what no ordinary horse should comprehend, the connection between himself and the rope, and he had refused to let the old man anywhere near the trailing length of nylon. Longe whip in hand, Grant had tried to corner the black. It was as useless as spitting into the wind. The black horse was fast and fearless. Finally, though he knew Bobbi would have a right to be angry at him if she ever found out, he had tried to rope the mustang. But the black was more rope-wise than any horse he had ever seen. Shane had made a monkey of him, all afternoon, and when Bobbi said she would put him in a stall, Pap opened his mouth and roared.

"You're going soft in the head!"

"I've been right about him so far," she challenged, "haven't I?"

But Grant Yandro was too bullheaded to admit that. And he didn't just want the black horse in a stall. He wanted to conquer him. He handed Bobbi the whip.

"You get over there on the right. Come at him that way while I grab that lead."

It was an order, given in the heat of action. Bobbi had never gone against such an order of her grandfather's in her life.

"No," she said, though her voice sounded far less than firm. But she followed the word by dropping the whip in the dirt.

Grandpap glared, then shouted, "Jesus shit! Goddamn it, girl! Why not?"

She would not admit, even to herself, that she did not want the black mustang to hate her. Though she knew she could have walked up and taken him by the halter, and he would not have resisted her by even so much as turning his head away.

"He's my horse," she said. It came out sounding bratty. Inwardly she groaned, for she could see Pap was boiling mad.

Rather than face him any longer, she turned away and jogged across the corral to where the big sliding door to the barn stood open, offering the mustangs shelter should they choose to accept it, though no escape. At the other end of it another door, closed and latched, blocked the way and the light. Stepping inside the shadowy aisle, Bobbi opened the door to the first stall. She did not have to look to see if the black horse was watching her; she felt sure that Shane was always aware of everything taking place around him, both because he was a wild stallion and because he was—himself. Without turning around and without raising her voice, she requested, "Shane, would you come and get into this stall, please?"

She could hear the black stud walking toward her across the corral. Without looking she could envision his catlike alertness, his desperado grace. She heard his steps steadily approach, then the slightest of hesitations; Shane was put off by her nearness. He thought perhaps she would try to touch him as he went past her into the stall. "Don't worry," she said sourly to the wall. "I wouldn't think of it."

He speeded his walk slightly, brushed past her, entered the stall and turned around so that he faced her as she closed the door. Bobbi felt a slight shock as her eyes met the eerie blue ones in the horse's strong, black face. Almost, she had expected a man's handsome, headstrong face, dark brows, straight nose. . . . Shane stood watching her intently.

"I won't latch it," she told him quietly. "You can just push it open if you want. But please stay in until Grandpap is done. He's not a bad man. Even the temper you've got him in, you'll see he doesn't hurt the horse."

She went outside, squinting in the brighter light of the corral. Grant Yandro was still standing where she had left him.

"The black devil's name is Shane," she told him.

Pap looked at her oddly. "I see," he said in a quiet, angry voice. "And when I want him in a stall I'm supposed to just hold the door open and ask him nicely, is that it?"

Bobbi said wearily, "Probably not. I think he just does it for me because I'm a girl." She went into the house.

More often than not, Pap made supper, but since he was busy with his horse Bobbi started some sausage frying on the little bottle-gas stove. While it cooked, she watched the corral out the kitchen window. The sorrel was so worn out it was not hard to catch. Grandpap got his horse by the lead rope and maneuvered the animal to the hitching rail near the barn, where he snubbed the sorrel tightly to the strong post. Then, for an hour, standing on the opposite side of the post and rail, he methodically rubbed and patted the sorrel's head, first one side and then the other, starting at the cheeks and working his way up to the forehead, ears, poll and upper neck. Each time he moved his hand to a new place the sorrel struggled, wild-eyed. Each time, it found that struggling was of no use and ended it by standing still. Sometimes its ears came forward, its expression curious as well as scared as it listened to the sound of Grandpap's voice.

From the darkness of the barn, Bobbi knew, Shane was watching, or at least aware, his blue eyes ablaze with hatred in his black face. True, the sorrel was not being hurt. But it was being forced, pushed, shaped.

Bobbi sighed and started to mix pancakes.

It was almost dark before Grant Yandro came in for supper. "You didn't latch the black horse's stall," he told Bobbi as he washed his hands. "He could have come out any time he wanted to."

"I know," she stated.

Pap stared at her with eyes as hard and gray as the stones long-ago glaciers had left in his horse pasture. But he said nothing more. He sat and ate in silence.

In spite of his gray hair, Grant Yandro had never seemed old to Bobbi. Stubborn, and set in his ways, but not old. Nor did he seem young. He simply was, like the mountains, and like them he weathered without seeming to change. Though Bobbi knew in her mind that he would someday be gone, in her heart she assumed he would always be there for her, like the hills, when she needed him.

"I called Doc Boser," he said after he had eaten for a while. "He'll be out a week from Monday to cut them mustangs."

Grandpap kept speaking, but Bobbi could not at first comprehend what he was saying. She heard only cut, mustangs, and the palms of her hands pressed against the table top to keep her upright; for the first time in her life she felt faint. "Cut" meant geld. Make the studs into geldings. Castrate them.

"He'll want to do it in the stalls," Pap was saying. "We got to get them halter-broke and stall-broke by then."

"You can't geld Shane!" Bobbi burst out.

She saw her grandfather's eyes widen in surprise, as well they might. Nearly every year of Bobbi's life there had been a horse gelded at the Yandro place, and she had never objected before. Nobody with any

sense kept a stallion unless they intended to breed it,
and had the special stalls and corrals meant for studs.
Stallions were considered too unreliable and just plain
dangerous to use as pleasure mounts around mares.

Bobbi knew these things. But—that was all before
she knew Shane. . . .

Pap sat astonished by her outburst, but, oddly, he
did not rear up and roar. Bobbi had spooked him
with so many surprises in the past two days that
perhaps, like a mustang snubbed to the hitching rail,
he was growing tired of struggling. Or perhaps he
was learning, out of necessity and quickly. He asked
quietly, "Why not?"

He was really asking. He was really ready to listen.
His tone touched Bobbi so that she nearly opened
her mouth to tell him. But she couldn't . . . how
could she share what she had so long kept secret, tell
him about the weird things she saw? Her reasons
were too strange for words. As crazy as her screwball
mother. Suddenly doubt numbed her. Thinking what
she did about Shane, was she—was she crazy? Ever
since she could remember, ever since the first time
she had visited her mother in the awful, screaming,
urine-smelling psychiatric ward, she had been afraid
of going ga-ga like Chantilly.

"You just can't," she said to her grandfather, but
all the fight had gone out of her.

"No reason?"

"Shane's . . ." But he would know she had gone off
the deep end like her mother if she told him. And,
anyway, how could she feel so sure? She faltered,
"Shane's . . . different."

Grandpap said, "I can see you and that horse got
something special."

It was a struggle for him to say it, she could see that, after he had been so set against her getting the black mustang. But fair was fair, and Grant Yandro was always fair. He added, "You planning to breed him, maybe?"

Pap was really trying to understand. Bobbi felt her eyes prickle with hidden tears.

"No," she said, "I wasn't planning on it." She had to be at least that honest with him. He was trying to be honest with her.

"I was going to say, ain't nobody going to breed to him, not with those walleyes. He's a real nice horse," Grandpap added hastily, "aside from that. Real light on the forehand for the way he's built. Moves nice." There was a grudging but genuine admiration in the old man's voice. He was recalling the way Shane had dodged his rope. "Faster on his feet than any horse I ever seen."

Moves like a cat burglar, Bobbi thought. Or a gunfighter with Indian blood. Or a drunken gypsy, for the gypsies only danced better and with greater splendor and defiance as they became drunk. Or a swordsman—no, a Jedi knight.

"Flashy. Good flex to his neck." Grandpap was still trying to be nice, but then the horseman in him took over. "It's plenty muscled up, Bobbi, maybe even a little too thick. You ought to get him cut if you're planning to show him. He might make you a real good barrel racer, quick as he is."

"I ain't thinking about things like that," Bobbi said.

For the first time her grandfather's voice rose. "Well, you ought to be! What the devil are you thinking about?"

Castration. Done at the proper time, it let a male

horse's bones grow longer, his neck grow more supple and graceful, more yielding to the rider's pressure on the bit. And made him more docile, and let him share the same pasture with the mares. But what would it do to—a man?

That was crazy. Bobbi felt the craziness of it twitch at her face.

"What ails you, girl?" Grandpap asked impatiently.

There was no proper answer Bobbi could give. "It just don't feel right!" she burst out, and she lunged up from the table and blundered out into the springtime night, up the dark mountainside, staying away from the corral where the weird black horse might make pictures in his eyes for her, leaving Pap to clear off the supper dishes.

Chapter Four

The next day Bobbi's grandfather told her, much too patiently, as if speaking to someone whose mental balance he held in doubt, that he would not have a stallion on his farm with his horses. There would be no more arguing with him, Bobbi knew, patience or no patience. Shane must be gelded.

Bobbi spent the next week floundering in a mental whirlpool she could not seem to escape.

If Shane was just a horse, then it was reasonable and customary that he should be gelded. And it was crazy to think that Shane was anything other than a horse. And no matter what she had seen and what she knew, she did not want to be crazy. Grandpap would get a court order and have her put away like her mother. She had to make sure nobody ever knew she had thought crazy thoughts. Shane had to be just a horse.

And yet, there was the form beyond the form. . . .

She had seen it only once, at the wild horse distribution center, and she did not want to see it again. She looked at Shane as little as she could, and when she did look, she made sure she saw black hooves, black hide, a tail swishing flies. A horse. A mustang. She made her eyes tell her mind that Shane was a mustang, and she would not allow words to the protesting part inside her that was going crazy. Grandpap was right. Of course the horse had to be gelded. She did not want to go against Grandpap. She had no good reason to go against Grandpap. He was right, and she knew it.

Why, then, did she feel so wrong?

Grant Yandro watched her as if waiting for the next shoe to drop. There was nothing he could put his finger on about her—maybe she was a little too quiet, but a person is entitled to be quiet—there was nothing, really, but just a feeling he had, that she was not done surprising him. She wasn't spending much time with her horse, he noted. "When are you going to halter-break that Shane?" he asked her cautiously over Monday morning's breakfast.

"What does it matter," Bobbi said right back, "as long as he'll go in the stall for me?" He could tell she had the answer ready. She had been giving it some thought.

"I'll have to hold him by the halter for the vet." Grant had arranged for Dr. Boser to come the following Monday while Bobbi was in school. He was old-fashioned enough so that he always did that when he needed to have a horse gelded. Bobbi had seen almost every other kind of vetting, but she had never seen a castration.

"Can't you just muscle him for a couple minutes? Won't Doc give him a sedative right away?"

"It's my body you're talking about here, girl!" Grant studied Bobbi closely, not really angry despite his tone. He knew he could manage the horse in the close confines of the stall. There would be a little excitement—he was almost looking forward to it, especially after the way the horse had made a fool of him. He would not mind putting a twitch on the black mustang's nose and making the animal stand still. But he couldn't understand Bobbi. He would have thought, as moony as she had been about her mustang, she would have wanted to prepare Shane and make the operation as easy as she could for him.

"Are you hoping he'll get away from me?" he demanded.

"Not really."

That was the truth. Bobbi knew her grandfather, and she knew better than to hope a horse could best him. Or even—something more, in a horse's body. The thought made her eyes wince and shift, and the way her glance slid away from his convinced her grandfather that he had hit on the truth.

"Well, he ain't getting away from me," he said in a hard voice. And because he felt a dare, he did not order her to gentle the horse. He only told her, "You put that mustang in the stall on Sunday night, and you make sure the door is latched, and you leave him there."

Bobbi nodded, got up and went out to tend to her chores. She didn't look at Shane or speak to him.

All that week Travis Dodd stopped by the Yandro place morning and evening, before and after school. The struggle inside Bobbi was wearing her out so that she did not have the energy to be rude to him. And because she did not want to be near the black horse for any longer than she had to—because she might see crazy things in those weird blue eyes again, or the mist-thin form hovering like a nimbus around the black shoulders, in the air—because of her problem, she nearly welcomed Travis. She let the neighbor boy help her carry hay and water to the mustangs in the corral. The water had to be hauled from the spring, bucket by bucket, and dumped into the wooden trough. Once the mustangs were tame enough to go out to pasture, they could drink from the run like the other horses, but as long as they stayed in the corral it was Bobbi's job to provide them with water. With other mustangs in the past she had enjoyed it, pausing between trips to talk to the wild horses, coaxing them to come nearer to her. But as things were with Shane, she hurried through the job as quickly and silently as she could, actually grateful for Travis's help, though of course she did not tell him so. She was so moody all week long that Travis sensed something wrong, and every day with clumsy questions he asked what it was, though he knew she would not answer.

Thursday evening, as she was lugging her third bucket of water into the corral, eyes down and fixed on the ground, a pair of dandy-small black hooves invaded her view, and the straight, slim black legs above them, and a broad expanse of chest. Standing square and still as if for a showdown, Shane put himself in her way.

Bobbi set down her bucket and made her eyes scan slowly upward, up the arrogant arch of the neck to the high head and the gunfighter-hard eyes looking

the aisle between stalls, blacker than night, and did
not turn on a light. She opened her horse's stall.
"Shane," she called, her voice only a little shaky,
"come here, please."

He came, but slowly. Something in her voice made
him hesitate. But a man of honor had to obey the
wishes of a lady, even a lady he detested. He came.

"I have to ask you to go into the stall, please."

The stall was clean enough that she could have
slept it in herself; she had seen to that. There was a
bucket of fresh water hanging on the wall, and hay
piled in the corner. Not that she expected these
things to make any difference to Shane. But they
made some small difference to her.

He went into his prison. He had to, because she
asked it of him. All she could see of him was a
glimmer of yellow lead rope, dragging in the dirt like
a felon's chains. All he could see of her was a dark,
slim shape in the night.

She closed the stall and latched the door firmly,
and imagined that she saw his head lift with uneasy
surprise.

"I have to," she told him, not trying any longer to
keep the tremor out of her voice. "I can't go against
Pap. I got to live with him, and he's—he's all—he's
the only one—"

All the family she had. The only one who—loved
her?

She could not feel love anywhere in the night.

She left Shane in the stall and went into the cabin.
Her grandfather was sitting in front of the TV and did
not look up as she passed him on her way to her
room.

Bobbi could not sleep. Early the next morning,

Monday morning, she did her chores and left for
school without speaking to her grandfather. But he
saw her walking down the lane toward the bus stop
and called her back.

He looked hard at her, and she met his stare
without expression. He wanted to say something to
help, somehow, but it came out sounding as hard as
his stone-colored stare.

"Time you get home," he told her, "it'll be done.
Now, don't fuss no more. Pay attention to your
teachers."

Bobbi nodded and left.

Three-quarters of the way down the lane she met
the vet's truck rattling up. Doc Boser waved at her.
She waved back, turned and watched him drive out
of sight up Canadawa Mountain.

Then she stepped off the lane into the woods, left
her schoolbooks and started back up the slope toward
home, at a run. She had no plan. In fact, she was
trying not to think. There was a knotted feeling in
her chest that she did not want to name. She told
herself that she was going to watch and see for herself
what gelding was like. Then she would know what—
what had been done to—

Shane's image shadowed her mind, black, no matter how she tried to send it away. She ran as if
wildcats were after her. Like a deer she crashed
through briars and underbrush. When she saw the
maroon siding of the barn through the trees and
slowed down to be more quiet, her heart would not
quit pounding. She felt half panicked. Skipping school
to watch something on the sly, a small rebellion,
should not have made her feel so scared. . . . She
quelled the thought. She did not dare think.

The big door at her end of the barn, the end away
from the corral, hung open. Bobbi slipped out of the
woods, edged along the barn wall, and risked a peek
inside. Shane. . . . The black horse had not yet been
touched. Relief washed over her, a feeling as dangerous as a thought; she sent it away, trying merely
to see what was happening in front of her. Doc and
Pap in the barn, working on the sorrel.

Take the easiest horse first was the horseman's
rule, whatever needed to be done. The horse that
was likely to give trouble always waited until last;
otherwise, his struggling would upset the others and
cause them to give trouble as well. Since the sorrel
was halter-trained, Pap and Doc were gelding him
first. In a way hidden even from herself, Bobbi had
been counting on that.

She eased her eye past the door frame and watched.
Both men were busy, and neither of them saw her.
Grant Yandro was just taking the twitch, a sort of
metal clamp, off the sorrel's nose after using it to
make the horse hold still while the vet injected the
sedative into the neck. The sorrel's head sagged;
Bobbi could see it through the stall door. Doc had
unbundled his instruments. They lay on a white cloth
on the stall ledge. Bobbi watched as the vet selected
a scalpel and disappeared into the stall. Most vets
laid horses on their sides to castrate them, but Doc
Boser preferred to do them standing up. Pap steadied the sorrel by the halter—the horse was standing
on tottering legs, nearly falling, much too weak and
shaky to struggle. Its head drooped nearly to Grandpap's knees.

The sorrel groaned.

Deep, heaved up from the inmost depths of the

horse's helpless pain, the groan trembled through the stable. Bobbi felt her fists curl. The knot in her chest turned into something that stung like smoke, burned like flame. The sorrel groaned as if it were giving up its soul. Something round and bloody, tossed out of the stall, landed in the dirt of the barn aisle. A cluster of stable cats gathered around it.

Deliberately Bobbi shifted her stare and looked at Shane in his stall at the other end of the barn, the corral end.

The door there stood open wide, like the one she stood at, for light. Bobbi could see the black mustang plainly, and she saw how sweat slicked his black hide, how the whites showed around the blue of his eyes, and she knew Shane's fear was not horse fear, made up of blood smell and strangeness, but man fear, because he comprehended what was happening and knew his turn was next. Shane, the outlaw hero who had hardly ever been afraid of anything . . . Bobbi saw his head turn as he scanned the stall walls, roof, floor, looking for escape. There was none. She saw him thinking, trying to plan where there was no hope. She saw the thinking and the hopelessness along with the fear in his eyes. She knew that, when they came to castrate him, she would see the form beyond his horse form, the man.

The second round, bloody morsel landed in the barn aisle for the cats to gnaw and drag about and pat with delicate paws. Doc Boser reached for his emasculators, a shiny, foot-long pair of tongs to crush what was left inside the sorrel.

And in her mind Bobbi felt an angry, fiery crackling, a snap or click as if something had either broken or slipped into place. She found that she could think again. All right, she thought, I'll be crazy.

She slipped away from the door and around the outside of the barn, quickly, quietly. She ducked through the bars of the corral, eased over to the barn door at the corral end and looked. Pap and the vet, still in the stall with the sorrel. Good. In three soft steps she was at the door of Shane's stall. Blue eyes turned on her and blazed in sudden hope.

"Run like hell," she whispered to the horse, and she opened the stall.

Shane ran. He was a swashbuckler slashing his way across a hostile courtyard; he was a tavern brawler; he was Han Solo against the storm troopers. He moved like a black thunderbolt. Grant Yandro shouted and started out into the aisleway the moment he heard the snick of the stall latch, but the black horse knocked him aside with one mighty shoulder. Before Pap could raise a hand, Shane was past him and gone, out the far door to freedom, and Bobbi was jumping up and down and yelling after him, "Run, Shane! Keep going! Don't stop till you get to Wyoming!"

And then her grandfather was standing in front of her, and the way he looked at her stopped her shouting. She could almost hear the storm wind rising in his mind, could almost see the bruise-black cloud growing, a thunderhead swelling atop a mountain of pure jagged granite. Bobbi had just sent Grant Yandro beyond mere anger into a state more like what the preachers called wrath.

He did not roar out any of the usual things: what the hun did Bobbi think she was doing, why wasn't she at school, what sort of idiot was she. He did not roar at all. Maybe because Doc Boser was there he did not feel he could shout. So what happened was worse. He spoke in a low voice, stone-cold and hard and hateful.

"Bobbi Lee Yandro," he said, "you had no right to do that."

She tried to argue. "He's my horse! I guess I can set him free if I want to." Though her voice choked on the words.

"I'm the one who signed the papers for him. The federal government says he's their horse for a year yet, and I have to let them know if he gets killed or gets away. I'm the one the Bureau of Land Management is going to come after."

Bobbi stood stricken. She couldn't speak. What had seemed right was crazy, which made it dead wrong, every other way you looked at it.

Her grandfather said in the same cold rage, "Now you get out of this barn. You go find that black son of a bitch and I don't want to see your face until you bring him back here."

Bobbi stared at him, feeling the loveless words sear their way into her brain as if they were branded there.

Pap said, "You don't find him, don't bother coming back."

She turned and walked out of the barn, off the farm and away from the place she called home.

Chapter Five

"Well, then," Bobbi muttered, because she was a Yandro and had a Yandro's pride, "I won't be back."

Since her head and heart were out of their whirling confusion and working together again, she knew several things very clearly. She knew gut-deep that Shane must not be castrated, and therefore she knew that she could not take him back to Pap. Her grandfather had no more give in him than a rock, experience told her. Shane had to get away. If someone took him back to Pap again, he would be gelded, sure as a dog gets fleas.

Her grandpap had told her not to come back without the horse. Well, then, she wouldn't come back.

Cleanly, calmly, as she ran, her mind started working on her own survival. She would need food. She would need a means of traveling, and she would need someplace to go.

First, though, there was one last matter to be attended to, if Shane was to get away for good. She had to find the black horse and speak to him once more, just the once, asking him to let her take the halter and lead rope off him. There had been no time, back in the barn. But the dangling lead would make Shane vulnerable to anyone who got near him. What was worse, the lead and halter could catch in the trees or rocks of the rough mountain terrain. Shane could starve to death.

She wouldn't let the thought panic her, not yet. But it had sent her running for all she was worth up the lane, upmountain, because Shane had gone that way.

The lane rounded a curve, and the shanty where Travis Dodd lived with his parents came into view. Bobbi slowed to a jog. The horse might still be within earshot. "Shane!" she shouted to the woods. "Shane!"

She stopped in front of the shanty, scanning the encircling woods, listening. Nothing happened except that Travis appeared at the shanty door in his ragged pajamas, looking surprised. Bobbi jumped back from him like a spooking colt. She had forgotten he would be home, sick, while both his parents worked. But there was no time to spare thought for Travis.

"Have you seen Shane?" she demanded.

Travis looked puzzled for a moment, until he tore his mind off Bobbi's presence and remembered who Shane was. "The black horse?" His face lighted up. "I thought I heard something! Must have been him. Went by here a minute ago."

"Shane!" Bobbi called to the woods. "Come here, please!"

"He get loose?" Travis asked. It was not the first time he had asked Bobbi a stupid question, though he didn't seem to have that problem with other people. He flushed, but, preoccupied, Bobbi did not notice.

"I set him free," she said softly, still watching the woods. Then, before Travis could gawk, she wheeled on him. "Travis, get me something to eat, please. Quick."

Startled, he didn't move for a moment.

"An apple, a couple slices of bread," Bobbi expanded impatiently. "Hurry up. I gotta catch him before he gets too far away."

Travis opened the refrigerator—it stood beside him on the shanty porch—and handed her his school lunch, packed the night before just in case he felt well enough to go. "Thanks," Bobbi told him. She ran on, and he watched after her as she disappeared into hemlock and mountain laurel. He thought the sandwiches were for the day, until she went home at nightfall. But she knew that this was her food for the foreseeable future, and Lord and the black horse only knew where darkness would find her.

She was a hunter. She knew how to look for sign. Skirting the Dodd clearing, she found the place where Shane had entered the forest, displacing the dead leaves and pine duff on the ground with his hooves. A horse leaves a plain trail in the woods, especially in the soft, moist ground of springtime. Bobbi followed as fast as she could, through grapevine tangles, down damp ravines where the hoofprints showed plainly, along the mountainside on slopes so steep that her feet slithered and she supported herself with her hands. From time to time she thought she heard a crashing noise in the brush ahead. But when she stopped and called, the black mustang did not come to her. Probably it was deer she was hearing. Shane must have been out of earshot. He could move far faster than she could. She had no chance of catching up with him.

But she continued to follow the trail, feeling fear swell in her and dampen her palms. A day, two days, three, and the trail would grow too faint to lead her. Sooner, if rain fell. After that, if Shane caught himself by the halter—

Damn double-thickness nylon halters wouldn't break for anything.

Years later, somebody might find the skeleton strewn at the base of the tree, the bones pulled apart by wild dogs or Pennsylvania coyotes, but the skull still hanging in the bright red halter.

Her mind shied away from the scene and started wandering as her feet carried her onward. She wondered what sort of a ghost a starved or savaged horse that was not a horse would leave. The ghost of a desperado stalking the mountains in his broad-brimmed black hat? She knew people who claimed to have seen ghosts in these hills: the ghosts of the lost children of the Alleghenies, two little boys, brothers, seven and five years old, who had died of starvation and exposure back in 1856. The bodies had been found after two weeks by a man who had seen them in a dream. People still heard the children crying on the hills at night. And there were the ghosts of a murdered hex witch, a man, and his murderer, his jealous wife, who poisoned his food then died shortly after him of his final curse on her name. Her ghost was supposed to haunt the woods in the form of a china cupboard, of all things. A cupboard full of fancy plates, dancing under the moon. What a thing to run into in the dark. Some people were crazier than she was, Bobbi decided, to think of such things.

The murdered man was the hex witch of Ness Hollow, Bobbi recalled from the stories. He had the evil eye and could seduce women without effort. She didn't want to run into his ghost. But there were other hex witches who were worse, and some who were far better. Old Nell the Hill Witch had lived for a hundred years and was reputed to have saved the lives of more than a hundred babies. Bobbi had heard of other witches still living in the mountains: the Buppsville Witch, the Hollis Corners Witch, the hex witch of Seldom—

Where the hun was Seldom, Bobbi wondered. She knew of many towns in Canadawa County with peculiar names: Good Intentions, Cold Bottom, Salamander. She knew where they were, and she had been to some of them. But she had never seen a road sign for Seldom, or known anyone who went there, or seen it on any map. Maybe it was a ghost town. The thought amused her. A ghost town. She could be in the middle of a ghost town right now, walking through the woods, and not know it. The way people talked, there could be a city's worth of ghosts all around her.

She didn't like to believe the stories. Horses that spooked at nothing, she joked, were seeing ghosts. Yet in a way the ghosts were as real to her as the dead butts of giant chestnut trees lying on the mountainsides, trees killed off sixty or eighty years before. Life was different in these parts. Old, like the hills. Deep, like the taproot of a pine. People remembered back a long time in Canadawa County.

Well, maybe they'll remember me when I'm gone, Bobbi thought darkly. Maybe they'll tell stories of how I was never seen again. Bewitched away by a black horse.

She followed the horse's trail through the day as fast as her body would let her, walking along the steepest slopes, jogging when the terrain allowed and the trail was plain. She stopped to drink at every clear-running spring, but she didn't stop to eat. She did not even look into the bag Travis had given her. A few times she crossed a dirt road or a snowmobile path, and a few times she saw the back of somebody's cabin or bungalow, but she never came out of the woods, and that didn't surprise her. A person could go for miles and days in these hills and still be in forest. The valleys between the mountains were mostly cleared for farms and towns, but the mountains didn't lie in neat ridges any more, not once you got west of Canadawa. They lumped and rumpled like a thousand wallowing pigs across the rest of the state, and except for right around Pittsburgh all their backs grew thick with woods.

Shane was heading that way. West, toward Wyoming.

Bobbi followed until it became too dark to see the trail and she was afraid she might lose it. In that last dark ravine, she had barely been able to make out the sign at all. Off to one side she had thought she saw oval prints, dark and moist, as if the black horse had just come down to the stream to drink. But she must

have been mistaken, must have been seeing shadowed
deer tracks in the dusk. She felt sure the black horse
was far ahead. Once out of the ravine, on the dryer
ground atop the bank, she sat down on the dirt. She
could pick up the trail again at first light.

She thought of the bag of food in her hand, and for
some reason her stomach turned. Just as well she
wasn't hungry, she decided. Likely she would be
ravenous by the next day. She would save the food
until then.

She sat, too tired to sleep, and tried to think
instead. Where was she going, once she and the
black horse had parted paths for good? She had rela-
tions scattered all over the map, her father's brothers
and sisters, her mother's brothers and their wives,
Aunt This and Uncle That. Half of them, she forgot
exactly where they lived. There were none of them
she felt anything special for or trusted not to send her
back to Pap. Then there was her mother, in her ward
with the other crazies. And her mother's parents,
Grandma and Grandpa Buige, who she sometimes
saw when they came to visit her mother on Chantilly's birthday and Bobbi was there too. They lived in
Louisiana somewhere, and always sent Bobbi Christmas presents that showed they didn't understand her
at all. She had never been friendly with them, because she had sometimes felt that they might like to
take her away from Pap. Huh. A good thing, now, if
they did.

The night had gotten very dark, and chilly. In her
unlined windbreaker and cotton shirt, Bobbi started
to shiver. The ground under her was damp. Somewhere spring frogs were chorusing: a sound that Bobbi

loved, usually, but this time it felt cold and wet to
her. In the cabin, Pap would be lighting a fire in the
woodstove to take the chill off the air—

She should not have thought of Pap in that way.
All in a moment the full extent of her anger and
hurting broke through, like a fire breaking through a
thin wall, and Bobbi could have screamed with the
sting of it.

I-DON'T-WANT-TO-SEE-YOUR-FACE-DON'T-
BOTHER-COMING-BACK. . . .

The words might as well have been branded on her
mind, and still smoking. She cursed aloud with pain.
"Jesus Christ!" she blurted at the night. "How could
he have *said* that! He might just as well have said—
have told me—"

That he didn't care about her. Go away, Bobbi.
You Have Done Wrong. I don't love you any more.

She put her head on her knees and cried. Crying
made her feel angry at herself as well as at Pap, but
she couldn't help it. She hurt all over, inside and out,
as if she had taken a licking. Pap had never done that
to her, but this was as bad or worse.

"Hell," she muttered to her knees when she was
mostly done crying.

Something howled in the woods, not unlike the
way she had been howling, but with an animal voice.
Her head jerked up. Pennsylvania coyotes had inter-
bred with Canadian wolves on their way east, and
they were big.

It howled again, farther away. This time Bobbi
paid no attention, for beyond the wash of tears in her
eyes she saw a whitish blur in the air. She dug at her
eyes with her knuckles. Her vision cleared, but the
blur was still there: a dim, floating face. Something

like Pap's, yet—not like Pap's exactly. Hazy. She did
not want it to become any clearer.

"I'm tired of seeing things," she said fiercely, aloud,
yet more to herself than to the face. The voice, when
it answered her, seemed to sound inside her head.

"Seeing things is your gift."

She knew him now, though the misty whiteness
in the night was no clearer than ever. She knew him
because she had heard the voice before, in her dreams.
Her father. Wright Yandro. She felt too heartsick to
be afraid; and why, anyway, should she be afraid of
her own father?

"Go away," she told him bitterly.

"But I can be with you, because of your gift! Why
won't you let me?"

"Gift, my eye! Look where seeing things has got
me. Grandpap—" She couldn't say any more.

"You've got to understand about Pap. He says hard
things sometimes, but he doesn't mean it. He's sorry
already, though he'd never admit it. He's so worried
he can't sit down, wondering where you are. He
won't be able to sleep tonight."

She found this news gratifying, but she only said,
"Serves him right. I'm never going back there."

"I'm not saying you should! You have to help Shane.
I'm the one who sent you to help him, remember?
And you have to follow where your gift leads you.
Pap never understood about me, either."

For the first time she began to wish she could see
him more clearly. Her own father. From his photo-
graphs she knew the look of his strong-boned face,
but—what was he like, really? The white blur in the
night told her no more than the newsprint blur had.

She could not see its eyes. When it spoke, no mouth moved.

It said, the words sounding inside her head, "But you have to understand, he loves you just the same."

"Who you trying to kid!" Suddenly she was furiously angry, and stiffly she struggled to her feet, and for the first time her voice rose. "Loves me, my eye! He can make me cry, but he don't cry. He can say all sorts of things, but I never heard him say he loves me. And he never—" She could not say it. "Hell!" she shouted to the woods.

Hell was feeling sure he never would.

She watched as the white blur, frightened, bobbed away into the night with a crashing of bushes and a soft scuttering of cloven hooves. "Jesus shit," she said to herself. "I'm loony, all right. I been sitting here talking to a deer's behind."

She wiped her nose with her fingers and sat again, curled up and shivering, trying not to think or see any more.

She did not expect to sleep, but after a while she did. She lay on her side in the pine needles, and every time she moved any part of her out of the small spot she had warmed, she half woke, and when the side of her not next to the ground grew too cold, she woke up completely and turned over. At first light she stood up and jogged in place and pumped with her arms, trying to come alive. She felt chilly pale, like the dawn sky. She felt empty with an emptiness food would not fill.

It was almost light enough to see the trail. She stood still and looked around her, and suddenly she felt warm as the colors of sunrise.

No more than ten paces away stood the black mustang, watching her.

"Shane," she whispered.

The horse did not move. He stood with his head up, his blue eyes wary.

"Shane," said Bobbi again, this time loudly enough so that he could hear, "Shane, I've got to get that halter and lead rope off you before they hang up on something."

His blue stare blazed into her, and Bobbi felt an odd, inward fear. She knew Shane would never hurt her. But she felt as if he was scanning her soul.

She was the one who had put him in the stall.

"Shane," she said with a small catch in her voice, "I know I haven't earned it, but you're going to have to trust me, or you might not get very far. You think maybe Pap made me change my mind and come after you, but that's not it. I just want to take that halter off you so you have a better chance of getting back where you belong. Then I won't follow you any more."

He stood in his gunfighter stance, looking down at her with keen blue eyes, and Bobbi saw him as if she were seeing him for the first time, or the last, saw the tangled mane tossing on his high-flexed neck over the white brand, saw the draggles of mud and fur still plastered to his sides and belly—she had never groomed them off as she had wanted to do. She had never touched the black horse. And now, if she had her way, she would touch him once and he would go back to his wandering life, like a gypsy, ragged but free.

"I know you don't like to be touched," said Bobbi.

"I won't lay a hand on you unless you come to me. And I won't ask it of you, because I know you feel you have to do what I ask. But I want you to let me be your friend, just this once. It'll just be for a minute, for me to take the halter off, and then you'll go away. You won't have to see me again."

Shane stood motionless, and Bobbi stood just as still, afraid to move, wondering what more she could say, watching him make up his mind.

Then Shane moved. He came forward, and the sunrise light caught on his head and made his black forelock shine white. He came toward her, not in the hesitant way a horse would, but like a man who has decided to risk something: steadily, firmly. He did not stop until he faced Bobbi within arm's reach. Then he planted his feet and stood like a captive soldier, unmoving.

Bobbi did not take any liberties. Her hand went to the halter catch. For a heartbeat, as she snapped it open, her fingers brushed the smooth hair over Shane's cheekbones. When she lifted the halter off his head, passing the crownpiece over his ears, her wrist felt for a moment the coarser touch of mane. Then the garish red thing was off, and she stepped back, letting it drop to the ground. She nodded to Shane. "Goodbye," she whispered.

He turned and cantered away up the next rise, his head high and the mane tossing on his neck. Bobbi watched him until he had topped the rise and gone out of sight. Her eyes stung. She felt sure she would never see him again.

Then she stooped, picked up the bag of food Travis had given her, and trudged off westward, the way Shane had gone. There was no sense in heading back toward home. She had some notion where she was going, but she didn't want to head that way yet, not when it would take her out of the woods. For the time she just wanted to stay in the woods and not have to cope with people.

She walked numbly, looking down at the ground in front of her feet, not taking much notice of the birds wildly singing or the sunrise colors in the sky. She made her way slowly to the top of the rise where Shane had left her sight. He would be a mile away by the time she got there—

He was standing in her way, confronting her as he had once confronted her in a corral, and as they had done that time, her eyes caught on his blue-black hooves and traveled up his tough, slim legs to his head and blue-eyed gaze that bored into hers.

"I'm not following you," she told him. "I—I guess I'm heading for Louisiana. Not that I'm looking forward to it. But I can't go back to Pap."

Shane stared at her a moment longer. Then with a sudden, imperious turn of his body, he put his side toward her and stood waiting.

It took Bobbi a moment to understand. Then it took her several moments longer to speak. The breath had caught in her throat. She was stunned.

"You—you want me to—to ride you?"

Almost unthinkable, Shane being what he was. But he turned his head and looked back over his shoulder at her impatiently, urging her to get on with it. Even when she placed one hesitant hand on his withers, he did not move away from her.

"You want to—take me with you?"

Still he waited for her. And although she had vaulted onto bareback horses many times, and Shane stood no taller than any of them, somehow Bobbi felt daunted.

But what she had to do, Bobbi Yandro generally could do. She took a deep breath, bent her knees and sprang. She bellied onto Shane's back, swung her leg over, took her place behind his shoulders. She held the bag of food in one hand and laid the other on her thigh, not daring to touch Shane's neck or take hold of his mane.

As soon as he felt her weight settle into place, the stallion started off, and at an easy, fluid lope he carried her away from the slopes of Canadawa Mountain.

Chapter Six

Whatever it was she had talked with the night before had told her some truth, Bobbi found. For within the hour she heard helicopters circling over the forested mountains and knew they were searching for her. She felt a dark satisfaction. Pap must have called the cops after all, and the volunteer firemen and the National Guard and whomever. So he was worried. He deserved to be worried, after what he had said. And she was not about to be caught or go back.

There was no need to say anything to Shane about choppers. The black horse—or whatever Shane was—had carried her under the densest cover of trees at the first sound of beating rotor blades in the distance. The broad-leaf trees, oak and sugar maple and ash and hickory, were mostly bare yet. So as not to be seen in the pale sunlight below their spidery, reaching branches, Shane took her into the pines. These mountains had been logged for white and yellow pine, but there was plenty of scrubby second growth of pine, and fir and hemlock and evergreen laurel. Shane traveled on, under the shelter of their dense boughs. When a chopper drew close—Bobbi could tell by the noise that it was right overhead, though she could not see it—Shane stopped under the evergreen canopy and stayed there until the danger had passed.

"Shane," Bobbi remarked in a low voice, "I guess there's going to be people on foot and ATV's and stuff after us, too. Maybe even dogs."

He flickered an ear in acknowledgement and went on. The going was rough, through scraping, prickly branches, over rock outcroppings and fallen tree trunks. Shane chose his own path. Bobbi would not have dreamed of trying to guide him. She balanced herself to his movements and tried not to be a bother to him. He went at the fastest possible gaits, often dangerously so. When he cantered through the trees, lunging across the choppy terrain, she tilted her body to the speed of the canter and went with him, her lips pressed together.

Through the racket of choppers in the sky, Bobbi did not hear the whoosh of cars. But Shane slowed and stopped. He had seen the glint of a pickup barreling along the blacktop. A road lay ahead.

Shane eased forward until he stood behind a laurel thicket near the road. Bobbi saw him watching and listening, waiting for his opening. Not a sweaty hair on him, she noted, except where her thighs pressed hotly against his back and sides. Shane made a cool-headed fugitive. He had been a fugitive often before, and not just as a wild horse stampeding through the sagebrush.

Bobbi felt his hindquarters bunch. He gave her just time to grab hold of his mane before he leaped. With choppers hovering in the distance, but no cars in sight, Shane shot across the pavement, hitting a gallop within a jump of the place where he had been standing still.

The pause behind the laurel thicket was the last time he stopped that morning.

He seemed tireless. He jostled Bobbi over some of the worst terrain she had ever seen, at speed. Yet his courtesy for her never failed. He slowed before going under low branches until he felt by the shifting of her weight on his back that she had seen the danger and ducked. Unlike a horse, he never tried to go under anything too low for her. Sometimes, though, she had to lie flat on his back, with her head pressed against his neck. That embrace felt like intimacy. She could not help a hot, frightened rush of emotion in her heart.

In early afternoon, Shane came to a fair-sized stream and stopped, turning his head toward his rider.

"Yes," Bobbi answered the unspoken question, "I'd better get a drink." She slipped off the horse, staggering a little until she got her land legs back, and kneeled on a rock at the stream's edge to drink. She saw Shane lift his head, listening for choppers before he waded in downstream of her and lowered his muzzle to the stream's surface to drink as well. Then he came over to stand in the pool by Bobbi's rock, letting her mount him more easily than she could from level ground.

"Thanks," she murmured. "Huh?"

Instead of crossing the stream as she expected, Shane was making his way up the middle of it, against the current, picking his way over the scarps of rock.

For more than a mile he waded upstream in rushing water sometimes chest deep. He came out of the stream at last onto a broad shoulder of rock, where he would leave no trail once his wet hoofprints had dried. He followed the rock away from the stream until it dwindled into brushy mountainside again. Then he lunged upslope, crested the ridge, and took off at speed down the other side, toward some distant goal.

It was even more difficult and dangerous to gallop down a mountain than up it or along it. Bobbi gritted her teeth and rode for all she was worth.

Shane had a purpose, she felt sure of it. She felt it through the long bones of her legs, felt it in the horse's sure movements. He was going someplace. But where? Wyoming? He could hardly expect to take her all the way to Wyoming. How would she find food?

She thought of food because she was hungry. And she stayed hungry, very hungry, all that day. Shane seemed to have no thought of stopping to rest or eat, and she would not have asked it of him, not for anything.

At nightfall he finally stopped. For the first time since she could remember, Bobbi stumbled and fell to the ground after dismounting. Riding bareback stretches every muscle. She felt stiff and aching and too starved to care. Not even bothering to move from the clutter of sticks where she had landed, she sat and ate until she felt better. Peanut butter and jelly,

thoroughly soggy by then. And a blackened banana.
And a Snickers bar, and more sandwiches; she made
herself leave them for the next day. Travis had packed
for a big appetite. Bless Travis.

Shane had gone off somewhere, out of sight in the
woods, to browse or perhaps relieve himself. She had
noticed days before that even in the confines of the
corral he never did in her presence any of the earthy
things that horses customarily do. It had been
an unintentional cruelty, keeping him in the corral where there was no privacy. Bobbi regretted
it briefly, then gave up thinking about it. Shane
was aloof, but not one to hold a grudge against
anyone less than truly evil. Knowing he would
be back when she woke, as surely as she knew
the sun would rise, Bobbi lay down where she
was and slept.

In the morning she could barely walk. Sleeping on
the ground without covering had not helped her sore
muscles. It took all the grit she had just to get onto
Shane again.

Her misery eased from the heat of his body and
the touch of morning sunshine after a while. Spring
was giving her its first warm day, strangely warm and
fine for the time of year. One other thing was good:
she had not heard a chopper. Shane had brought her
into the next county, she felt sure, far away from the
focus of the search. Nobody would be looking for
them this far west.

Shane must have felt the same way, for when he
and Bobbi came to a power line angling south and
westward, the horse cantered down the grassy road
that ran underneath it. Dirt bike trails spiderwebbed
in and out of the pole line, and snowmobile trails,

and logging roads. When Shane found a logging road that veered due west, he trotted onto it. Soft dirt, shady and wide, it made far easier, faster going than the deer paths on the mountain ridges. After a while Shane slowed to a walk, and Bobbi was able to eat the rest of her sandwiches as she rode. She stuck the Snickers bar into her windbreaker pocket for later, zipped the pocket closed, and gratefully tossed the bag away. She had been carrying the crumpled thing so long that it seemed her hand had grown into the shape of the brown paper; she flexed her fingers. On Canadawa or the mountains since, where searchers might find it, she had not left any trash. But these woods people had filled with their garbage. She saw it everywhere.

She saw more of it over the next hour or so, as Shane passed from logging road to dirt bike trail to abandoned strip mine access road to snowmobile trail to mine road again, and as he passed from walk to canter to trot and walk and canter. There were junked cars along the roads, dumped tires, rusted-out refrigerators and freezers, even somebody's falling-down trailer and an old armchair with the stuffing coming out. There were beer cans and broken bottles and a naked doll with its arms and legs torn off. There were dumped garbage bags, torn open by animals, their contents strewn and smelly and indecent.

Then, on toward midday, Shane and Bobbi encountered the real garbage. The human trash.

They had been hearing motorcycle buzz for some time. It echoed through the woods, maybe near, maybe far, hard to tell how far or the direction either. Several times Shane had turned off the trail, picking his way through rusting metal to take cover, only to hear the racket fade away along some other path. The area was networked with trails.

This time, when the noise grew louder, Shane laid back his ears and kept on walking the way he was going. Bobbi sensed the change in his mood as surely as if he had spoken to her. Fugitive he might be, but he would not be turned aside from his path any longer. He would take his chances.

And as chance would have it, three dirt bikes roared around a turn of the old mine road and shot toward Bobbi and her horse, their riders staring.

She knew right away that these men were trouble. It was not just the way they looked. Bobbi had nothing against long hair and dirty jeans. Lots of men around Canadawa were as dirty and unshaven as these three. But any courteous motorcycle rider cuts his motor and stops his bike when he sees a person on horseback. These men were goons. They grinned and revved their engines louder. At increased speed they rocketed straight at Shane.

"Hey!" Bobbi yelled, angrily, uselessly.

It was a game of chicken, and Shane didn't give an inch. He held to his portion of the road and kept walking. At the last moment the bikers swerved aside and zoomed past with shrill yells that should have scared any horse into a frenzy. Shane didn't flinch.

"Bastards," Bobbi said furiously to the world at large. "Pigs. Some people don't deserve to live." She was not frightened, not on Shane, but she knew that if she had been riding a horse that really was a horse she would have been in serious trouble. The thought made her outraged. "Shitheads," she declared.

She heard the mutter of their engines fading away.

Then she heard it grow louder again. They were coming back.

"I don't *believe* this!"

The first one pulled his bike up beside her and stayed there. She felt all Shane's muscles harden under her, but the horse kept walking.

"Hey, girlie! Where'dja learn to ride?"

There were yips from the other bikers to show that this was meant as mockery. The man had placed a leering slur on "ride." Bobbi looked down at her questioner with distaste, seeing the things he wore to mark what he wanted to be: boots, leather vest, earrings, tattoos, dirty hair stringing back from his unhelmeted head. Seeing also the marks of what he really was: graying strands in his scraggle of beard. Flab bulging above his belt, though muscles bulged in his arms. No form behind the form. This man was like a flat thing, all surface, nothing beyond. She wondered briefly where he had misplaced his soul.

"Get lost," she said.

"Hey, tell ya what! Get down off that horse a minute. C'mere. I'll give you a real ride." He laughed smuttily, and so did his friends.

It had not occurred to Bobbi yet to look frightened. She hadn't reckoned on the way these bikers would react to her, a teenage girl out on a black horse that was walking along without saddle or bridle or even a halter, and neither horse nor girl acting scared.

"Stuff it," she said.

The man made a grab at her leg, trying to pull her off Shane.

Bobbi reacted quickly, swinging her booted foot to

knock the man away. But Shane was even quicker than she. Before her boot could connect with its target, Shane whirled and let fly at man and motorcycle with both hind feet. There was a crash as bike and biker landed in the dirt. Bobbi heard, but didn't see, for Shane had stretched out into a gallop.

And she heard the buzz as the bikers came after her. And she knew not even Shane could outrun them on the road.

Even as she thought of it, she felt Shane gather himself, and she grabbed at his mane with both hands. Three junked cars hulked beside the road at a curve, coming up fast. Shane cleared the middle one in a long, strong jump—Bobbi winced, feeling her stomach flip. She was not used to jumping anything bigger than a fallen log on the trail. She'd been coon hunting on a mule that would leap a barbed-wire fence, but her job then was to get off first, duck through the wire, drape her jacket over the top strand and clear the terrain on the other side. . . . No telling what sort of rock or sharp metal might be on the other side of this junker. But Shane landed in weeds and was off at a hard gallop. He knew what sort of men these bikers were. He knew they would find a way around the abandoned cars and be after him quicker than they could curse.

At reckless speed Shane snaked through the woods, taking a twisting way between close-spaced saplings and giant oaks, crashing through brush, jumping rocks and fallen trees, trying to throw the bikers off. Bobbi flattened herself over his neck and shielded her eyes against branches with one hand. Behind her she heard yells much like the yelps of hunting dogs. Wheels spun, engines whined. The bikers were enjoying the chase. They liked tearing up the forest with their tires. They enjoyed destroying things. If they caught her, they would enjoy the—what? The kill?

The bikers roared closer. Bobbi recognized the shouting voice of the biker who had wanted to give her a ride.

"Tight ass!"

She did not look at him or reply.

"Bitch, you wait! I'll show you a couple things."

"Damn," Bobbi muttered into Shane's mane. She was beginning to feel frightened, though not for herself. She knew Shane too well for that. Not only the black stallion Shane, but the man, or more-than-man, the legend. She had lived with it almost since she was born, in her dreams, in the stories she read for school, in a hundred TV shows, even before she had met Shane in her father's notebook. She knew what was likely to happen, and it frightened her. What was sure to happen, if the bikers left Shane no choice.

They were fanning out to either side of the black mustang, finding themselves easier terrain than what he chose for them, catching up with him. Soon they would try to cut him off.

A thick fallen tree blocked the way. Shane leaped across; the bikers veered around. Then—

"Shane!" Bobbi gasped aloud.

A rocky ravine a good twenty feet deep sheered down at their feet.

There was no time to stop. There might have been time to turn aside, to skid slantwise down the steep slope or run along the edge, easily brought to bay either way. Shane had no intention of doing either. Even clinging to his neck as she was, Bobbi felt the powerful spring of his hindquarters, and it seemed to propel all the breath out of her. With an energy, a focus, a concentrated force like nothing she had ever felt in man or stallion before, Shane leaped toward the far side of the ravine. But it was a crazy leap; Shane had to be crazy. No horse could jump so far—

Too scared to scream, Bobbi hid her face in black mane. Shane had carried her into midair, with nothing but his body between her and the rocks below, and the curve of his leap flew forward into nothing, and he and Bobbi were falling, falling—

Shane's reaching forefeet struck about halfway down the opposite bank. His hooves dug in, his forelegs curled like the arms of a fighter landing a punch, his shoulder muscles bulged, and he surged upward. His hind hooves grabbed. Hindquarters bunched, then sprang. Bobbi's hands tightened around the base of his neck, feeling the sweat break out on Shane's chest as he brought her up the side of the ravine and over its lip to the more level floor of the forest.

Without even a pause to catch his breath, Shane galloped on. Bobbi moved her hands to his mane, raised her head and stole a glance behind her. Even before she looked, she heard the waspish buzz of motors and knew. The bikers had found a way through or over the ravine. They would run Shane until he dropped.

Shane dug in his forefeet, slid to a stop and whirled.

Bobbi understood. He frightened her, but she understood. She sat straight on his back, sharing his defiance. Shane had given these men every opportunity to give up, go their own way and let him be. He had tried to spare their lives in every way he knew. He had run from them as long as he was going to run. Now it was showdown time.

Shane stood squared off and rock firm, neck arched but low, head extended in a stallion's threat gesture. The warning was clear. This was to be a duel to the death.

The bikers understood as well as Bobbi did. Engines faltered, cycles muttered to a stop. At a safe distance the three of them sat their mechanical mounts, eyeing Shane.

"You stupid no-neck fugheads!" Bobbi yelled. "Go away, or you're going to get killed!" Her voice shook on the last word. She did not like what was happening any better than she liked the men who had been pursuing her.

The one who had tried to grab her pulled a knife from a sheath at his belt. His face, Bobbi noted, was sweating above his graying scraggle of beard. "Come on!" he ordered the others. "The horse is wore out. Let's get her!"

"You get her," the man next to him retorted.

Even from the distance Bobbi saw the flush of anger redden the first biker's face. "Christ!" he yelled. "You scared of a girl on a *horse?*"

"That ain't no horse," the third man said in a low voice. "Look at its eyes."

"Jesus shit!" The one with the knife didn't look. He spoke with the scorn of a frightened man who won't acknowledge his own fear. "All right, you two scumbags watch. I'll show you how it's done. I'm going to kill that horse. And then I'm going to lay that tight-assed bitch, and you two dickless wonders don't get a piece of her."

He revved his cycle and roared toward Shane.

The black mustang waited until his enemy had

gained some speed. Then Shane also sprang forward into a driving gallop. The biker saw him coming, spun his cycle sideways and lifted his knife. He meant to slash as Shane charged past him. But Shane was quicker than any dodge or any knife. He lifted into a low rear. One deadly hoof struck the man's uplifted hand, sending the knife flying. The other smashed into the man's head.

Bobbi shut her eyes.

She heard the motorcycle fall and lie sputtering in the dirt. With momentum still carrying him forward, Shane cleared it and the body in one leap. It took him a few strides to come to a stop.

Bobbi looked at the other two bikers. Close in front of her, they sat without moving, white-faced, their eyes staring. They would not hurt her.

Shane turned and left that place at an easy lope, knowing that only silence would follow.

Bobbi's fingers twisted and clenched in his mane as she rode. Her insides felt sick. She had seen dead bodies enough in her sixteen years, rouged and laid out amid flowers in funeral homes, but she had never seen a man killed before. She tried not to think of the smashed-pumpkin sound his head had made, or of the color pink. Instead, she thought of what he had meant to do to her, and felt at the same time better and worse.

She noticed that Shane was making his way through woods again instead of taking one of the many logging roads and snowmobile trails. The black mustang was keeping to the densest cover.

"Right," she said aloud in a hoarse voice. If she and Shane had been fugitives before, they were doubly fugitives now. The police would want to know who had killed that biker, and how. Maybe the man had belonged to a motorcycle gang, the Pagans or the Hell's Angels, and the gang might come after them.

"I bet even the blasted federal government is after us," she said to Shane, "because you're a mustang."

She felt badly shaken, and reached out to Shane without thinking. A scared horseman always moves to calm his horse. She stroked Shane's neck. She reached up and laid her hand on the white scars of his brand, and Shane did not pull away.

Chapter Seven

Shane nosed her awake in the middle of the night.

Sleepily stirring in her nest of dead leaves and hemlock boughs, Bobbi did not at first know where she was. She dreamed that the touch was Grandpap's, that Pap was shaking her to awaken her before dawn for a day's hunting. Then she shivered and woke up, and there was the black form of Shane standing over her, looming in the chilly night.

"What is it?" Bobbi asked groggily, too sleepy to show surprise that the black horse had touched her of his own accord. Just as well, she knew later, thinking back on the moment, that the night was dark and that she was too numbed by sleep to feel much. Shane would not have wanted to see the flush of joy on her face.

She sat up without waiting for an answer. There

could have been one from Shane's eerie eyes, but she did not want that, and instinct told her such answers were not for the small questions. She listened and looked around for her own answer. There was no sense of danger in the night. Shane stood by her, waiting.

"You want to go on? Now?"

It would have been better to go on in the daytime, when Bobbi could see what she was doing. But she got up, flexed her aching body and scattered her bed, hiding her traces as best she could in the dark.

"I guess you have your reasons," she said.

Shane stood by a log, making it easier for her to get on him. He kept to a walk through the woods, over the uneven and unseen ground, and Bobbi laid her head down on his neck, closing her eyes and covering them with one hand to protect them from branches.

After a while she began to hear distant traffic noise. The rumble of trucks carried clearly on the night air. She sat up and looked at the headlights strobe-flickering through the trees. Traffic was light at the time of night, but she could tell it was a big highway. A four-lane.

"You knew this was here," she said to Shane in amazement. "But how—no. I won't even ask."

After a moment she added, "I take it we have to cross." Shane had brought her to the expressway in the dead of night, when it was least likely they would be seen.

Steep embankments topped with chain-link fence flanked the highway, making it a ravine that not even Shane could leap. After a moment's pause he turned leftward, picking his way along the top of the bank, just behind the fence. It was unlikely that anyone would see a girl in dark jacket and jeans riding a black horse up there in the black of night.

Bobbi kept silent, wincing each time headlights swept over her, or seemed to. She could not think how they were going to cross. Even if they could get through the fence, sheer rock fell below.

She felt Shane's head come up. He was looking at something ahead.

"We're in luck," Bobbi breathed. In the headlights she could see the concrete span of a bridge crossing the highway. Better yet, no neon signs glared. No gas stations, no fast-food huts.

As Shane walked closer, Bobbi could see why. A small secondary road overpassed the four-lane, with no access. No cloverleaf. No exits. The chain-link fence curved toward the bridge and joined with its railing. The narrow blacktop ran through woods, over the highway, and into woods again. At the time of night, traffic on it would be nearly nil. For two fugitives, it couldn't have been a better bridge.

Shane stopped to study it.

"Go for it!" Bobbi whispered to him excitedly.

He tossed his head in annoyance and did not move. In a moment Bobbi understood that Shane was waiting for the traffic to clear on the highway. It was a slim risk, that somebody passing under the bridge might notice the dark horse and rider overhead, but it was a risk he did not want to take.

For what seemed a long time, but might not have been more than five minutes, girl and horse-man waited. Bobbi felt herself grow tense with impatience, felt Shane's body between her legs filling with tension of the same sort. At last she felt him bunch for

his run. Another moment and the sky over the highway would be dark . . . it was. Shane burst from
a standstill into a canter and clattered onto the bridge,
running for the other side . . .

Out of the woods ahead of them rattled a mud-
splattered pickup. Headlights swept onto the bridge,
caught them in high beams. Even Shane could not
dodge them. There was nowhere to go. Trapped on
the narrow road between railings, all he could do was
keep running. Atop the black horse, Bobbi passed
the pickup so close that in the greenish glow of the
dashboard she could see the startled face of the man
behind the wheel as he stared back at her.

Shane barreled into the woods on the other side.
Ducking branches, Bobbi swore, "Damn." It was not
strong enough. "Oh, crap, damn, SHIT."

The search would be hot after them again.

"There wasn't a single car on that road the whole
time we sat there," she grumbled to Shane.

She blamed herself for not watching the side road
while he was intent on the expressway. She could
have watched, she could have said something. Only,
Shane had taken charge from the beginning, and she
had gotten used to sitting on his back, carried away,
swept away into adventure. . . . Riding Shane was
utterly unlike riding a horse. It was more like riding
a romance. But now she blamed herself for not putting reins on him, taking control of her own life. In
woods behind her was a man lying dead by a downed
motorbike, when maybe she would have handled it
differently. . . .

Or maybe she would be raped, mutilated and dead
instead of riding on a black mystery at midnight.

Closer to morning, now. Dawn was lightning the

sky, and as soon as he could halfway see his footing Shane settled into a distance-covering lope. He would put as much forest as he could between Bobbi and the bridge before six kinds of cops swarmed out and the choppers started flying over. Bobbi tilted her weight forward, rocked like a baby by the rhythm of the canter, but her thoughts were uneasy. She was not used to being protected. That was one thing she liked about Grandpap. He always treated her like a man. Well, almost always.

Shane stumbled, regained his footing, and surged on. Hit a hidden hole or a root beneath the dead leaves on the ground, most likely.

Bobbi's stomach was nagging her with hunger, and there was nothing for her to eat. The Snickers bar had been last night's supper. By the time the sun was up, she felt so ravenous she could think of nothing else but how to find herself some food. She wished she had paid more attention when Grandpap and his cronies had talked about the wild-growing foods they used to gather. Too early in the year for most of those, anyway, even if she knew them. She would have to risk stealing from someone's kitchen. If she could get Shane to take her there.

Shane faltered in his lope and slowed to a walk.

The going was really too rough for a lope. No ordinary horse could have managed it. And the heavy flat-tire sound of a chopper vibrated in the distance. Bobbi turned her attention that way, and Shane speeded his gait to a trot, heading for the cover of some hemlocks.

Only the one copter appeared. Bobbi felt nearly insulted. As the day wore on, either it flew away or they left it behind, and they no longer had to hide from it.

She and Shane had struck a sort of flat-topped,
leaf-strewn mound, a long mound that ran straight as
a rifle barrel through the woods. It made much easier
going than the rumpled slopes of the mountainsides,
and Shane followed it. Trees grew out of it from time
to time, but not as thickly as they did elsewhere.
Creeks and ravines cut across it at intervals, and in
those cuts Bobbi could see the remains of stone pil-
ings. The mound was, in fact, an old tram bed, the
built-up roadway for the tram line that had taken
lumber out of these hills years before. It ran on
southwestward for miles.

Thinking as she was of her stomach, it took Bobbi a
while to notice that Shane was moving along at walk
and jog trot, when this would have made a better
place than most for a gallop. It was only half a day
since the man in the pickup had seen them, and she,
for one, still sweated at the memory; she would have
thought Shane would be moving at top speed. But
the mustang was picking his way down the sides of
the streambanks, walking across the bottoms and trudging up the opposite slopes—and this was the same
horse who had leaped a fifteen-foot ravine the day
before! The thought struck her, making her stomach
knot more sharply than hunger could, and she exclaimed aloud.

"Shane! Your hooves!"

Those small, black hooves, small as a dandy's polished boots, not really wide enough to carry the
weight of a rider . . .

Bobbi leaned over and tried to look. She couldn't
see whether they were cracked, or worn, or which
one, or how. Shane was unshod, of course, and the
rocks he had come across, the leaps he had taken,

should have lamed any horse before now. But Bobbi
had been thinking of him as more than horse, and
she hadn't realized . . .

"Shane," she demanded, "stop." She wanted to see
how badly his hooves were damaged.

The stallion responded only by speeding his walk
into a trot. Hooves struck the ground in hard-driving
rhythm. Bobbi felt the slight unevenness of that
rhythm.

"You're going lame," she stated. "Let me down.
I'll walk."

Shane lifted his head angrily and trotted faster.
Bobbi put her arms around his neck, slid down over
his shoulder and hung there, dragging her heels in
the dirt until the horse came to a stop. Then she
stood up, wobbling a little. Shane faced her with his
blue eyes blazing, plainly furious. He stamped his
hind feet.

"Kick me if it'll make you feel better," Bobbi retorted, and she stooped to examine his hooves. "God,"
she added in a different tone. "I could kick myself."

All four hooves were worn and ragged, but the
front ones were the worst, because they bore the
most weight. Shane's front toes were worn so short
that his hooves stood almost upright, straining his
pasterns. Far worse: up his left front hoof ran a crack,
and the pressure of every step widened it and forced
it longer.

"I bet that started yesterday. I should have seen it
before. I shouldn't have been riding you. Now it's
worse."

Bobbi turned away with tears stinging her eyes and
began to walk. After a moment Shane followed her
down the overgrown tram road.

By midday, with no food in her stomach, Bobbi was reeling, but she kept stubbornly on. She stopped being aware of the forest around her and saw only the ground beneath her feet. Another damn creek. Down the bank, slosh through the water, don't bother to find the driest way, up the other side, good. Shane, following her, stepping clear of the rocks in the creekbed, plodding through the water. Cold water probably felt good on those hooves. They had to hurt. . . . She didn't look at his head, his eyes, only glanced back at his legs from time to time as he followed her. She felt her feet starting to stumble and tried to correct them, but it was all she could do to put one in front of the other. She concentrated on that. Left foot step, right foot step, left foot again. Staggering a little. No longer much aware even of the black-horse-not-a-horse behind her—and then a gentle nudge in the middle of her back sent her toppling onto the ground.

It was soft as a bed down there, springtime-damp and leafy. Bobbi lay blissfully still a moment before she realized what had been done to her and pride made her move.

"Hey," she protested weakly, rolling over to scowl at Shane.

Looming above her, he seemed gigantic. His eyes, a blue glow—no, white. Shane was the world. Shane-blaze took her, she saw nothing else, and in it, in his eyes, she saw—the gypsy dancers, the dragon with gray hair, the old woman with the walking stick that moved, the young beauty in the flounced and ruffled dress, and—and the man in the black shirt. He had turned to look straight at her, and his eyes under the broad brim of his black hat blazed piercing blue, fire and ice. The shirt glistened; silk. Something white glinted at his neck, under the open collar.

"Bobbi," he said.

She felt her mouth fall open in astonishment. "Shane," she blurted, "you can talk to me!"

"Sometimes. Listen. There's no need for this. Get up on me and ride. It's not much farther."

"But you weren't meant for that!" Still lying on the ground, looking up at him, too weak and dazed to care that she was being crazy and seeing things again, Bobbi said, "You were meant to be the rider. You had—a big horse, the best in the world. You rode—"

"Hush," he said. His face was youthful but not boyish; it was hard, clean-shaven, lean and sunburned. The lines of his brows and nose and jaw were straight, with a set look about the jaw. Small weather-marks showed around his eyes; perhaps he was not young after all, but ageless. His mouth was strong, somber. The form behind his form was that of a horse, a black mustang. Bobbi had no trouble thinking of him as man and mustang both.

He said, "I've been eating. I can go for the little while longer it will take. You can't. Get up and get on me."

"The crack will get worse." Bobbi's eyes never left his.

"It will be only for a few hours. Until the tram line ends."

"And what is there?"

"A friend. Shelter, food."

Bobbi had not blinked, but the blue-white blaze vanished, and with it the man in the black silk shirt. She was staring up at Shane the wild horse, and the mustang had turned his head away.

Bobbi rolled to one side and got up off the ground with an effort. She steadied herself with one hand against the nearest tree.

"I hate to do it," she told Shane. "If I had any choice, I wouldn't."

There was no fallen tree nearby, and she knew she couldn't vault on from the ground this time. She walked as far as the next cut, holding onto Shane's mane at the withers to support herself. Then he stood partway down the bank and she eased onto his back from above.

That afternoon seemed very long.

Giving up her pride, Bobbi had laid her head on Shane's neck when she felt his already-slow walk turn yet slower, then stop. It took her a moment to gather the strength to sit up and open her eyes.

Shane stood within the last fringe of trees before a tiny mountain town: just a dozen tumbledown buildings, half of them empty, strung along a narrow, winding dirt road that vanished back into forest again. It was dusk. For some reason Bobbi noticed with great clarity the minute, white spring flowers blooming in the woods trash at Shane's feet. Yellow light glowed gently from the windows.

The woods pressed on the town the same way they pressed on the Yandro farm, so that the trees seemed to push the shacks and trailers, the vacant single-room store and the square wooden post office down the steep slopes toward the road and creek at the bottom. The nearest house, a plain, two-story frame house, stood half in forest. Its front porch faced the downhill slope and the town. Its back stoop stood hidden in laurel, and taller trees fingered its roof, leaving mossy marks.

Shane looked at the lay of the land a moment, then drifted forward as silently as a mountain cat toward the back stoop, that house.

Though she could not possibly have heard them coming, a square-built old woman came to the back door, the one facing the woods, and looked out at the twilight. She stood in the doorway with the light streaming through from behind her back; Bobbi could not see her properly, only her housedress and her smooth silver hair. Shane had stopped. The old woman turned her head, and Bobbi knew she had somehow perceived the black horse standing in the nightfall, and though Bobbi could not see the old woman's eyes, she felt as though they had looked on her naked.

The old woman beckoned, reached inside the door and turned off the brightest light, leaving the porch in near-darkness. Then she went back inside.

Shane carried Bobbi forward.

Straight up to the stoop he took her, and the fast, half-frightened beating of her heart gave her strength to dismount lightly, stand on her own and slip quietly in at the open door. The kitchen door. In the soft light coming through an inner door from what seemed to be a parlor, she could see the oilcloth-covered table, the ladder-back chairs. A good smell of cooked chicken greeted her. "Set down there at the table," a throaty old voice told her. But Bobbi froze where she was, on the braided rug. The old woman standing at the cookstove was the one she had seen in Shane's eyes.

Shane came in behind her, up the wooden porch steps and right into the house, and the old woman scuttled over and shut the door behind him.

PART 2

Witch Hazel

"The trickster must first win trust," the bearded man whispered to his wand at midnight. "It is tiresome, I know, my beauty, but 'twill be worth it in the end. And the years are short to an immortal."

The wand lay in his callused hands without moving or speaking. It was made of wood stolen centuries before from a tree in a cemetery in Italy, a cypress then already old, with its roots deep in the dead heart of a Borgia, stolen in the dark of the moon, rumor said, with a sacrifice of human blood. The staff was black with age, thick as a blacksmith's arm and very powerful, but still and mute as the tomb.

Bearded nearly to his waist, but with no mustache on his upper lip, the whisperer turned the death-wand in his hands. He caressed its steel-clad head between his palms. He murmured to it as if to a lover. Overhead hung a single dim, bare electric bulb, casting a sheen in the polished metal. The whisperer held the wand upright between his two hands, scrying in the steel, and there he saw a black stallion with a white brand on his neck and a tired girl on his back. And he saw an old woman in a mouse-colored hickory rocker, waiting.

He smiled and lowered the dark cudgel so that his shadow fell across it and the sheen in its metal sheathing dimmed. "I knew he would come to her when he needed help," he whispered. "I knew it before she knew it herself. Simple-minded old woman. Stupid with her own goodness." Whispering, he sibilated the words, sending forth stealthy, snakelike sounds into the night.

"Soon," he whispered to the wand. "Very soon, now. Goodnight, my beauty." Then with casual ease he passed one hard hand down the length of the wand while he held it in the other. Without even looking he laid it down, turned out the light and went away, out the large barn door, up the unlit yard to the house.

In the dark a cypress-handled hammer lay where he had left it, on the anvil.

Chapter Eight

Bobbi looked around uneasily for the walking stick and saw it in the next room, standing near the front door in a green ceramic urn shaped like an elephant's foot, along with several umbrellas. She turned her eyes away quickly and did not look at the staff again.

"Set down, Bobbi," the old woman repeated. "Ain't you hungry?" She placed a large bowl of homemade chicken corn soup on the table, then brought saltines.

Bobbi stood where she was, staring because she saw the form moving behind the form. More plainly than ever before, she saw it, and her head fuzzed in confusion; a stumpy old woman in a housedress stood before her, but another woman stood there as well: hunchbacked, in a robe of white calfskin edged with the fine fleece of lambs, in a pointed hat and lappets of white fox fur. A veil covered her face. Her flowing silver hair rippled down her back to below her waist, a thick waist rounded by a belt of silver links; on each link was etched a mystic sign. From the belt hung a gleaming silver knife with no scabbard. On her spraddling feet were tall, white boots, fox-furred and leather-laced. In her white-gloved hand she held the sensate staff.

Though it neither moved nor spoke, Bobbi shook her head hard at the sight of the staff, sending her own hair flying across her eyes. When she blinked and looked again, only an old Pennsylvania Dutch woman stood on the braided rug, holding a box of crackers. But what she had seen—it was like nothing she had ever seen before, or imagined. She could not possibly have dreamed it out of her own mind.

"I know you're hungry," the old woman insisted, taking Bobbi's gesture for refusal.

Bobbi still didn't move, but for some reason she blurted out, "Shane has a cracked hoof."

"I know it." The old woman's eyes, Bobbi noted now that she could see her clearly, were of an odd amber-brown color, almost yellow.

"Epsom salts," said Bobbi breathlessly. "You have any Epsom salts? He should soak it in a bucket of warm water with Epsom salts in it."

"I'll take care of it. Stop your fussing." Rotating her whole thick body, the old woman turned toward the horse. "Go straight on through to the parlor, Shane. The drapes are drawn in there. One of them nosy neighbors of mine might see you in here wunst I turn a light on."

Shane walked through into the next room.

"This here's Seldom," added his hostess with rue-

ful amusement, "and folks watches out for each other
all day long. Seldom anything better to do."

Bobbi trailed after Shane. She felt spooked and did
not want to be separated from the horse, but what
she saw in the parlor spooked her more. Loose hay
lay strewn on the camelback sofa. Bales of it stood
stacked behind the glass-topped end tables, sweet-
smelling and greeny-gold under the glow of ginger
lamps in velvet-swagged shades. A metal bucket of
water and one of oats stood on the carpet. Shane
swung his haunches past a breakfront full of knick-
knacks, lowered his head to the oats and started to
eat.

Standing there and gawking, Bobbi felt more woozy
than ever. She wobbled back to the kitchen, sat
down in front of her cooling soup and started to
shovel at it with her spoon.

"Here," said the old woman rather sharply, "let
me heat that up for you."

Bobbi shook her head, then thought of being more
polite. Better be very polite to this person. "No,
thank you," she said, gulping soup with an effort.
"It's fine." Her voice came out strained and mumbling.

The old woman scooped the bowl away from in
front of her with a motion like that of a bear clawing
for grubs. Bobbi held her dripping spoon in one
hand, afraid to put it down even on the oilcloth. She
caught the drips in the palm of the other hand, and
she sat that way without moving as her hostess re-
heated the soup, tasted it, then finally stumped over
to the table and gave it back to her.

Bobbi ate. The old woman ponderously circled the
table and turned on a plastic wall lamp with a faded
motto on the shade, "Let there be light." Bobbi

watched her the whole time. The old woman was built like a cookstove: not fat, but short, flat-bosomed, thick-waisted and broad, with a capacious belly. Her legs, poking out from under her housedress, were set so far apart that they seemed like cookstove legs, canted, bowed and attached to her corners. She wore nylon stockings rolled brownly down to the tops of cheap, black vinyl slippers with a seam running up the center from the toe. A segment of her sturdy legs showed white and hairy between the nylons and the hem of her cotton housedress. She had three chins arching down her neck; wisps of caked cornstarch lay in the creases. Bobbi noticed that and the safety pin holding the front of the housedress together. She tried not to stare at the safety pin as the old woman sat down across from her and watched her spoon the soup.

"You want a glass of milk?"

"No, thank you." In fact, at the mention of milk she felt weak with longing, but the sharp, yellow-eyed gaze on her frightened Bobbi, making her feel as if that old-woman stare could see everything about her. Maybe it was the effect of food after extreme hunger, but she felt half sick. She set down her spoon in her bowl and demanded, "Who are you?"

"Hazel Fenstermacher's my name."

"Mrs. Fenstermacher—"

"Just call me Aunt Witchie. Everybody else does."

Bobbi stared, her breath taken away, as if someone had hit her in the stomach. After a moment the old woman understood and laughed, a quiet laugh, not unkind. "It ain't like that, Bobbi. They called me Witchie from little on up, because my name is Hazel,

see? Witch hazel." Witchie got up and brought her
the glass of milk anyway, even though Bobbi had said
she didn't want it. Aunt Witchie's arms swung out-
ward when she moved. She carried things with her
elbows pointing sideways.

"Thank you," Bobbi mumbled. She drank the milk
and finished her soup. Witchie sat on the rocker near
the cookstove.

"You can stop worrying about that motorcycle rider
Shane killed," the old woman said after a while.
"Them kind ain't going to the police. They buried
that body deep, and good riddance."

Bobbi set down her spoon, on the oilcloth this
time. "If you're not a witch," she burst out, "how do
you know so much about me and Shane? How come
you were expecting us?"

"I never said nothing about what I was or wasn't,"
Witchie replied. Her voice was low and filled with
phlegm, as gruff as her manners. "But for the matter
of knowing things, how did you know Shane's name?"

The abrupt question and the hazel-eyed stare that
came with it made Bobbi sweat and start to stammer.
"It—it's just—what I called him."

The old woman looked back at her out of a softly
folded face with shrewd eyes that knew better. "It's
what he is," she said. "Or part of him. It's his name.
Or one of them."

"But—what—"

What is he? she was going to blurt out. But Shane
appeared at the doorway between the kitchen and
the parlor, his blue eyes on Witchie, ears at a troubled sideward angle.

"He don't want us to talk about that right now,"
Witchie told Bobbi. "You want something else to

fress?" Eat, she meant. "I got some sweet bologna here, and red-beet eggs."

Bobbi shook her head.

"What's the matter, girl? Your tongue need scraped?"

It was hard to think of a reply to that. Bobbi said nothing. She really did not want anything more to eat. Her stomach, long deprived, was making an uproar over what she had already put in it.

"I guess you're tired. Better have a bath before you go to bed. Give me them filthy clothes, I'll wash them. What you want to sleep in?"

Bobbi said, "Anything." She ruefully expected that her hostess would loan her an old woman's nightie, frumpy and several sizes too large. At home—but it wasn't her home any longer, she remembered, her gut twisting; too much food, she told herself—when she had a bed to sleep in, she usually slept in a man's teeshirt in the summer, boys' flannel pajamas in the winter. The pajama legs always twisted up around her crotch, and she hated them.

Witchie was looking at her. Almost defiantly, Bobbi looked back.

Abruptly, and without another word, Witchie swung into action. She heaved herself out of the rocker and beckoned Bobbi to follow her upstairs. While Bobbi waited uncertainly in the cluttered spare bedroom, she stumped up another steep flight of stairs to the attic and came down a moment later carrying a gown that took Bobbi's breath.

"I can't wear that!" she exclaimed, though in fact the gown called to something unacknowledged inside her and her body sent up a warm flush, a tingle of excitement, in answer. A long spill of rose-colored satin . . .

"Why the hun not?" Witchie snapped. She dumped the gown on the bed as if it were so much clean laundry, and waited to take Bobbi's clothes away for washing. In her bent old hands, Bobbi noted, she held a brand-new, large-size cannister of Epsom salts, brought down from the attic under the nightgown.

"Jesus!" Bobbi wailed. "I forgot!" She started out of the room, bound downstairs to tend to Shane's cracked hoof.

"Get your bath and git to bed!" Aunt Witchie barked. "Crimony, girl, I can heave a bucket of water. I ain't a cripple yet."

After taking her bath in the big, claw-footed tub, after combing her wet hair and carefully French-braiding it and using the toothbrush Witchie had given her, Bobbi put on the long nightgown. The rounded tops of her breasts showed bare over dusky-rose lace. Satin seemed to embrace and caress her belly, buttocks, thighs. She knew without needing a mirror that she was beautiful. She went to bed, warm under the cathedral-window quilt, and placed a hand on her breasts and one on the small mound between her legs before she thought of Witchie. Then she moved her hands away from the places that felt good and waited for sleep, trying not to think any more about the strange old woman who seemed to see into the hidden places of her mind. . . .

When she woke up in the morning she found lying across the foot of her bed a pair of slim-cut jeans, a western shirt, buckskin moccasin boots, blue socks and blue nylon briefs, all brand new and all like something out of her dream image of herself, though she had hardly known until that moment that she had one. No bra. How did Witchie know she hated bras? She stared at the clothes a moment, then let them lie and stomped barefoot downstairs in her low-cut satin-and-lace nightgown. Shane was just coming back into the parlor from outside—through the back door, screened by brush, he could go out to relieve himself without much danger of being seen. He lifted his head when he caught sight of Bobbi and looked at her intently, but Bobbi paid no attention. She had forgotten how she looked; she wanted only to confront Witchie.

In the kitchen she found the old woman mixing batter, just somebody's gray-haired grandmother, a puttering old woman—Bobbi refused any longer to be fooled.

"You looked inside my head," she accused.

"Huh," Witchie acknowledged. "Do them things fit?"

Bobbi stamped her bare foot, hurting it on the linoleum floor, then suddenly stopped being angry. Instead, she felt oddly desolate, and confused. "I give up. I don't understand you. Where did you get them?"

"Where I got your nightgown. In the attic."

Brand-new size-eleven Jordaches, with the tags still on them, in the attic? Bobbi felt cold and tried to joke. "You have a shopping mall up there, or what?"

The old woman just looked at her with those strange yellow eyes.

Bobbi whispered, "You're a witch."

"I'm just an old pow-wow woman, Bobbi." A healer, she meant. The Pennsylvania Dutch called their old-style healers pow-wows. "I'm the seventh daughter of a seventh daughter. I got Indian blood in me, way

back. Have some scrapple while you're waiting for
the pancakes."

"No," said Bobbi. Fear made her sound rude, but
Witchie seemed more amused than offended.

"You think I'm trying to fatten you up before I pop
you in the oven?" Witchie laughed. Her laugh, low-
pitched and pleasantly husky, sounded quite unlike a
cartoon witch's cackle. When she was done laughing
she said, "I won't eat you, Bobbi. If you burn yourself I can draw out the fire, and if you cut yourself I
can stop the bleeding. I can pow-wow warts and
children's ailments. Sometimes I help people when
the doctors can't, and sometimes the doctors help
them when I can't. I don't deceive nobody nor take
their money. I don't hold with burnt chicken feet
buried under the eaves and *Himmels-brief* charms
and all that gibberish. I can dowse for water and
things people lost, but people don't always like me. If
they ask me, I tell them the truth, not what they
want to hear. A witch has to refuse money to be
honest. I do curses, but not for pay or nobody's
say-so." Her tone turned dark but quiet, like a still
river under tall trees. "Wunst I am sure, I hex what
is evil."

Witchie was strong, Bobbi felt sure of it. She heard
it in the dark, quiet voice. Witchie had powers she
wasn't telling.

The thought frightened her into a cold sweat. Even
her own strange visions had never frightened her as
much. She turned away, not knowing where to go,
and found that her bare feet were carrying her into
the other room, where Shane was. She hurried up to
him and laid her hand on his hard, black shoulder for
protection, like a chased child in a game no longer

fun, as if touching her base would make her safe. "Shane," she appealed to him, and his head came up from his hay, his vivid eyes met hers, but there was nothing in them to still her fears.

Witchie followed her into the parlor, wiping her hands on her flour-sack apron. She said, "It ain't easy for him to talk to you. Takes a lot out of him. Just wait a minute." Elbows out and swinging purposefully, legs taking wide strides, Witchie crossed the room to the umbrella urn and reached for her walking stick.

Bobbi felt her legs turn weak, and clutched at Shane's mane for support. "No!" she gasped—and then her fear was lost in astonishment, for Shane had turned his handsome black head and gently nuzzled her. Telling her not to be afraid, that did not surprise her, but . . . there was something of affection. . . .

And then Witchie was holding the walking stick up in front of her, though not too fearsomely close. Above its silver ferrule the small, round, smoky-clear handle seemed to glow and swirl. Roundness disappeared; Bobbi saw something like a soft gray mist swirling and glowing in a quiet sunrise. And then she saw the man dressed in black.

That was all she was to remember about his clothing afterward: that it was black and fitted his broad shoulders and slim legs beautifully. The broadbrimmed black hat, was it the hat of a Spanish rider, a western gunslinger, a riverboat gambler, a gentleman from the deep south? Did he wear a cloak, or some sort of elegant jacket? She couldn't remember. She did recall a glint of white at his throat. But for the most part her gaze was caught on his face, the face she had seen only once before, and on his ice-blue, fiery eyes.

"Bobbi," he said.

It was as if he stood before her at a small distance, in a misty place she could not name, an anyplace. Walking stick, horse, hay-cluttered parlor and Aunt Witchie had all disappeared, and though Bobbi still felt mane and hard muscle under her hand, she was not conscious of them.

"Bobbi," the man in black said, "you were never afraid of me, and I've killed more men than Mrs. Fenstermacher."

She swallowed. What was he saying, now that they could finally, truly talk? "Shane?" she faltered. "Is that your real name?"

"As real as any of them."

"But—who are you?"

"I never tell anyone that. Not even you, Bobbi."

"He's Shane." Aunt Witchie's voice sounded plainly to Bobbi, though she either couldn't or didn't see her standing nearby. "He's the gunfighter who gave away his heart. Besides that, he's Zorro. And Rhett Butler. And Paladin, the black knight, and Hal, the tavern prince, and a hundred more."

Stories. Misty legends, tales told around hearthfires, forms in the flames, no more. Insubstantial forms seen beyond what was real. Yet Shane was as real as the hard, supporting withers under her hand. And Witchie—what was Witchie?

"Even in movies." The old woman's voice sounded dry and disapproving. "Han Solo and them. Copies."

"They're entitled," said Shane, or said the man with the blue eyes blazing under the black hat.

"They're miserable shadows."

"It doesn't matter." Shane's eyes held steady on Bobbi, like blue flames with no wind blowing, and in a crazy moment she knew that he was even stronger than Witchie, yet more vulnerable. She knew that she could hurt him—no. Fear clawed her at the thought. But she knew that someone had hurt him, sometime.

"Why are you a mustang?" she whispered.

"How else can a man roam free any more?"

She knew that there was more to it than that, much more to drive him to the harsh life of a wild horse running on the upland plains of Wyoming. In an eerie, wordless way, yet as clearly as she knew anything about him, she understood that his being a wild, black stallion had something to do with women, or a woman. She knew it because she stood beside him in a low-cut, rose-colored gown. She was not a woman yet, not really, but a virginal girl still, horse-crazy; she had never wanted anything to do with men. But the way she loved wild horses . . . intuitively she knew the truth: it was the same way women loved a certain sort of man.

Wanting to touch him and tame him and make him their own, heart and soul, and no one else's. . . .

She pressed one hand to her head as she clung to black mane with the other, pressed her palm against her forehead and eyes as if trying to force down what she was seeing and thinking.

"Bobbi. What's the matter?"

"Shane . . . Nothing."

He said, "Tell me. It's my fault you're in this mess."

"It—it's not that. I feel like I'm going crazy."

Witchie's throaty old voice came through to her again, like the voice of an offstage narrator. "A person has to have madness or poetry in them to see in my walking stick. You got both, Bobbi. Your father was a poet, did you know that?"

"No," Bobbi mumbled, though she did know, if only lately, though in fact it was her dead father and his poetry who had gotten her in "this mess." No, she said, because at that moment she wanted nothing to do with madness or magic or any of what was happening to her. She had closed her eyes, leaning against the horse, and everything looked as black as the black shoulder under her head.

Shane the man-legend said, "You were the only one who could see me, Bobbi. Who could see what I am."

Witchie said to Shane, "She needs time, Dark Stranger."

Bobbi heard the old woman's slippers shuffling as she crossed the room to return the walking stick to its urn. Opening her eyes, Bobbi saw hay-strewn parlor again, and a black horse, and found that she was clinging to the mustang's neck with both arms. Abashed, she turned away and went up to her room to put on her new clothes.

They fit perfectly. She went back down to the kitchen, where she and Witchie ate scrapple and pancakes with maple syrup Witchie had made herself, boiling the sap from the huge sugar-trees that nodded over her roof. Bobbi changed the soak for Shane's foot, and watched for a moment as the black mustang set his hoof in the bucket of fresh warm water and Epsom salts, carefully, so as not to upset it on Mrs. Fenstermacher's parlor carpet. Then she went and offered to do the dishes. Witchie turned on a huge, old TV in the parlor and settled into a front-room rocker, a cane-and-ladderback one, to watch the late morning news.

Time, Bobbi was thinking. Sloshing around with her hands in warm dishwater soothed her, and so did her full stomach. Her aches from too much bareback riding were disappearing. Time was a heal-all. It took care of things no pow-wow woman could.

". . . Bobbi Yandro," the TV said, startling Bobbi so badly that she squeaked. At first she thought the television was—bewitched, though she hated even to think the word. Peculiar, as some other things in this house seemed to be. Talking to her. But then, peering through the door to the parlor, she saw her school-picture face flashed on the screen as the familiar Pittsburgh announcer went on with the news story about her.

". . . no recent developments in the disappearance of the Canadawa County girl. State police have expanded their search to include the Scubber's Creek and Parsimony areas following a report by an area man that he saw a girl on a dark-colored horse crossing I-72 on the Bell School Road overpass in Blessing Township early yesterday morning. The massive search effort in the Canadawa and Mandawa Mountain area has been called off, since it is now believed that the girl is not in fact lost, but ran away following a dispute with her grandfather. Anyone who has seen Bobbi Yandro, or who may have information concerning her whereabouts, is urged to contact . . ."

Bobbi found that her feet had carried her into the parlor as she listened. Shane had gone rigid, his head lifted high. Witchie turned the set off. "They'll be

putting your picture on milk cartons next," she remarked to Bobbi. "And grocery sacks."

Bobbi asked, "How far from here are those places?
Scubber's Creek? Parsimony?"

"Not far."

With a dry mouth Bobbi said, "We don't have
time, then. For Shane's foot to heal. For whatever it
is that I need time for."

Chapter Nine

Witchie did a peculiar thing. She heaved herself up out of the rocker, whisked the oilcloth off the kitchen table and plopped it in a corner, then got four new, white candles out of the drawer of a huge, carved, claw-footed, great-bellied, oval-mirrored, dark-veneered, monstrously imposing piece of furniture called a buffet. She put the candles in star-shaped glass holders, the kind sold at McCrory's, and set them at the corners of the square slab of oak, the tabletop.

"Girl's right," she remarked to the house at large, perhaps to her walking stick or to Shane. "There ain't much time. By tomorrow old Ethel Schroyer next door will be on the phone wanting to know why don't I pull the parlor blinds, am I sick. And when I tell her I got the grippe, she'll be over here with some fool thing to eat, in a bowl I got to wash and return. And she don't miss much, so she ain't likely to miss noticing a horse in the parlor. Bobbi, come here. Set there."

She placed Bobbi in a chair at the table, facing the window. She lit the candles and turned on the lamp that said "Let There Be Light."

"This is to tell you what you ought to do," she explained to Bobbi, "or to help you make up your mind what to do, however you want to look at it." Out of the buffet drawer Witchie pulled a deck of cards.

They were the oddest cards Bobbi had ever seen. They were circular. And as Witchie fumbled through them, looking for something, Bobbi glimpsed pictures on them, and the bright-colored, symmetrical hex designs she had sometimes seen on old barns.

Witchie found the circle she was looking for and handed it to Bobbi. It was a perfectly plain, empty white circle of rich-feeling, heavy rag paper. A white nothing. A naught.

"That's the innocent," Witchie told her. "The petitioner. That's you. Put it in the middle of the table. Smack dab in the middle, now."

Bobbi turned the white circle over and around in her fingers, feeling serious in spite of herself. "Does it matter which side is up?" she asked Witchie.

"That one, no, it don't matter which side or how you turn it, long as it's right in the middle."

Bobbi placed the card. It lay like a white zero against the dark wood, and Witchie handed Bobbi the rest of the cards.

"Don't look at 'em. Look at the light while you shuffle 'em."

Bobbi mixed up the cards as best she could. It was hard to handle them. Their circular shape made them seem to have minds of their own. "Is that enough?" she asked after a while.

"I can't say," Witchie replied. "You say."

Bobbi glanced at her. The old woman's face was set in quiet folds, and her braided hair lay calm and sleek in loops around her head, but her yellow eyes glinted bright as sunlight. Bobbi handed the cards back to her, and Witchie laid them out.

She laid them with care in a certain pattern and order. When she was finished, they made a large wheel with twelve spokes, and Bobbi's white card formed the hub.

"Tell me what you see," Witchie said to Bobbi.

There were faces on some of the cards, or stylized drawings of people, animals or birds. Some of the cards were simple discs of a solid, bright color. Others were painted with vivid hex designs or the primitive, exuberant flower-forms called fraktur lilies. Also, Bobbi saw later, there were pictures of a crown, a six-pointed star, a sun, a moon, a water cup, a five-pointed star and a black heart. But at the time she noticed none of those. Her glance was caught on one circle which showed a man in black clothing riding a black horse. Even in the tiny ink drawing she seemed to see the fire of blue eyes.

"Shane!" she exclaimed to Witchie, pointing.

The old woman nodded. "The hero in black. He's at the juncture of a spoke. He's important, but you've put him off to one side. What else do you see?"

Bobbi scanned the dazzle of bright colors and designs, searching for something familiar. Then her finger shot to the image of a veiled, hunchbacked woman

with some sort of stick or staff in her hand. "That's
you," she said.

"Huh," said Witchie, taken aback but not caring to
show it much. "That's the sorceress, all right. How'd
you know?"

"I saw her! Or you. Right when I first came in."
Bobbi felt cold, telling Witchie what she had always
hidden from everyone else, but she could not seem
to stop herself. "In a white robe with fleece on it, and
pointed hat and veil like that, and a silver belt with,
like, hieroglyphics."

"Runes." Witchie was giving her a sharp look. "My
stars, girl. You have the sight. That's how you knowed
Shane, ain't it, by seeing him in his true form. What
else ain't you telling me?"

Bobbi jerked her gaze away from Witchie's and
looked down at her hands, not speaking.

"You see things like that often?"

Bobbi didn't say anything. Witchie peered at her.
"You saw yourself, I'm the white witch," she complained. "I ain't going to hurt you."

"I don't want to talk about it!" Bobbi flared.

"Whatever." Without reacting to Bobbi's tone,
Witchie turned back to the cards. "Where were we.
You found me, and I'm ascendant. That means I'm
not real important to you right now, though I could
be. Pay attention, Bobbi. What else do you see?"

Bobbi blinked and looked at the cards again, pointing to the first one that caught her eye. "Who's that?"
Her hand hovered over the picture of a straight-
browed, golden-haired young man.

"That's the golden hero. He's ascendant, too. So's
magic." Witchie indicated the five-pointed star, located midway up one of the spokes.

"There's the distelfink." Bobbi had spotted the familiar bird.

"That's your luck, and it's low right now." The bird was located at the base of a spoke near the bottom of the wheel. "The old trickster, the villain, he's at the rim, and I don't like that." Witchie indicated the black heart. "But you've put him in opposition to Shane, so maybe that's all right."

The villain. "Grandpap," said Bobbi darkly.

"Guess again. Look who you put right at the top. The most important person in the world to you."

Bobbi looked, and saw the picture of a dragon perched on a mountaintop with strong handlike claws, a dragon with gray hair and a face through which a human face looked, form behind the form—she knew that face. She felt a jolt and a rush of fear, anger, hatred, something else, a tangle of emotions so strong that it set her shaking. She started to jump from her chair to run away—Witchie's bent, bony hand on her shoulder prevented her.

"Grandpap," Bobbi whispered. And she saw, plainly drawn on the heavy circle of paper, the form she had seen behind his form so many times, misted with her own fear. The huge thing jagged as the mountains. The dragon.

"The old man of the mountain," said Witchie, nodding. "Grant Yandro don't know himself what he is, or he won't. The dragon is strong and *dickeppich*, stubborn. Wrongheaded sometimes. Be glad he is not your enemy, Bobbi."

"But he is!" Bobbi shouted. "I hate him!"

Witchie pointed. Between Bobbi and the old man, ascendant on the spoke, lay the bright red heart of love.

"It's a lie! He don't love me, or he couldn't have said what he did." Tears stung Bobbi's eyes at the thought. Angrily she blinked them back.

"Huh," Witchie grumped. "I guess you never said nothing you didn't mean."

"Not like that! Not to hurt somebody."

"You're hurting him a lot worse, and punishing him, by staying away from him, and you know it."

"I don't care! I won't go back to him. I hate him!" Her own vehemence made Bobbi start to sob, though she hated to cry in front of anyone. Shane put his head through from the parlor and looked at Witchie as if to tell her to ease off. The old woman glared back at him.

"She's got to hear the truth!" Witchie declared.

From the parlor came a low, flat voice. "She needs time. As you said before."

Bobbi stiffened and stopped crying instantly at the sound of the eerie voice. But Witchie was outraged. "Kabilde, you just keep out of this!" Mrs. Fenstermacher shouted at her walking stick.

The same voice said, "Try to make me. And stop trying to tell the girl what to do. She will go back to her grandfather when she is ready."

"I couldn't go back to him even if I wanted to!" Bobbi burst out. "He would geld Shane!"

A peculiar silence settled over kitchen and parlor. Shane stood without moving. Witchie breathed heavily, but the angry color faded out of her face.

"What I would like to say," Witchie said to Bobbi at last, very quietly, meeting the girl's eyes, "what I thought I could say, is, Shane ain't your concern. I know the Dark Rider. He's a loner. He prefers to take care of himself, and he don't want anybody looking out for him, least of all a slip of a girl. But I can't say none of that, because of this."

Her forefinger, knobby with age, pointed at the card lying between Bobbi's and Shane's. Thin ink-strands on it made a convoluted knotwork pattern Bobbi did not understand.

"What's that?"

"Entanglement."

"What's it mean?"

"Your life is tangled up with his somehow."

I could have told you that, Bobbi thought.

Leaning over the table, Witchie studied the bright-colored circles of cardboard a while longer, moving her hand slowly from one to another.

"You got a gift, girl," she said to Bobbi with a thoughtful look out of hooded, hazel-colored eyes. "More than you know. You've put almost all the Twelve of the Hidden Circle on the rim. At the junctures of the spokes, yet. See, here's the poet. That's your father."

The picture was that of a unicorn drawn in the Pennsylvania Dutch style, big-browed, puppy-eyed and winsome. Bobbi studied it silently. It told her no more than any image of Wright Yandro ever had.

Witchie added, "And here's your mother, with the lightning bolt linked to her. That means either madness or inspiration. And here you are, the virgin. At least I expect you're a virgin. You've put yourself in the same spoke as the golden hero."

"I thought I was the innocent," Bobbi objected.

"Can't you be more than one thing? One time or another, you'll be most of them, won't you? Here's the king and the jester down at the bottom. But this puzzles me." Witchie fingered a circle of bright, featureless red. "It mean anything to you?"

Bobbi shook her head. The red circle lay at the juncture of a spoke with the rim, the next such juncture down from the image of the hero in black.

"It should be linked with something, but it's not. It's off by itself. And it's important. Think, youngster."

Bobbi said, "All it makes me think of is blood."

"Death is not in the ascendant."

"Thank God," said Bobbi sourly. She felt bone tired, though it was still morning. Her mind was so full she couldn't think. Witch Hazel looked at her for a moment, then said, "Huh. I guess that's the best we're going to do, and it's not as much help as I had hoped. Blow out the candles." Carefully the old woman gathered up the cards and tidied them into a cylindrical deck.

"I wish I could do for Shane, too," she muttered, "but he can't mix the cards. And I doubt he would let me even if he could."

The middle of the day passed in an odd, becalmed silence. Shane stood motionless in the parlor, resting his cracked hoof but not dozing. The walking stick named Kabilde stood in its urn. An old, wooden, mission-style clock ticked on the wall. In counter-rhythm to it, mouse-colored rockers creaked under Witchie's weight. Bobbi went upstairs and lay on her bed for a while, then came down and helped Mrs. Fenstermacher make macaroni salad for lunch. She and Witchie ate it along with brick-red honey bologna and beet-red pickled eggs and applesauce brown with cinnamon, all in near-silence. Afterward, Bobbi did the dishes and Witchie sat in the kitchen rocker again, rocking some more.

Bobbi went and got the bucket Shane soaked his foot in off its towel on the parlor carpet, dumped the

water that had cooled in it, refilled it with very warm
water and put in a generous sifting of Epsom salts.
She lugged it back to the parlor and remained crouching by it as Shane came toward her to soak his foot.
The black mustang was scarcely hobbling.

She said to him, "Let me see."

Another time, maybe, he would have argued the
matter with her in his way. But there had been
enough tumult in the day. Without demur, he placed
his cracked forehoof on her knee for her to look at,
and she reached up and turned on a table lamp so
that she could see it better.

The day before, she knew, the crack had been
oozing pus and blood. And even considering the drawing action of repeated Epsom salts soakings, she knew
it had no business looking so clean, so soon. She had
seen hoof injuries before. They took days to treat.

"Aunt Witchie!" she called toward the kitchen.
"Did you pow-wow this hoof?"

Shane took his foot off her knee and placed it
carefully in its bath.

"Course I did." The old woman's voice floated back
crankily, as if Witchie had been awakened from a
doze. "Might help, and can't possibly harm. What of
it?"

Bobbi's Yandro upbringing told her that fair was
fair, and credit belonged where credit was due. She
got up, went to the doorway where she could look at
the old woman and said, "I've never seen a hoof dry
up so fast."

"Huh," said Witchie, gratified and grumpy. "For
all the good it'll do. He can't walk far on it, can he?"

Bobbi shook her head. If he was going to be a
horse, Shane needed the attention of a good farrier.

Even if he could stay in one place and rest until his hoof had grown out, he would need trimming. If he could not stay in one place, he needed to be shod. But that was impossible. Any farrier who watched TV would turn them both over to the police. Bobbi shook her head again and turned her attention to what was possible.

"You got a brush and comb I could use on Shane? If he'll let me."

"Look up in the attic."

The attic. A glint in the old witch's eye. Bobbi sensed a test, turned without a word and went. She felt edgy, climbing the steep stairs. It was dim up there in the attic. Why old people insisted on using 25-watt bulbs in ceiling fixtures, she would never understand. In the jaundiced light, Bobbi saw cardboard boxes, a hideous old lamp, a cane chair with the bottom broken through, a few more pieces of furniture. Nothing that looked like brush or comb, and certainly nothing that looked like brand-new clothing her size. She groped at the top of an old dresser. No comb. She opened the dresser's top drawer.

There in the drawer lay three kinds of expensive, leather-and-natural-bristle horse brushes, and two sorts of metal horse combs. And nothing else. In the very first drawer she had opened. It was uncanny. What would Hazel Fenstermacher be doing with horse brushes, anyway?

She took the things out of the drawer, closed it, and stood thinking. After a moment she opened the same drawer again. It was empty, but what had she expected? She opened another. It was empty.

If I had any sense I'd get out of here, Bobbi

thought. But she did not leave. She felt nettled, as if someone were daring her.

Hoof treatment, she decided. She opened the top drawer again. A small, unopened can of hoof oil awaited her.

"Yah!" Bobbi exclaimed involuntarily. She left the petroleum-based hoof dressing, took the other things and hurried downstairs. But before she came within sight of Witchie again, she took care to regain her poise.

"Shane," she asked urbanely, entering the parlor with brush in hand, "may I?"

He turned his head toward her, and his eyes gave assent.

She spent most of the afternoon and part of the evening grooming him. Though it took hours, she combed all the tangles out of his mane and tail. She went back to the attic for a currycomb, curried all the rough and ragged places off his shoulders and sides, then brushed him smooth. She borrowed Witchie's smallest scissors and trimmed his fetlocks and whiskers. She made him shine like silk, then used the hoof dressing and oiled his hooves, even the cracked one, until they shone as well. She made a dandy out of him. Shane held his head low, his neck flexed toward her, and Bobbi hummed as she worked, feeling the sweet touch of intimacy.

There was nothing new on the evening report about the missing Bobbi Yandro and her horse. Going to bed that night in the rosy satin nightgown, Bobbi slipped its long skirt up around her hips and lay with her hand between her legs, her other hand at her breasts under their flimsy covering of dusky lace, no longer caring what Witchie knew. She fell asleep that way and dreamed of Shane. Not the mustang. The stranger dressed in black.

Chapter Ten

On the morning news, also, there was no new development regarding the missing Canadawa County girl. Bobbi felt an odd, floating sensation, a suspension, an abeyance, as if she might not have to run any farther, she could stay hidden in Witchie's house forever, finding food and whatever she needed in the dresser drawer in the attic—and all the time knowing the feeling was false, she was becalmed in the eye of a storm, something could happen at any moment to hurl her back into the cyclone outside. Moreover, hiding was not what she wanted of her life. She knew that, though she had no idea what she did want. Her future seemed less real than her trickster hope of being let alone.

She ate hot sticky buns with Witchie for breakfast. Then the old woman sat on the hickory rocker while

Bobbi cleared the few dishes off the table and rinsed the syrupy plates.

Witchie said suddenly, "Bobbi." She waited until Bobbi turned and looked at her, wet plate in hand, before she went on. "Leave them dishes," she said. "It's been a long time since anybody's helped me with my hair. I wonder if you would. Comb and brush are up on my vanity."

Bobbi said, "Sure," dried her hands and went. The comb and brush sat just where Witchie had said they would be, on the rosewood hand mirror atop the dressing table in her room. The comb was carved out of real tortoiseshell. The brush was marked "pure bristle." Both were perfectly clean. Bobbi looked at them a moment and at the bedroom with its wedding ring quilt and dust ruffle and hand-embroidered dresser scarves, remembering her own messy room in the Yandro cabin, her plastic comb always gray-brown with hair crud, the purple brush she had bought at a discount store. Then, feeling as if she should light candles, she took brush and comb downstairs along with the rosewood mirror.

Black metal hairpins gathered into a pile on the kitchen counter. Witchie's gray hair, when she and Bobbi let it down over the back of the rocker, reached nearly to the floor and shaded from silver-white near the scalp to a dark ashy gray at the trailing ends. With gentle, quiet motions of her hands, Bobbi combed and brushed Witchie's hair while the old woman sat with her own knobby hands lying like sleeping kittens in her lap. The hair smelled faintly of Witchie, just as a horse smells of itself; it was not an unpleasant or unnatural smell. Bobbi brushed it for a long time, until it lay smooth and took on a pewtery sheen. Finally she parted it to braid it.

Witchie said, "I wonder could you start the braids up top, the way you do yours. I'm curious how you do that."

French braiding. Bobbi smiled, pleased to be able to show Witchie something the old woman didn't know. She did her own hair in a single, thick French braid starting near her forehead, but she would do Witchie's with a braid on each side. She straightened the center part and started the first braid. The silent working of her own fingers put her in a sort of trance, and she found, without much thinking about it, that she wanted to ask the questions that had seemed too fearsome the day before.

She asked, "Aunt Witchie, who are the Twelve of the Hidden Circle?"

Witchie said, "Them's the dark hero and the golden hero and the king, the virgin, the madonna, and the old sorceress, the villain, the fool, the poet, the old man of the mountain, the jester, and Lady Death."

"But—Shane's the dark hero, and he's real. You're the old sorceress. I'm the virgin, you said, and Grandpap's the old man of the mountain, and we're all real."

"What else would we be?"

"You know what I mean."

"There's lots of us right around here," Witchie admitted. "Something about these mountains. Old bone in them. Goes deep. People remember, the dead haunt."

"Is Shane from around here?"

"The Dark Rider is one who went away from wherever he was born, so long ago nobody knows where he's from. Far away. He's a wanderer by nature, the Stranger. *Schooslich*. Restless. Wherever he comes, he don't stay for long."

Bobbi plaited silver-gray hair in silence.

"But there's more to the Hidden Circle than the Twelve," Witchie added. "And we're everywhere. We're in all the people who dream, all over the world."

Bobbi finished the braids, crossed them and coiled them, pinned them in place, and handed Witchie the mirror. "They make a sort of crown," she said.

Witchie looked and nodded with a wordless grunt of satisfaction. She said, "Makes it a little easier to believe I used to be pretty when I was young."

Bobbi was feeling somehow better than she had in days. She said, "Tell me about my father."

"I didn't know your father, Bobbi."

Bobbi stared. Something had made her think Witchie did.

The old woman said, "I knew of him, was all. I read his poem in the newspaper, and I knew he understood, he was one of the special ones. Then I read a couple of years later where he died."

Bobbi thought. "He didn't write about you," she admitted, "but he wrote about your—stick."

"He understood, is all. You got to keep in mind, Kabilde is as—as various as Shane. Its name means, 'Cunning Man.' It's been a necromancer, a doctor, a con artist, a—"

Interrupting, Bobbi blurted in horror, "You mean, it has a—a human form, too?"

"Of course. We all do."

Wild thoughts swooped through Bobbi's mind. If

she was looking at Witchie's human form, then what—no. She didn't want to know.

With a soft clop of unshod hooves, Shane came from the parlor through the kitchen and nosed his way out the back door. Bobbi watched after him until the black horse, flanks shining since she had groomed him, disappeared in the woods. Turning her head with difficulty on her stumpy body, Witchie looked after him too.

Witchie said, "The form Shane's in right now, it belongs to him, same as you belong to you. But there's a problem. He's—well, he's stuck."

"How'd that happen?" Though she had just seen Shane go out, Bobbi kept her voice low, as if the mustang-man still stood in the next room, his foot soaking in a bucket. "How come he's stuck being a horse?"

"I can't tell you, Bobbi, I can tell you my story, or your story, but you'll have to ask Shane to tell you his."

Bobbi said, "Tell me yours, then. How did you come to be a—a—" Something Yandro in her choked on saying "witch."

"A pow-wow?" Witchie smiled a dry old smile, wrinkling her face into soft folds. Then the folds smoothed as she eyed Bobbi soberly. "It come to me late in life," she said. "I think a person has to go through a sort of choice. I was married to Abe Fenstermacher near to forty years, and never had no children, and never did nothing but do for him, and when the black lung took him I figured I might just as well die myself."

Bobbi was still holding the tortoiseshell comb and oak-backed brush, staring at the old woman, who looked gravely back at her. Witchie nodded. "Them was bad times," she said. "I near to done something foolish. But I had a choice, you see, and it come to me that I might better live and be myself, my whole self, since I couldn't be the better half of Abe Fenstermacher no more. And then I begun to feel the power."

"I see," said Bobbi faintly, though she didn't really, and the word "power" frightened her.

"That was ten years ago," said Witchie.

Shane nosed open the back door and came in again, looked at Bobbi a moment with his head held high, then went on into the parlor.

Bobbi said awkwardly, "Just ten years? I mean, the stories I heard made it sound like you'd been here a long time."

"Must have been another hex witch of Seldom," Witchie said.

It seemed odd that so small a place would have had more than one pow-wow. But Bobbi had had enough talk, and did not pursue it. Turning away, she took the comb and brush and rosewood hand mirror back upstairs to Witchie's bedroom. When she came down, the old woman was sitting in the parlor rocker. And near Witchie's feet, flat on the carpet, lay the walking stick.

Bobbi stopped where she was, staring like a spooked colt at Kabilde, the stick that spoke.

"Step over it," Witchie told her.

Bobbi gave her a look. "What for?"

"Just do it. You afraid?"

The dare was so blatant that Bobbi continued to balk. "No! But why should I do what you say?"

Witchie harrumphed, but before she could speak

Kabilde cut in from its place on the floor. "So the crazy old termagant will let me up, is why." Its voice was dry, stinging and without texture, like smoke. Nothing about it moved or changed except the tiny mouth of the carved hazelwood snake. "Do what she says, youngster. It won't hurt one way or the other."

Bobbi liked the sound of that last even less than she liked stepping over the weird stick. Yet she found herself walking forward. She stepped over the staff squarely, at its middle—pride would not let her do otherwise. And as she passed over it, an odd, dislocated sense washed through her body, something not at all painful yet so uncomfortable that she squeaked and her hands shot up. She could see them for an instant, hovering in front of her face, her hands—but they were not hers. They seemed made of mist, curled and curved and white as crescent moons, and they—they belonged to someone else—

Then she was over Kabilde, and herself again, and furious at Witchie. "What's the big idea!" she demanded, backing away from the staff.

"Just as I thought," Witchie said as if to Shane or Kabilde or the parlor walls, not reacting to Bobbi's anger. The old woman picked up Kabilde, got up from her rocker with a grunt and crossed the room to replace her walking stick in its urn before she said more. Then she turned and stated, "You're a potent one, youngster. You can do things I can't."

Bobbi grew more puzzled than angry. Witchie looked very serious, yet she couldn't understand what the old woman was talking about. She said with only a small edge to her voice, "Like what?"

"My golly days, girl!" Witchie shuffled back to her rocker, irritated. "Ain't you noticed you got powers?"

"All I've ever noticed is I got craziness."

"That's part of it. You stop shrinking back from that, Bobbi, and learn to use it, and you'll be able to do just about anything."

Shane stood with his foot in its warm bath, listening, and Bobbi felt a sudden tingle of hope. Including —healing Shane's cracked hoof in one moment, as if it had never been hurt? Including—bringing him back to being a man again?

If she could do those things for Shane, it would all be worth it, whatever she had to go through.

"How?" she demanded. "How do I learn to use it?"

Witchie's soft old face moved almost into a smile. She leaned forward in her rocker and started to speak.

The telephone rang.

Shane's head came sharply up from his hay. Bobbi stiffened, staring at the phone. Witchie looked at it as if it were a buzzing, poisonous black insect sitting atop the white lace doily of her drop-leaf table. Then she reached out to answer it.

From where they stood, listening, Shane and Bobbi heard the cicada-noises of the voice on the other end. Then Witchie pointed and rolled her eyes. It was Ethel next door, wanting to know what was wrong at the Fenstermacher place, that the blinds were drawn and yesterday's newspaper still on the front porch, as if no one had been in or out.

"I'm entitled to be sick and lazy!" Witchie complained. "Yes. The grippe. No, I don't want you to pick up my mail. It's never nothing but bills. Just let it set."

After more of Ethel's shrilling, she grumpily declined all assistance and hung up. Bobbi let out her

breath as if she had been holding it. She looked at
Witchie, then at Shane; the two of them were staring
at each other. But oddly, it was Kabilde who first
spoke.

In its glassy-smooth voice, as startling as a snake
coming through the parlor, the walking stick said,
"Time you three decided what this side of hell you're
doing."

There was a sound like a small explosion, and the
smoky-glass handle of the cane started to glow, and
Shane the man appeared in it as if on a tiny television
screen. "No need for Witchie to do a thing more," he
said. "She done enough."

"I'll speak for myself," Witchie snapped at him.

As if he had not heard her Shane said, "I'll be
moving on. I'll be out of here before daylight."

"Where to?" Bobbi protested. "You can't travel on
that hoof."

"I been taking care of myself a long time, Bobbi."

"Would you have some sense? You got a brand on
your neck. Even if you was to get all the way back to
Wyoming, anybody who sees that brand knows you
belong to the government. They caught you once,
they can catch you again, and you'll be gelded for
sure next time."

"The girl's right, Dark Rider." Witchie's voice
sounded oddly gentle, for her, old witch that she
was. "There's only one way out that I can see."

A long pause. Shane, when he spoke, sounded
reluctant.

"What way?"

"You know what way, good as I do. Be a man
again. Not likely anybody will mess with your balls

then." Witchie was making up for having spoken softly a moment before.

"Just my heart," said Shane. "And my soul. And my mind, and my life."

"Who would do that?" Bobbi demanded. The horse looked sidelong at her. When the small Shane in Kabilde's crystal did not answer her, she insisted, "They'll be looking for a black mustang, not a man. Who would mess with you?"

Shane did not reply. His image in Kabilde's globelike handle clouded and disappeared. The mustang Shane carefully removed his foot from its bath, set the hoof on the towel a moment to dry it, then walked to Witchie with scarcely a limp and looked at her.

"I can only do it if you really want me to," she told him. "Heart and soul and all."

He lowered his proud head and let his face rest against the old woman's flat bosom.

"You're stronger than me," Witchie said to him. "You have to help me. I'll try." Her hands came up to rest on either side of the long, black head. She closed her eyes. Shane had already closed his. Both of them stood very still for what seemed a considerable time to Bobbi, so long that she wanted to find a chair and sit down, but she did not dare move. She watched intently. Shane and Witchie looked as if they had stopped breathing, but their limbs trembled with tension. And Witchie's hands—when had they started to move? So slow, might have been forever ago. They crept up Shane's smooth cheekbones to his poll, the seat of every proud horse's soul. They met at his forelock, and Witchie's mouth moved, she started to whisper. Shane's ears quivered and lay back against his neck. With an angry swish his tail lashed against his hind legs.

Witchie opened her eyes. "I can't help you unless you want it," she said in a toneless voice, and she stepped back from Shane and sank down in the ladderback rocker. Shane's head hung low. Bobbi came and laid her hand on the black shoulder.

A knock sounded at the front door.

Bobbi went rigid, feeling Shane jump beneath her hand. But there was nowhere to run to and no place to hide a horse. Witchie bawled out, "Who's there?"

"It's me!" announced the high-pitched voice of the overfriendly neighbor.

"Ethel, I ain't decent!" Witchie yelled. "Or the house, neither!"

"It don't matter! I just want to give you some rice soup!"

"Holy gee, I got to go to the pot again!" bellowed Witchie with convincing desperation. "I got the trots, Ethel. Just leave that there and I'll get it later!" Witchie thumped up the stairs. Bobbi and Shane stood where they were, not daring to move, staring at the glass parlor doorknob. Ethel tried to come in; the knob rattled and moved. But the door was locked. With relief, Bobbi heard Ethel walking down the porch steps—

"Jesus shit!" she swore softly. Ethel was going around back.

Bobbi saw the neighbor's shadow cross the side window and thought wildly. Shane could move out of eyeshot of the back door, but there was no way she could move all the paraphernalia, the hay, the oats, the water bucket, the Epsom salts bath in time. And

she would make considerable noise if she tried. And—
and there was no time.

Determined to come in and leave her soup on the
kitchen table, Ethel was at the back door. It would
just have to be locked.

Bobbi stared. Through the parlor archway she could
see the kitchen door, its inside knob, the ornate brass
dark with age and shiny with wear, and she watched
the door, the knob, with widened eyes, picturing the
mechanism within her mind, willing it to be locked.
The knob stirred. Be locked. Be locked—

It was.

For a while there was silence, and then Bobbi
heard Ethel set down her offering of soup on the
back steps and go away.

But—that door could not possibly have been locked.
It was a wonder it was even latched. Shane had come
in from outside, pushing it open with his head. No
one had been near it since.

Witchie came down from upstairs. "I told you,"
she said mildly to Bobbi, "you put your mind to it,
you can do—"

Bobbi felt half panicked, and not only on account
of Ethel's persistence. She cut in, "We're leaving.
Shane and me got to get out of here as soon as it's
dark."

Shane swung his head and gave her a look as if to
say, Speak for yourself. She ignored him.

"I got to fix up his hoof somehow so he can travel,"
she went on. "You got any duct tape?"

Of course she did, in the attic. But Witchie shook
her head irritably. "That's no good. You go to Samuel
Bissel."

"Who?"

"An old Amish blacksmith, lives not far from here. He's one of the Circle. You'll have to go along with Shane and tell him I sent you. Then he should help you."

"A horseshoer?" Bobbi was astonished, not because there was a farrier nearby, but because he was—what Witchie said he was.

Witchie grumbled, "My stars, girl. Smiths have had powers since the day metal was born. Don't be afraid of old Bissel, or he'll know it. I'd come with you, but I got to stay home and have the grippe." Witchie's tone filled with disgust. "Ethel's sure to call again."

Bobbi stood feeling chilly. A farrier with—what, a magic hammer? Another sort of witch to deal with.

"Good Lord, Bobbi." Aunt Witchie sounded annoyed and tender at the same time. "Anybody who can stare my back door silly don't need to be afraid of Samuel Bissel."

Chapter Eleven

Old Bissel (or the old pisser, as Bobbi took to calling him in her mind) lived half a mile up the Seldom road and back in the woods. She and Shane did not take the road, of course, but walked through the woods, Shane with one hoof in a heavy sock, Bobbi at the horse's side. They had to keep close enough to the road so that they could find their way, but hide from the headlights of the occasional car that passed. Between cars, the night was very dark. Bobbi rested a hand on Shane's shoulder so as to stay with him. The other hand swung empty. Witchie had packed spare clothes and some food in a brown paper bag, but the old Dutchwoman had been so generous with the food, making the bag so heavy, that Bobbi was to stop back for it. Bobbi thought of Witchie with mingled affection and annoyance, remembering the

supper of rice soup, the goodbyes complicated by
gifts of bananas and cheese and bread and corn chips
and Lebanon bologna. Witchie had distracted Ethel
with a ringing telephone while Bobbi and Shane had
slipped out into the night, just in case old eagle-eye
Ethel might see anything. . . . The day had been
tiring, too full of danger and decisions and weirdness,
and it was not over yet. Stumbling over rocks and
stumps in the dark . . .

At a small distance, in the black interstices of the
woods, Bobbi saw something drift whitely.

"No," she muttered. It hovered ahead, the way
she and Shane had to go, and it seemed to be waiting
for them.

"Bobbi." The voice sounded inside her head—her
father's voice, which she had never heard. Not in any
real way. Just in this ghostly farce. She couldn't stand
it. Too much.

"No," she said aloud. "No more. Not today."

"Bobbi!" Urgently.

She didn't like people talking inside her head, and
with a surge of angry energy she sent the voice away.
Her anger crackled in her mind. She had her own
urgent business to attend to.

"I tell you no!" she shouted at the woods. "Not
now! I ain't talking to no buck's behind now!"

Scared, the deer bobbed away. If it was a deer.
She didn't hear anything above her own noise, and
she couldn't tell. A deer wouldn't have waited for
them to come so close . . . she didn't care.

Shane swung his head curiously when she shouted,
then continued on his way. She wondered briefly
what he had seen or heard. Too much trouble to ask
him. She stumbled on through the dark.

Her feet found open flatness, the grit of gravel. Samuel Bissel's long driveway. A relief. But the stones were sharp underfoot; Shane hobbled. Bobbi felt the hitch in his gait through his shoulder, where her palm still rested.

The house loomed dim ahead. No electric lights for the Amishman. Though he was no Amishman in fact, Bobbi knew, but one of the Circle in that form, if she understood correctly.

Old Bissel came out to meet them like a shadow in the night, standing on his rickety porch with a candle in a lantern. He had heard them coming, or perhaps he knew by other means when there were visitors about. Bobbi saw the wild, white bristle of untrimmed beard growing right up to his sharp, dark eyes. She saw the baggy black coverall trousers, a rusty, nearly formless black, not at all like the crisp and shining black clothing Shane wore. She saw the plain green shirt, the homely black hat. She heard no sound in the night except the crunch of Shane's hooves on stone. Samuel Bissel held the lantern and said nothing.

Bobbi said, "Mrs. Fenstermacher sent us. She wants you to care for this horse's feet and be quiet about it."

Samuel Bissel said, "The forge is banked for the night."

Something about him made Bobbi afraid, and because she had fear to hide, she spoke brashly. "Fire it up again! We have to be in the next county by morning."

She saw a movement of the wild white beard. The Amishman was smiling, a sour, knowing smile. He turned, strode the length of the rotting porch, stepped down off it and with the lantern led the way to the forge.

From what Bobbi could see, the place used to be a farm, but cedars and scrub trees were taking it over. The forge was in the barn. Samuel Bissel flicked a switch; a bare electric bulb flared overhead, and he blew out his lantern. A few renegade Amishmen might use electricity in the barn, Bobbi knew, but no Amishman would let his house rot or his land go to scrub. She wondered if Bissel had a wife. He should not have grown a beard until he had taken a wife, and there should be many children, keeping the house trim, making the farm shine. . . . The smith, the immortal with magical powers, did not seem to fit into the form he had taken the way Shane fit into a wild horse's black form.

She bent and slipped the protective sock off Shane's injured hoof, then stood and studied Bissel. Now that she could see him better, she saw no more than before. His flat hat shadowed his sharp eyes, his bristle of beard hid his face, baggy clothing hid his body. Except . . . she could see form beyond the form. Dark . . . no. It was just barn shadows. She was too tired to see more.

Samuel Bissel studied the horse's hooves with a shadowed and glinting glance.

"Too small," he said curtly. "We'll spread 'em. Quarter crack in the off fore. It'll take clips."

He said nothing of the strange fact that Shane was standing in his smithy loose, without halter or lead line or even so much as a rope looped around his neck, and with blue eyes blazing.

Bobbi nodded. She did not want to make conversation with this man. She and Shane waited in silence for a considerable time while Bissel heated up his forge. He used a huge, old-fashioned, coke-burning forge, and worked the bellows with his foot. And unlike every other farrier Bobbi had ever met, all of whom started with pre-shaped, factory-made horse-shoes, old Bissel started with bar steel. While the first bar was heating red-hot in the white-hot forge, he trimmed Shane's hooves level and even. A good job, Bobbi could see that; Bissel knew what he was doing. But he knew something more, and she could see that too. He picked up Shane's feet without a word or a pat, without preamble, as if Shane was a jointed toy, not a horse that could kick a kneecap to smithereens, break an arm or smash a skull. As if he knew Shane would not harm him. As if he knew Shane was no horse at all.

Just as well, Bobbi decided. Shane would not appreciate patting and sweet talk the way a horse would.

She stood watching the black stud, watching the straight, alert lines of his head and shoulders, knowing she would be with him yet a while. Wearing horseshoes, he could not go off on his own. He would need her or some human to take them off when his hooves grew long. The shoes would have to be removed, the hooves trimmed, and the shoes reset two or three times more before the crack grew out entirely and was gone. Bobbi would stay with him that long, at least.

With tongs and hammer Samuel Bissel shaped the first shoe. Sparks flew, the sound of metal striking hot metal rang through the night, and the hammer shone, flashing in air with every blow; Bobbi had never seen a hammer head shine so, like a mirror. Hazily she watched it dazzle. When the smith put the hammer down and held the hot shoe to Shane's hoof for fitting, a burning smell went up and smoke poured off, cloaking Bissel like a fluid shadow, turning his face and beard dark with soot. His eyes gleamed through the smoke, and Bobbi took a step back, as if she had seen a devil.

Bissel lifted the shoe away from the hoof, studied the dark mark it had left, and went back to his forge to further shape the shoe.

It was all part of hot shoeing, Bobbi knew, though she had never seen it done before. The scorch on the hoof told the shoer what yet needed to be done, and it did not hurt the horse. It was the best way to shoe, the old people said. Yet she found that she was shaking.

Bissel cooled the first horseshoe in water—it hissed like a hundred snakes and clouded the forge with steam. The Amishman came back to Shane and nailed it on, and as he worked he began to whisper to the mustang.

Three more shoes he forged, fitted and nailed, taking the most time shoeing the cracked hoof. On that shoe he pulled clips out of the hot metal, one at the toe and two at the sides of the hoof near the heel. They would steady the hoof and keep the crack from lengthening. All the time, as he shaped the shoes, as he fitted them and the stinging smoke poured up, as he tapped them into final form and as he nailed them on, he whispered to Shane.

Bobbi could not see his face as he bent over his work. His voice came muffled out of his beard, low-pitched, murmurous as wind in the trees, so that at first Bobbi did not notice his whispering. Then, when she grew aware of it, she stood as close as she dared and listened, but could not understand a word of it. Bissel might have been whispering in some foreign language. German, perhaps.

He thought Shane was a horse after all, Bobbi decided, her mind sluggish from smoke and weariness and the rhythmic coruscation of the hammer. He thought Shane might bolt, and he was trying to gentle him. She had heard about horse tamers who worked that way; people called them "whisperers." There was once one in England people thought was a wizard. He could go into a stall with a killer, a horse everyone else had given up on, using nothing but his voice to tame it, and come out leading it by the forelock. No matter. Nothing like that could work with Shane—

Bobbi's half-lidded eyes snapped open, and she jerked rigid, staring. Shane's head was nodding at the level of his shoulders. The horse's lower lip had gone as loose as that of an old plug pulling a junkman's wagon. The blue fire had faded out of his eyes.

"Shane!" Bobbi yelled. "Wake up!"

Shane did not move. Only Samuel Bissel moved, straightening up from pounding the final nail in the last shoe. He loomed tall and terrible in his dull black coveralls and his soot-blackened face and beard, with eyes gleaming red in the ruddy light of the forge and teeth flashing, bared in a grimace or grin. He held his hammer in one hand, and with the other he grasped Shane by the forelock.

"Stop it!" Bobbi shouted. "What do you think you're doing?"

The Amishman brushed past her without replying, walking toward the door, and Shane plodded placidly where the man led him. Bobbi stood thinking wildly.

What could she do? Knock the man away from Shane?
He still had his hammer; he could defend himself
from anything she did to him. And the hold he had
on Shane was not merely one of the hand.

Samuel Bissel and Shane were disappearing into
the night.

Bobbi ran after them. "Shane!" she called again.
But Shane did not seem to hear her. That Bissel, she
would like to—

Something crackled inside her mind.

"You Samuel Bissel!" she shouted so fiercely that
the Amishman stopped and turned to face her. "Let
go that horse! I'm telling you by the Twelve of the
Hidden Circle."

She saw darkness swirl in the night, as if Bissel
stood cloaked in smoke again, even though there
could not have been any. Something flashed like fire
or lightning: the terrible bearded man's eyes, or his
bared teeth. . . . Bissel raised his hammer, its handle
blacker than the night, its metal head shining fit to
blind her. Sparks flew as if it clanged against hot
steel, and though she stood a good ten paces away
from the smith, Bobbi fell down as if she had been
struck. There was no pain, but the great weakness
she felt was as bad as any pain. She could not move,
no matter how her heart ached and struggled. The
man, the devil, trickster, villain, blast and damn him,
he was leading Shane away. . . .

She blacked out for a short while, then opened her
eyes again and blinked at the blackness of night.
Shakily she got up on her hands and knees. Somewhere not far away she heard a rattling sound and the
rhythmic clop of hooves. A lantern swayed, hanging
from a buggy hood. The black Amish buggy passed

Bobbi, a spidery shadow in the night, and between the shafts trotted a horse in full harness and bridle, bit and blinkers, stretching out briskly into a smooth trot—and at the crest of its neck, glimmering in the lantern light, Bobbi saw a white brand.

By the time Bobbi had wobbled to her feet, trying to stagger a few steps after the buggy, it had disappeared far down the lane. The rattling of its hard, spoked wheels and the ringing of hooves were fading away swiftly, and she knew she would never be able to catch up to them.

She forced herself into a lurching run, bound back toward Seldom. Even if she could have caught the buggy, there was no way she could deal with Samuel Bissel. She needed Witchie.

Her heart hurt, but not with running. Her breath rasped in her chest.

Inside her mind a voice said, "I tried to tell you."

Eyes straining straight ahead through the tunnel of the night, she had not noticed the pale, hazy face floating to one side. "Go away!" she screamed at it. "You're the one who got me into this mess!" Father or not, she hated it. Its presence seemed the utmost insult to her heartache.

"Bobbi—"

With a surge of self-will she shut her mind against its voice so that she could no longer hear it. Anger combined with her panic to send her into a strong run, and she did not look back.

Not bothering to hide any longer, she pounded into Seldom on the main road. She darted straight toward the Fenstermacher house, thudded through the side yard and slammed in at the back door.

Witchie sat waiting in the hickory rocker, holding

the overstuffed brown paper bag, heaving herself up when she heard Bobbi coming. "The police was here," she said, "right after you left. Going house to house, asking. It's a good thing I had just cleaned up the parlor. I put some more deer bologna in here, and some apples, and—"

Between panting breaths Bobbi burst out, "That man took Shane!"

If she had known how hard it was to dumbfound Witchie, she would have savored the moment more. To the end of her acquaintance with the pow-wow, she was never to see her nearly so taken aback. But at the time the old woman's floundering amazement made her stamp with impatience.

"That Bissel!" she shouted. "He put some sort of a spell on Shane! He whispered at him and led him away like an old plow horse! When I told him to stop, he blasted me with his hammer!"

"There's got to be some mistake," Witchie declared, regaining some of her usual forcefulness. "The smith would never go against me. I'm one of the Twelve, you know."

"Ha! I told him stop by the Twelve of the Hidden Circle. That's when he knocked me down. Then he harnessed Shane to a buggy and drove him away."

For a moment Witchie's face turned as pale as her hair. Then she flushed red, her nostrils flared, and she turned and strode strongly to get her walking stick. Or, more properly, her sorceress's staff.

"This is all I need," she snapped at Bobbi. "Heft that bag and let's go."

Witchie did pause long enough to grab her over-size, baggy purse and a white cardigan sweater off a kitchen chair. And she turned off the lights and locked the door after her, fishing the key out of the vast depths of the purse. Ethel next door was peering out of her window over a rank of potted African violets. Mrs. Fenstermacher waved at her, more of a defiant salute than a wave, then led Bobbi across the steep side yard to where the garage squatted half in the woods.

"Ethel has something to talk about now," Witchie remarked grimly. "We'll take the car."

She said that last with a certain panache, as if taking the car was an act of reckless daring. She heaved the heavy, wooden garage door open with a rumble, and with flair. Bobbi gawked at the vehicle inside.

"What *is* that?"

"A Kaiser."

Massive, monumental, blimp-like, the color and somewhat the shape of a huge June bug, the Kaiser left scarcely space in the garage for Bobbi and Mrs. Fenstermacher to scrape through and embark. Once inside its capacious cabin, perched on the plump rondure of the front seat, Bobbi felt disoriented, dwindled, as if time had somehow turned backward and she was a little leg-dangling girl again. Witchie placed her sweater, bag and stick on the seat beside her with seemingly yards to spare. She unlocked the steering wheel, and her right foot stretched toward the starter pedal on the floor. She got the monster running, sent it bumbling backwards out of the garage and down the steep, rutted driveway to the road. Then her right foot clawed again to reach the accelerator and her cornstarched neck accordioned to its fullest stubby length as she tried to see over the steering wheel. She gave it up, peering through the narrow segment of glass available to her under the top of the wheel and over the swelling dash. Majestic, the Kaiser progressed out of Seldom and cruised through the woods, taking up the entirety of the narrow road.

"Now," Witchie commanded as she drove, "you take that there pow-wow cane in both your hands and tell me what you see."

The wooden snake on Kabilde's shaft turned its head to look at Bobbi.

She felt cold with fear of the weird thing. But she was so miserably afraid for Shane that she did not hesitate. Softly, so as not to anger the snake, she picked up the staff—the wood felt warm and muscular to her touch. She held Kabilde vertically in front of her, between both her hands.

The small globe of the handle began to glow pearl gray, then swirl. Then it cleared, and in it she saw the black buggy passing through the lighted streets of a town with the black mustang trotting between the shafts. It was so wrenching, unthinkable, to see Shane tamely in harness that for a wild-minded moment she believed it was not him, that she was mistaken, Bissel owned another black horse and had driven it off on some errand, they would find Shane safely in a stall in his barn. But the walking stick, seeing or sensing her doubt, showed her Shane's head, the white brand at the crest of his neck just behind the bridle's crownpiece, the blue eyes, vacant and staring, behind blinkers.

"That there is Parsimony," Witchie said, glancing over to see the town going by behind him, and where the dirt road ended on a paved one she turned right. "You can lay that stick down awhile."

Bobbi did, and the light from its handle faded. For some time Witchie drove in silence down a mountainside beneath dark trees. The crowned Pinchot road sent the Kaiser listing sideward as if in heavy seas. Bobbi hung on, feeling half sick.

"That ain't no smith," Witchie spoke up suddenly, grimly. "That's the old villain, the trickster. And I should've knowed it long since."

Bobbi had closed her eyes, and behind the lids she seemed to see a wheel-shape of bright-colored circular cards laid out on the darkness. But they would not stay still so that she could comprehend the pattern. They shuffled and swirled, changing like a kaleidoscope. And she, herself, was more than one thing at once—

"What fooled me," Witchie went on, "that Amish business. A person gets so used to thinking of the Amish as the people of peace. Hard to think of anything in Amish form as evil."

The word chilled Bobbi. She opened her eyes and shook her head in the darkness as if Shane and Bissel and all that had happened were a dream she could shake away, she would wake up in her Grandpap's cabin. But she could not wake up. She was still blundering through darkness in a huge old car with a witch at the wheel.

"I wish I knowed what Bissel thought he was doing," the old woman said. She did not sound grim any longer; her tone had turned shrewd, scheming, contemplative. "The way he's heading, looks like he's going to the Hub. Must be he means to use Shane somehow to give himself power in the Twelve."

Bobbi asked, "Where's the Hub?"

Witchie seemed suddenly to realize that she was thinking aloud. "Never mind," she snapped.

Bobbi was not put off. She had been raised by a Yandro, and Witchie's curtness no longer impressed her. "Use Shane how?" she asked.

There was a considerable silence. "As a hostage, maybe," Witchie said at last, thoughtfully, "or maybe . . . I hate to say. The trickster's got even more power than I thought, if he could take control of Shane."

"It wasn't fair! Shane was off his guard. He wasn't expecting an enemy."

"I know that," said Witchie.

Chapter Twelve

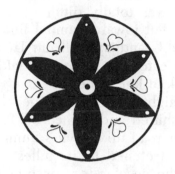

The Kaiser bumbled through Parsimony, and Bobbi held the walking stick again. This time it showed Shane pulling the buggy through darkened, featureless woodland. Shane was still trotting, but his black sides were slick and white-lathered with sweat. His cracked hoof had to hurt him still, Bobbi knew, though the shoe would keep the injury from worsening. . . . The buggy whip snaked out and flicked the horse, and then Bobbi understood "villain." To the bottom of her heart she loathed and hated Samuel Bissel. The trickster, the liar, the black heart. The man was evil.

"Croyle's Summit," said Witchie after a look at Kabilde's globe.

"How can you tell?"

"My glory days, girl. How can you tell a friend's

face, when you see it? That there's Croyle's Summit,
all right. Next left and then a two-mile hill."

And Bissel was making Shane take it at a trot.
Grandpap would never have done that. Bobbi had
thought she hated her grandfather, but in the darkness of that night she knew that her feeling toward
Grant Yandro was totally different from the horror
and wrath she felt toward Samuel Bissel. How could
she have called Grandpap a villain? He was no villain.

"We'll soon catch up to them," said Witchie, the
grim note back in her voice.

Straining mightily to reach the clutch, the old
woman downshifted and turned off Parsimony Road
onto the wider road up Croyle's Summit. Then with
her right leg stretched to its fullest stumpy length
she pressed the accelerator, pushing the Kaiser as
fast as it would go on the hill, which was not much
faster than a fast horse's trot. And every moment
Shane suffered longer.

Bobbi demanded, "Do we have to catch them?
Can't you just hex Bissel or something?"

The Kaiser's throaty roar hit top volume, faltered,
coughed and died away into a silence that screamed.
There was no chugging sound when Witchie pushed
the starter. The big car drifted along a few yards
further, noiseless as a floating shipwreck, then stopped.

"Looks like he put the hex on us instead," Witchie
said. She picked up her sweater, purse and stick and
clambered out of the car into the late-night darkness.
Bobbi took the paper grocery sack and did likewise.
The screaming sound in the silence, she realized, was
inside her mind. She let go with a yell.

"Jesus!" she burst out at Witchie or the world.

"Just one of his humble servants," said the old woman mildly.

"SHIT! Can't you do anything?"

Witchie stood patting the Kaiser just above its left headlamp, like a cavalryman patting a fallen steed. "Curse Bissel, you mean? Not if you want Shane ever to be the same."

Bobbi felt the yelling drain out of her. "You mean—if Bissel goes, he'll take Shane with him?"

"Smart girl," said Witchie acidly. She turned her back on the Kaiser and started at her spraddle-legged walk upmountain, up the berm of the road, holding her walking stick like a long flashlight in front of her. Kabilde's globular handle glowed softly, giving her light. Bobbi jogged to catch up, then strode along beside her. The old woman moved surprisingly quickly, considering her cookstove-like build. Bobbi had to push herself to keep up.

"What now?" she asked after a while.

"You got an idea?" Witchie sounded annoyed, as well she might, after losing her Kaiser.

"No."

"Then just walk and hush up."

There was really no choice but to follow Shane, even afoot. Bobbi walked and kept quiet.

"We got to catch up to him somehow," the old witch added curtly after a while, "and we ain't going to do it this way."

Bobbi kept her mouth shut.

"And if we can't do nothing else, we got to get to the Hub when he does. The others are likely to catch wind of this and come, or we can summon them, or he might."

"The Twelve?"

"Of course." Crabbily.

"They'll help?"

Witchie didn't answer, and Bobbi realized the old woman wasn't sure what might happen.

The two of them walked out the rest of that night in silence, leaving the road from time to time to hide from the headlights of cars. They topped Croyle's Summit and toiled their way through a convolution of ridges beyond, and made the long downgrade before daybreak. By sunrise they had come to the turn in the road where they could see the little town of Veto sulking in the valley below.

"Time to rest," Witchie said, the first words she had spoken in hours.

Bobbi thought so too. And she was desperately thirsty, though her Yandro pride kept her from admitting it.

Witchie huffed up a steep slope into the woods, and Bobbi followed. Once the two of them had gone well out of sight of the road, Witchie stopped at a halfway-level place behind an outcropping of rock. Bobbi helped her heave away a few fallen limbs, and the old woman seated herself amid the twigs and dead leaves. She settled her faded, frumpy cotton skirt and her belongings with an air, as if making the place her home. "There," she said.

Bobbi sat down and began listlessly to search in her paper bag for the bologna. Then she stopped and watched what Witchie was doing.

The old woman was unscrewing the handle of her cane at the silver ferrule. Out of the interior of the cane she drew a glass flask, long and nearly as fat as the staff itself. The globular handle of the walking stick formed the stopper of the flask. As Bobbi watched, wide-eyed, Witchie pulled the stopper off, raised the flask to her mouth and downed the contents in a single long and evidently satisfying draught.

The old hag had not even offered to share. Bobbi felt herself flush with fury. More than furious; she was nearly berserk, watching.

"Ah!" breathed Witchie. She replaced the stopper on the empty flask, put it back into the walking stick, and turned contented eyes on Bobbi. "Want some?"

"Now's a fine time to ask!" Bobbi raged. "Now it's all gone!"

Witchie smiled and pulled the flask out again, full. Bobbi did not take time to be surprised. She grabbed it—not even her Yandro pride could keep her from grabbing it. She drank. The beverage was as cold as if it had been kept on ice, crystal clear but faintly tangy, like spring water with a slice of lemon in it. When she finished she found that it had cooled her temper as well as her throat. She handed back the empty flash with a feeling of well-being.

"That was good," she said, and she pulled a stick of deer bologna out of the bag and began gnawing at it.

"My stars," Witchie chided. "Where's your manners?" She put the handle back on her staff, took it off again, and pulled out an ornate dagger with a long, slender blade. Kabilde's globe formed the butt to its hilt.

Bobbi stared, too amazed to be hungry for a moment.

Witchie was hungry. With an impatient click of her tongue she took the bologna away from Bobbi and expertly sliced it between her blade and her thumb so that the pieces dropped into her lap, where her skirt caught them. Then she put the dagger back into her walking stick and started to eat. Bobbi came out of her astonishment with a start, gathered her share and ate greedily. There was a loaf of Stroehman's Sunbeam Bread in the grocery sack also; she and Witchie each had several slices. Bobbi folded and compressed hers into little squares and popped each slice into her mouth all at once. It amused her to do this with soft breads. Fish baits, she called them. The loaf of bread was half gone before she stopped. Then she pulled out the bananas, already blackened by their confinement in the paper bag. Witchie had one, and Bobbi had three.

As if to signal that the meal was done, Witchie produced a gold toothpick from the shaft of her walking stick and began to pick her teeth.

Bobbi eyed the pow-wow staff, no longer astounded, but warily curious, like a colt. "What else do you have in there?" she inquired.

Witchie looked severe and did not reply. Instead, the old woman replaced the toothpick and unscrewed the round handle again. In her hand she now held a small cut-glass vial. She removed the stopper, inspected the contents, and a beatific smile creased her broad, soft face.

"Cornstarch," she said.

Ponderously swiveling her broad backside in the dead leaves and forest loam on which she sat, Witchie turned her back on Bobbi, opened her dress and began applying cornstarch to herself.

"Got to put some under my breasts every day," she told Bobbi, "or they gall. My lands, they gall till they bleed."

Bobbi thought of several possible replies to this, gave up on all of them, stood up and went off in the woods to relieve herself. When she got back, Witchie had made herself decent again and was replacing the vial of cornstarch in her staff. Bobbi lay down to get some sleep, squirming around in an attempt to settle herself comfortably on the rocky ground.

"I don't suppose you got a sleeping bag in there," she said wistfully to Witchie.

"In a walking stick?" the old woman scoffed in utmost scorn. "Good heavens, girl."

"Or a pillow." Ignoring her companion's sharp tone, Bobbi sat up again, got all her spare clothes out of the bag and bundled them into a makeshift pillow. After a moment she unwrapped the bundle, divided it into two and silently offered a share to Witchie. Instead of taking it, the old woman suddenly smiled at her, a warm, mischievous smile, and thrust Kabilde at her.

"Here," Witchie said, "you try it. You can get horse brushes out of my attic, maybe you can get a four-poster out of this here stick."

Bobbi looked hard at the old pow-wow witch before taking it. Witchie would not hurt her, she felt sure by then, but Witchie meant to laugh at her. And Witchie did. In succession Bobbi pulled from the walking stick a small, elegant fishing pole with glass-globe handle, a silver flute, an umbrella, a tiny kaleidoscope, a cheerleader's pom-pon on a stick (in the colors scarlet and black), a flag of truce, a blowgun for shooting poisonous darts, and a long, slender sword.

Witchie had stopped laughing. "Bobbi," she said in a tone the girl could not read, "you have a peculiar mind."

"What's my mind got to do with it?"

"Everything." Witchie gestured her to put the sword

away. "That's enough," Witchie added, taking the
walking stick away from her. "Tired?" she asked ten-
derly, as gently as Bobbi had ever heard her say
anything.

Touched to her heart, Bobbi blinked back tears.
No one had ever spoken to her like that, not since
she could remember. Maybe her mother, when she
was a tiny baby, had loved her enough to talk to her
that way—

Jesus shit. The old woman was talking to Kabilde.

Gently, carefully, Witchie set the pow-wow staff
upright in a crack of the rocks, as if it were standing
in its urn at home. Bobbi lay down on the ground
and turned her face away to hide her burning eyes.
The surge of angry mortification she felt was very
much like her feeling for Grandpap, which she had
formerly called hatred—but she had felt real hatred
now, and knew the difference. It blazed, but it did
not sting like this—this disappointment. And thinking of her grandfather, Bobbi felt the stirring of some
feeling deeper than chagrin, something that hurt.
Something that she did not want to face.

To send it away, she went to sleep.

When she awoke, sometime in the afternoon,
Witchie was sitting up and peering at her as if she
had been watching Bobbi's dreams. Bobbi's daytime
sleep had been floating, disjointed, uneasy, and once
again she felt as if Witchie herself and everything
about the past several days ought to be gone once she
woke up. Sometime in her sleep, when she was off
her guard, the sense that she should be home had
overtaken her. She rubbed it away, rubbing her face.
She had no home any longer, and only one thing
mattered to her.

"Where's Shane?" she demanded of Witchie, for she saw that the old woman held Kabilde between her gnarled hands.

"Quite a ways from here." Witchie heaved herself up off the ground and stood adjusting her voluminous underclothing. "I been thinking, young'un, it's no use we should pussyfoot around any more if we're going to get anywhere. So let's hit the road."

"Now? In daylight?"

"No time better for a person to see where they're going."

The old hag had settled on some sort of scheme, Bobbi decided. There was a bright glint in Witchie's yellow-brown eyes. Silently she helped Witchie gather up sweater and purse. Bobbi took the paper bag, and Witchie held the walking stick, and the two of them headed westward.

They walked straight through the little town of Veto on the main road. It was Sunday afternoon; there were plenty of people around to stare at them. Some old men were sitting on the benches near the war memorial. Some old women were rocking at their windows. Children were playing in the yards. Parents were sitting on the porch swings for the first time of the year in the mild weather. They all stared. Witchie plodded along, seeming to be in no hurry, paying no attention. Bobbi kept her eyes on the ground.

Someone lost no time in calling the cops. The state police caught up to them halfway up the next wooded hill after Veto.

"Don't run," Witchie ordered just as Bobbi was about to, as the cruiser pulled onto the shoulder behind them. "That didn't take long," she added, looking back smugly.

"What the hun do you think you're doing?" Bobbi whispered between clenched teeth. The question was rhetorical. No way could Witchie answer it with a big-bellied Smokey ambling toward her.

"We ain't hitchhiking, Officer," Witchie chirped at the man. "We're just walking." She folded her face into a big, bedentured smile.

The trooper paid no attention to her. He was looking straight at Bobbi, and he called her by name. "You're the Yandro girl, aren't you. Bobbi Yandro."

"Why, that's my granddaughter Hepzibah!" Witchie informed him. "Hepzibah Snort."

The name startled Bobbi so badly that she managed to remember it. But the policeman seemed hardly to notice it. "Your granddaddy's been going crazy with worrying about you," he said to Bobbi.

The words made her feel a sudden pang of longing for Grandpap. She smothered it quickly.

"I'm not her," she said in a small, wispy voice such as she imagined a Hepzibah might use. "My name's Zibby."

"That so," said the cop. He regarded her sourly, unbelieving and unamused. "Zibby."

"That's short for Hepzibah," said Bobbi wispily.

Witchie abandoned her beaming smile. "You got no call making fun of her name!" she complained.

The state trooper did not even look at the old woman. "Come on." He motioned Bobbi toward his cruiser. "Into the car."

"No!" Bobbi exclaimed, abandoning wispiness. She couldn't go back to Grandpap, not yet. Too much

unfinished business, too many things she needed—
she needed to know . . .

Witchie clutched Bobbi's arm with one knobby
hand and shook her stick with the other. "You can't
just haul off my granddaughter away from me!" she
shrilled.

Bobbi picked up her cue. "I ain't leaving my
grandma!" she wailed, grabbing Witchie around her
stocky middle.

The cop finally acknowledged Witchie's unwelcome
existence. "Both of you get in," he said to her. "I
expect the investigators will want to talk to you, too."

"We ain't done nothing!" Witchie screeched.

"Just get in before I arrest you for vagrancy. You
too, Hepzibah," the Smokey added sardonically. He
took Bobbi by her elbow and propelled her into the
back seat. In a moment Witchie thumped down beside her. As soon as the trooper closed the car door
and turned his back to go around to the driver's seat,
Witchie nudged Bobbi and winked.

Something unexpected was going to happen at the
end of this ride. Bobbi felt sure of it.

But meanwhile she found it long, silent, and tense.
She could not help thinking of the man lying dead on
Mandawa Mountain and feeling that he was a guilty
secret she had to hide. They would put her in jail if
they knew. . . . The cruiser took the Appalachian
hills like a ship breasting small waves. It passed
through the little towns between them, mere channel
markers, without a change in speed. Since the two
vagrants had been picked up by the state cops, they
were being taken to the state police station, clear at
the western end of the county. Miles washed by. The

sun sank low. Witchie looked out her window with an air of satisfaction.

Bobbi knew the state police station at once, without looking at the sign. It looked just the same as all the others: a low brick-and-concrete building set amid a sterile expanse of grass and blacktop, level and open and starkly out of place amid the wooded hills. And gray. Night was coming on. Everything looked gray in the dusk.

"Here we are," Witchie declared as if arriving at a long-awaited destination. Eagerly she readied her sweater, stick and purse as the cruiser pulled up to the concrete apron in front of the door.

The state trooper got Bobbi out of the car first, and kept a firm grip on her arm. Witchie heaved herself out as soon as the cop made room for her.

"Thank you for the lift, Officer," she said brightly. "We'll be on our way now." Appearing to hurry, the old woman tottered off.

Bobbi, who knew how fast Witchie could scuttle when she really wanted to hustle, did not understand at first. Why was Witchie so slow? Then she saw. Witchie was the mother pheasant drawing the fox away. And the Smokey was no smarter than the average fox. He was fooled.

"Hey!" he yelled, and he grabbed for the old woman. He had not wanted anything to do with her, back there along the side of the road, but now that he had brought her in he was determined to keep her. She had moved just out of his reach. Old bat, who did she think she was? "Hey! You stop right there!"

Not too smart, that cop, but he was smart enough not to let go his grip on Bobbi. He pulled her along with him as he lunged forward and caught Witchie by the arm. "Hands off, young man!" Witchie snapped, and she gave the big fingers curled around her elbow a smart rap with her walking stick. Bobbi felt the cop catch his breath, but his grip on her arm only tightened, though he snatched his other hand away from Witchie's arm in a hurry. He glared at Witchie, intent on subduing her.

"Hand over that cane!" he ordered.

"I'll do no such thing!" Witchie shrilled. The cop at the desk inside looked up, then heaved himself out of his chair and ambled toward the door.

"Hand it over, or I'll have you for assaulting a police officer!"

Witchie raised the stick as if assaulting the man sounded like an excellent idea. The trooper got hold of Kabilde by the shaft, then did something no police officer should ever do when merely threatened by an irate old woman. He screamed.

The snake on the staff was writhing under his hand. The snake's head darted at his hand and bit him.

Bobbi saw the wooden head dart and bite. Its eyes shone red, like tiny rubies. The inside of its mouth was the soft, pulpy color of balsa. She glimpsed the thornlike teeth. She heard the cop scream, a high-pitched, startled scream. The weirdness of the thing made him scream, not any pain. He snatched his hand away; his other hand left Bobbi's arm; he stepped back. He stood white-faced, and the other state trooper, coming out of the building, froze where he was and did the same, and the snake on Witchie's staff glared and hissed at them both while the globe on the handle blazed eerily in the twilight.

"Now, as I was saying," Witchie told the officers

sternly, "me and my granddaughter will be on our way." She walked off, not too fast, with Bobbi at her side, and the men didn't follow them. Glancing back, Bobbi saw them still standing near the cruiser, looking stunned.

"Take them a while to figure out how to report this," Witchie said.

Bobbi grumped, "Did you have to tell them my name was Hepzibah?"

"What's wrong with that?" Bobbi heard the quirk behind the injured innocence in the old woman's tone. Witchie had some private joke.

"What's wrong with it! God! If I had to have a name, I wish you would have let me pick it. Now I'm stuck with Hepzibah Snort."

"That was my mother's name," Witchie said. "You should feel honored. I've made you kin, giving you that name, girl."

Something warmer than laughter in Witchie's voice . . . Not knowing how to respond, Bobbi fell silent. At Witchie's side, she headed straight across the state police station's broad expanse of grass to the woods beyond. As soon as the trees hid the two of them from the station, Witchie accelerated into her fastest scuttle. Bobbi had to trot to keep up with her. Kabilde's angry flare of light faded away into a faint glow, just enough to light their way through the shadowy woods, and the carved snake on the shaft settled back into its usual attitude.

"Can you ride that thing like a broom?" Bobbi asked, panting from fighting her way through the woods.

"Have some respect, girl!"

Whether her idea was insulting to Mrs. Fenstermacher or to Kabilde, Bobbi wasn't sure, but it didn't much matter. She said, "What I mean is, those cops won't stand there and shiver for long. They'll be after us. We're going to have to do better than this, somehow."

"Alls we have to do is get to where our friends are," Witchie said, "and that's less than a mile from here."

Witchie had taken the two of them on that risky ride with the police because—

"Shane?" Bobbi gasped.

"No, child." The old hag sounded regretful. "Shane's quite a ways from here still."

"Who, then?"

Witchie didn't answer, and Bobbi knew without seeing the glint that was in the old scamp's eye. Witchie wanted Bobbi to beg and pester, but she would never tell.

"Huh," Bobbi muttered, and she kept stubborn silence as they struggled through the benighted woods.

Chapter Thirteen

Firelight.

Campfires, quite a few of them. And as she and Witchie walked closer Bobbi could see the cars pulled up on the abandoned strip site, the tents and camper trailers, the people. She blinked. The cars were Cadillacs and Mercedes. The people: dark men with kerchiefs knotted around their throats, darkly beautiful women in low-cut blouses and long skirts which dragged on the ground as they squatted beside the fires. Ragged, half-naked children ran everywhere, screaming. Dogs, nearly as many dogs as children, set up a din as soon as Bobbi and Witchie stepped out of the woods that surrounded the place.

The men turned away from their talking and looked: the men with their proud heads, their flashing eyes, their bright-colored, tattered clothing. And the smooth,

long, raven-black hair of the women, their many
golden bangles and chains . . . Bobbi knew these
people as if she had met them sometime in a dream.
Beyond their campers she seemed to see the forms of
brightly painted wagons; beyond their expensive cars,
the forms of horses: magnificent horses, the best
horses in the world. As they had done for over a
thousand years, ever since they had dispersed out of
distant India, these people wore gold and rags, and
camped wherever night found them, and begged and
pilfered and told fortunes by way of living off the land
as nomads always had. The whole world was theirs
for the wandering.

"Gypsies," she breathed.

"Indians, they'll call themselves to outsiders," Witchie
answered in a low voice, "but they're gypsies, right
enough."

Gypsies did not welcome outsiders. The children
swarmed around Witchie and Bobbi, dirty and rude,
impudently begging in order to drive them away.
The women squatted sullenly by the fires and did not
look at the newcomers. The men stood and smoked.

"Go introduce yourself, girl," Witchie told Bobbie.
"Your real name."

She stared at the old woman, wondering what
Witchie's mischief was this time, sensing a dare.
Then she rolled her eyes, pushed her way through
the children as if through a thicket and walked past
the haughty women and up to the group of men,
choosing one at random—for none of them looked
more important or prosperous than the others; all
stood like royalty, and all wore rags.

"Hello," she said to the man she had singled out,
"I'm Bobbi Yandro."

The women who crouched near enough to hear sprang to their feet with excited cries. The men exclaimed among themselves in a language Bobbi did not understand. All in a moment the whole camp was astir, all the women conferring, the children screaming louder than ever, the dogs barking madly. Because I am a runaway, Bobbi thought. They listen to the news, they have heard my name, they want the reward. . . .

She was mistaken. "Grant Yandro's son's daughter?" a gypsy man asked her, and all the others stood shoulder to shoulder, awaiting her answer. At her nod, one of them took a step forward. A tall, fiercely handsome man in a tattered yellow terrycloth hat, he took the role of their leader.

"Kinswoman," he said to Bobbi, "welcome."

Then the tall, beautiful women were shouting to each other and tossing chains of gold over her neck, and the children were hanging back shyly, gazing at her with huge, dark eyes, and someone pressed a small silver cup into her hand. She gulped. The liquid seemed to burn its way to her ears and smolder there. After that, all was more than ever confusion.

Witchie had come up beside her sometime, carrying Kabilde, and the staff's globe began to glow and swirl. "Cops are coming," Witchie said crisply as Kabilde showed her the cruiser nosing its way nearer through the woods.

Confusion to Bobbi, but to the gypsies, simple enough. They were accustomed to magic and used to police. A man swept open the capacious trunk of the nearest car, urging Bobbi inside. Where Witchie went, Bobbi did not know, but as she clambered into her hiding place she saw all the women resume their places by the fires and their sullen silence. The silver cup had disappeared. The men smoked. From the darkness of her refuge Bobbi heard the shrieking, begging voices of the dirty children as they besieged the state trooper. She heard the trooper question a few of the women. They answered him in their own language, shrilly, angrily. When he questioned the men, they spoke English and seemed eager to help, but gave useless, muddleheaded answers. They smiled winningly and scratched themselves as if for lice. The officer soon went away.

The trunk lid flew open. Many hands helped Bobbi out. "Come," a voice said, "we feast!"

There was no resisting the onslaught of the gypsies' hospitality. It was like an elemental force, a gale. Bobbi moved where the swirling winds took her. Through the dark to a creek, to wash herself. Back again to a seat on somebody's ice chest, a place of honor. Witchie sat on another one beside her. The men sat on upturned buckets, stumps of firewood, the ground. Some of the young girls started a dance. Their bright-colored skirts swirled out in circles, whirling, shape-shifting, kaleidoscopic. The men and their guests drank more liquor, gave toasts, made speeches. Bobbi secretly poured most of her liquor out onto the ground, but grew groggy on the small amount she sipped. After a seemly interval of talk the women brought the food, huge quantities of food, and the children hung back and watched. The strange, spicy cooked food burned in Bobbi's ears like the liquor. She could not eat much of it, and the women pressed other kinds of food on her in a near-frenzy, ransacking the campers for candies, Graham crackers, Pop Tarts. Witchie ceremoniously brought forth

the contents of her paper sack and offered them to
the gypsies. They refused vehemently; Witchie
insisted; they accepted and ate with delight. Rather,
the men ate. Then one by one they belched loudly
and declared themselves replete. Bobbi, dazed and
half drunk, failed to do the same until Witchie nudged
her and emitted a resounding belch. Then she managed to do the same, and as if at a signal the women
and children swarmed over the food, screeching and
fighting each other for what remained.

Some things had come clear to Bobbi from the
conversation, the toasts, the speeches. Sometime,
generations before, some of the gypsies had stayed
for a few weeks on Canadawa Mountain. Later, a
non-gypsy girl of that mountain had found herself
pregnant. Not an unusual situation, after gypsies had
passed through, for gypsy youths are darkly handsome and charming. But this was a girl of unusual
spunk. She went after the father of her child, and
found him, and (so the gypsy storytellers said with a
sort of awe) seduced him as he had seduced her,
making him love her so that he gave up his wander-
ings and his people and went back to live with her
and marry her according to the laws of her kind. The
name he gave her was Yandro.

Since those times the farm on Canadawa mountainside was known to the gypsies as a place of friends in
the enemy camp, a place where messages could be
telephoned and letters sent, a safe haven, though a
gypsy might not come that way more than once in
several years. But these gypsies knew the name
Yandro. Grant Yandro had helped them circumvent
the state's unnatural and incomprehensible laws re-

garding death, once, by putting together a coffin for a
lost gypsy child.

"Huh," Bobbi said. "Nobody ever told me."

"Your grandfather would have told you soon." It
was the man in the yellow terrycloth hat. He seemed
to be the leader, the one who took the best seat and
made the most speeches. "He kept it from you when
you were younger to protect you. The authorities,
they do not understand gypsies."

The gypsy girls still danced, a shifting circle of
colors bright as a hex sign. The women had joined
them. Some of the men had started a dance of their
own. The gypsy men, Bobbi had decided, did not
understand their women and children except to use
them, to show them off or order them around. No
wonder Grandpap treated her that way sometimes. It
was a wonder he talked to her as much as he did. She
kept silent.

"We will take you back to your home in the morning," the gypsy said as if assuming that was what she
wanted of him.

"No!" The words startled Bobbi out of her bleary-
eyed slump. She sat up straight. "I must find Shane!"

"Shane?" the gypsy said softly. "The wanderer in
black?"

"He's a horse right now. A black mustang." Because of the liquor, Bobbi said the words before she
realized she could not expect them to be believed.
But the gypsy showed no surprise. "You know about
Shane?" she asked him.

"Oh, yes. We gypsies know the dark stranger."
The same soft, thinking tone. "What has happened,
that you must find him?"

Witchie helped her explain. By the time they had

told the entire tale, most of the gypsy children had fallen asleep in heaps on the ground, like puppies, and Bobbi was falling asleep as she talked, and even the bright-skirted dancers were slowing. It was late. But never, by the glint in the gypsy's eye, too late for derring-do. Somehow all was settled before Bobbi fully comprehended, and she was stumbling into the back seat of a Mercedes. Witchie took the front seat, next to the driver, with Kabilde in her hand.

"He's somewhere down around Crown Stone, last I seen," Witchie told the gypsy.

The town name was familiar. "Pap and me go through Crown Stone," Bobbi said sleepily, "going to see my ma."

They both ignored her. "West of there would put him on Bupp's Knob somewhere," Witchie said.

And the gypsy was looking into the glow of Kabilde's globe. "Ah," he said softly, "I know that place. We have camped there. If I can only think where it is . . ."

And the Mercedes started off through the night. To Bobbi it seemed to float like a magic carpet. It was taking her to Shane.

Her body lay down on the back seat, wanting to sleep. Her mind circled and swirled, dancing with thoughts of Shane. She dozed, jolted awake, dozed again but remained aware of the two in the front seat; sometimes she spoke with them. And when that night ride was over she knew Shane's story, but she never knew whether she had dreamed it or whether the gypsy had told it to her.

He was a nomad, like the gypsies. A wanderer. But instead of bright colors he wore black, and instead of gold he wore a gun. This was the old west. There was sometimes occasion for a gun.

He was a gunfighter, the best who ever lived. As a young man he had aimed to be the best, and learned, and worked, and dared, and challenged. He killed his older rivals proudly. Later, young men came to challenge him, and as he wounded or killed them he began to regret his dream. He traveled, he wandered to leave it behind. He still wore black, but he no longer wore a gun. He no longer used his right name.

He came to a town in Wyoming, Red Bull Basin by name, and stayed there awhile because he liked the country. He gambled for a living and kept to himself.

There was a young woman whose name has been forgotten, though she was very beautiful and the mayor's daughter. She had dark hair, dark eyes, and people said she had a gypsy's soul, though the gypsies know better. A gypsy knows the meaning of loyalty. But what people meant was that this young beauty was wild at heart. She loved dangerous horses, and she rode them to race the wind. She loved the man in black the first time she saw him on the board sidewalk in front of the saloon.

She knew wild things. She knew that at the first scent of the trap he would be away and running. So she dressed like the lady her parents wanted her to be before she walked by. Out from under her ruffled parasol and her dark eyelashes she raised her eyes to him, and then, although he did not yet know it, her noose was around his neck. She had only to dally him in, like a wrangler dallying a bronc.

It took a while. And with every day it took her to win him, she loved him more. She meant to be true to him forever, once he was hers. And the night came at last, the night of her dreams, under a starry sky, when he declared his devotion to her. This strong, dangerous man kneeled beside her and reached for her hands, and laid his head in her lap.

Later, she mounted him.

He was hers, heart and soul. He dealt that way with life. What he did, he did heart and soul or not at all. If she had said to him, Die, he would have done it. If she had said to him, Kill, he might have done that as well.

Such being the case, she lost interest in him.

She loved to tame wild horses and teach them to eat from her hand. But she ceased to love them once they were tame. And once she had tested her powers, and proved them, once the gunfighter had kneeled before her, she ceased to love him.

For a while she was kind to him, out of compunction. Then the sight of him began to annoy her. A gypsy caravan had camped outside of town. She had gone with the other young women to have her fortune told, and the brightly painted, high-wheeled wagons seemed to call to her. A dark, proud-standing man with a kerchief knotted around his neck had caught her eye. She felt herself being dallied in, like a bronc on a lasso, and she did not resist. Being swept away was different, exciting.

But the man in black looked at her with troubled blue eyes. He would follow her when she went away with her lover. He would be a nuisance to her.

The gypsy was clever. It was he, the trickster, who suggested to her what to do about her cast-off lover.

She went to the sheriff, a friend of her father's. With curvetings and a few tears she told him the man in black was a killer, wanted by the law. She named names. The gunfighter himself had told her some of them. The trickster had told her others. The sheriff did not want to go up against the gunslinger himself, but he wasted no time in gathering a posse.

So it was that, when the gypsy wagons rolled away with the mayor's daughter hidden under a red quilt in one of them, the gunfighter was running like a hunted deer across the tableland with the black gunbelt, the pearl-handled pistol, once again riding on his hip.

And as he rode his big roan horse, running it hard, it came plain to him what had happened, and how his fate was to be always betrayed by the woman he loved, and his passion seemed to burn his body away into smoke.

He stopped his horse, unsaddled and unbridled it as it stood puffing in exhaustion. He sent it away with a yell. He laid the gun and gunbelt on the saddle. When the posse came, they found those things. They found odd footprints leading away. They never found their man.

That night as she flirted with her gypsy lover, who would so soon discard her, under the stars, the mayor's daughter saw a black mustang stallion standing at a small distance, watching. Glorying in wild things as she did, she walked toward him with her hand outstretched, coaxing. She knew he would run away before he let her touch him, but she had to try to touch him, even so.

But the black mustang did not run away at once. He reared with an angry scream and struck at her with his forefeet, almost killing her where she stood—almost. The stallion swerved just before his deadly hooves struck her head, her breast. Then he turned his back on her and thundered away.

That was a hundred years ago. And the mayor's daughter had long since died, her name forgotten except, perhaps, by one living being. But the black mustang had run on the tablelands and mesas since. He was of the Twelve. He would not die, only take different forms.

So the tale ran, or the dream—except it sometimes seemed to Bobbi that she had it wrong, that the man in black was a Spanish gentleman in old Mexico, or a riverboat gambler, or a British earl, though his fate remained the same—

But that was absurd. How would a British earl have come to Wyoming?

Bobbi jolted fully awake because Witchie reached back and prodded her with Kabilde. She sat up, peering into darkness. It was still night, the darkest, most eerie time of night, the time when all sane people are asleep. Without needing a clock she could feel that.

The gypsy turned off the engine. Silent, the Mercedes drifted to a stop. Without speaking, without slamming the car doors, the three of them got out. Bobbi stretched and looked around her. Trees. Steep ridges going up to either side of the road. Overhead, night sky.

"The new moon holds the old moon in her arms," the gypsy muttered, very low.

Bobbi also was looking at the sliver of crescent moon overhead, the gray-black form of the full circle visible in its embrace.

"It is a bad omen," the gypsy said, real fear in his voice, though he still kept it low. "Come, let us go back. We feast you again."

"We can't go back," said Witchie, just as softly.

"What can you do against the trickster under the dark circle?" the man pleaded. "Hazel lady, come away."

Bobbi had made out the dim line of a rutted lane leading into the woods. "Is Shane up there?" she whispered to Witchie.

"Yes."

"Then come on! Let's go find him!"

But the gypsy would not go. No matter how much he wanted to atone for the misdeed of one purported to be his ancestor, he could not make himself go. In the end it was just Witchie and Bobbi who walked up the shadowy lane where Samuel Bissel had taken Shane.

Chapter Fourteen

They walked up the rutted lane under the ominous moon.

"Is this the Hub where we're going?" Bobbi asked Witchie.

"My golly days, no, girl."

"Well, where—"

"Hush. Quiet from now on. Chances are better if we catch him by surprise."

The old woman walked on, slowly, taking her time, as quietly as an Indian, a cat. Bobbi felt big-boned and clumsy behind her, following her up the steep lane through woods.

It ended in a clearing of sorts, an abandoned, half-overgrown hilltop farm. Moonlight and shadow made a crazy quilt of the former pasture: a jumble of cedars, blackberry, sumac, and the boulders piled where long-ago glaciers had carelessly left them. In the middle of the pasture stood a black, boxy shape: the buggy.

Bobbi and Witchie drifted close—no easy matter, on the terrain—then crouched behind rocks to reconnoiter.

"Bissel's sleeping underneath the buggy," Witchie breathed, very low.

Bobbi did not answer or look. She was staring at the horse the Amishman had tethered out to graze. Though food grew within reach all around, the animal stood without eating, motionless in the gray moonlight, head drooping almost to the ground. And even to Bobbi's eyes the mustang seemed nothing more than a small horse, almost runty, underfed and dead tired. Nothing more. No hint of the black sheen, the stubborn pride, the blaze of blue eyes.

Fiercely she whispered to Witchie, "That man must have trotted him all night and all day and half the night again. He's exhausted!"

Witchie nodded, putting a dry old hand to Bobbi's mouth to shush her. "I know," she whispered much more quietly. "I can't expect any help from him."

Witchie's braided hair shimmered silver in the moonlight, making a sort of halo on her head, almost as if she were someone holy. Her faded cotton housedress no longer seemed dowdy, but merely soft, like the shadows, and old, like the hills. Crouched behind her concealing boulder, she sighed and laid her forehead against the globe of her cane for a moment, gathering herself. Then she lifted her head and laid her purse aside. She buttoned up her thin white cardigan sweater, a lacy old-woman's sweater, as if adjusting armor. She took up her walking stick in both hands and whispered to Bobbi, "Stay here."

Witch Hazel Fenstermacher stood up and strode forward to combat the trickster. "Renegade!" she challenged. Her old voice resounded in the night like a throaty trumpet call.

Bissel slithered out from under the buggy and loomed to his feet, like a drab black shadow growing out of shadow.

"Apostate," Witchie charged. "Traitor. Judas. You have broken faith with the Twelve, and grasped for power."

Something shot red sparks, and Witchie cried out. Her cane flared, and in the white burst of light Bobbi saw the smith's upraised hammer. It might have been moving, but to her it looked motionless, towering, awesome. And the white fire of the pow-wow staff wavered, for Witchie was staggering. Then Witchie shouted, "Kabilde!" The staff's light blazed so brightly that even behind her rock Bobbi cowered, and in that white flame she saw—the snake, the serpent's head, cat-tawny and growing, growing, and darting and reaching toward Bissel, looming up in the light, and it was the trickster's turn to stagger back.

"Necromancer! Give the dark rider back his soul!" Witchie's voice sounded puissant and terrible in the night. She was a crone old as earth, holding a serpent the size of a python by the tail.

But Bissel had not lowered his hammer. Blood-red fire it flamed, forge fire, and it battered at Kabilde, and Kabilde flattened his hazel-yellow head and shrank back. For the first time the trickster spoke.

"Try to take it from me," he said, and Bobbi glimpsed the glint of his grin in his beard, and his

voice was more dangerous than Witchie's because it
was darker. This man was the villain, all greed, his
heart blacker than the night all around.

"Give the dark rider back his soul!"

"Just try to get it."

And the black-handled hammer changed in Bissel's
callused hands. It was the black staff, the death wand.
And then Bobbi saw looming behind the Amishman
his more true form, saw the long robes black as his
heart, and she knew another of the trickster's many
names. The warlock. A necromancer is one who deals
in death. Witchie risked more than her power here.
She risked her life—

Witchie attacked.

"By all the mysteries of the ancient Twelve!" she
invoked in a strong voice. "By the three highest
names!" And the white light redoubled, seeming to
blaze as much from her stumpy body as from her
staff, and the golden serpent Kabilde swelled taller
than the scrub. Light and serpent beat against Bissel's
power. But the black staff, the death wand, though it
never moved, exuded an essence, a choking aroma,
that they beat against in vain. It clouded like an
umbra around Bissel, a black shadow that even the
whitest of light could not penetrate, and Witchie
could not seem to gain. Witchie would wear herself
out, and then it would be the trickster's turn.

Bobbi found that her hands were clenched, her
fingernails digging into her palms. Witchie had said,
she, Bobbi, had powers. She had to do something;
she couldn't just stay hidden and watch. Even though
Witchie had told her to stay where she was. Even
though she was scared.

At the edge of the battle Shane stood dully, taking

little interest. Not even spooked, as any proper horse
would be by the clamor, the weirdness, blaze brighter
than any lightning, chilling scent of death in the air.
Not Shane any longer, not even a mustang. Something—tamed. Something—castrated . . .

Shane!

Bobbi burst from her hiding place and ran to the
horse, her back to Bissel—she didn't care any longer
what he did to her. She could think only of Shane.
Those blue eyes, so dim and clouded. . . . She had to
save him. Facing the horse's head, she placed her
hands one on each side of it, by those eyes. "Shane!"
she begged.

Nothing happened. And if Bissel had been holding
his hammer he would have blasted her by now. She
didn't care.

In her mind she recalled a sweep of black hat brim
over eyes that blazed with blue fire, so much unlike
the hurtful, spiritless ones before her. . . . Thinking
of that rider clothed in black, the man with a straight-
browed face and broad shoulders under a black silk
shirt, she laid her forehead against the black mustang's forehead and cried out, "Shane!"

Something exploded inside her closed eyes. Something exploded under her touch.

She sprawled to the ground, and Shane the black
horse was rearing up over her, gigantic in the night,
breaking his tether, springing forward, but not at
her—he was charging, an embodied vengeance,
straight at Bissel, and though he was black in the
black night he shone, he gleamed in a way the shadowy villain he faced never could; he lustered like
silk. Bissel gave a barking shout and stood with his
hammer in hand again; he swung it. A bloom, a

blood-red chrysanthemum of sparks spread at its sheen-
ing head, and even where she lay on the ground
Bobbi felt the numbing shock, as if the smith had
made her and the whole world his anvil to strike.
Witchie shrieked. Kabilde writhed, convulsing. Shane's
head plunged as if he had taken a slaughterhouse
blow on his forehead. The horse crashed to his knees.
Bobbi thought he would go down all the way and lie
still, a mustang killed for dog meat, a body on the
concrete floor. She wanted to help him somehow,
but she had no strength, she could not move—

Except to cry out. "Shane!" she yelled.

And he was up again, lunging at his enemy, and
Bissel's hammer was upraised again, this time close
enough to strike with hard steel and a blacksmith's
strength. But Kabilde was there, huge, his ivory-
colored fangs fastened onto Bissel's arm, and Witchie
was there, and Shane was rearing, striking out with
iron-shod forehooves. And the hammer flew away
into the blackness of night somewhere, and Bissel fell
and lay still.

For a moment everything seemed to stop. Shane
stood by the body. Witchie stood dwarfed by her
own magic, awash in white light, holding a giant
serpent. Bobbi stared, not comprehending very well
why the red fire and the black smell of death were
finally gone.

Then she struggled up and went to Shane, running
her hands over him as if checking him for injuries,
unbuckling the halter with its length of dangling tether
from his head and hurling it away. He was puffing,
his nostrils flared nearly into circles, but she could
see he was more roused than exhausted now. He was
Shane again, and he was all right. And when Bobbi

looked around her, Kabilde was a carved walking
stick again, Witchie was a spraddle-legged old woman
again, her white light gone. Bobbi saw her by the
light of the stars and the new moon.

The new moon holding the old moon in its arms,
the bad omen. "It must have been for him," Bobbi
said to Witchie, pointing briefly at the moon and
then at Bissel.

Lying at her feet, the man groaned. Bobbi jumped
straight backward farther than she would have thought
possible.

"He's not dead," Witchie scoffed. "Land's sake,
girl, it would take more than that to kill the trickster.
We would never have got the better of him if we
hadn't come on him in his sleep."

"Good grief." Bobbi stared at her, not wanting to
believe it. The battle had been terrifying enough as it
was.

"He would have changed shapes if he'd had time to
gather himself." For the moment, Witchie's voice
had gone glassy dry, like Kabilde's. "He would have
had some of his deceptions ready for us. As it was, all
he could do was stand and fight."

"I—I wish he was dead, but I'm glad Shane didn't
kill him."

"He has killed men for less," said Witchie darkly.
"But this one is for the Twelve to deal with."

Shane swung around to face Bobbi and nuzzled her
briefly. His nostrils were quieting. Bobbi's hand went
to his forehead and rested there a moment. "You
were awesome," she said to him.

"Speak for yourself, girl," grumbled Witchie. Bobbi
ignored her.

"Where are you going to go now?" she asked Shane

softly, knowing he would not answer her. "What are you going to do?"

Witch Hazel Fenstermacher stumped up and stood in front of her, peering at her. "The question is, girl," she declared, "where are you going to go?"

"With him!" Her hand still lay on Shane's forehead. But at her words he tossed his head to shake it off.

"You can't stay with the dark rider for long," Witchie said. "Nobody can. He comes into your life, and then out he goes again."

"But I have to take his shoes off!"

"Shane can take care of himself. Always has."

And I have to turn him back into a man, she was thinking. Whether he wants it or not. So he'll be safe. Or . . . maybe other reasons . . . She did not say what she was thinking. She said only, "The entanglement . . ."

"Them cards was laid a while ago. Things might have changed. Think, Bobbi. Think about yourself. Are you still so dead set against making your peace with your grandpap?"

She felt a storm of nameless, muddled feeling at the mention of her grandfather. Not hating, she knew that, as she knew Grant Yandro was not evil. Far from it. He had done nothing worse than say some hurtful words. But—but . . . There was something she could not get past.

"I can see you ain't ready." Witchie looked around at the dimly moonlit night as if for a clue. "I wish I had the cards. Bobbi, think."

Wearily Bobbi did. The sight of Samuel Bissel lying unconscious on the ground distracted her. She felt as if he was somehow going to get up and hurt

her, and she didn't know where to go to get away
from him. "There's nowhere," she said. "There's
nobody."

Nowhere in the world she wanted to go, nobody in
the world who—who—

There was one who had loved her once, maybe,
when she was a tiny baby.

"My mother's not far from here," Bobbi said. "But
she's no use." A hidden bitterness hardened and
twisted her voice. "She's loony. She thinks she's
Scarlett O'Hara."

Witchie swayed where she stood, and for the first
time Bobbi saw Mrs. Fenstermacher use her walking
stick as such. The old woman steadied herself with
Kabilde, as if her props had been knocked wobbly,
and her mouth dropped open, and she seemed to be
having trouble getting her breath. Shane stretched
his long head toward her anxiously, and for a panicky
moment Bobbi tried to remember things she had
heard about CPR. Then Witchie found a gulp of air
and gasped, "That's it!"

She lurched forward. Bobbi grabbed her by the
arm, afraid she was actually going to fall, but Witchie
seemed not to notice. "That's it!" she repeated. "The
red card!"

"Huh?"

"Huh, hell! The red card!" Annoyed, and therefore
much more herself, Witchie pushed Bobbi's steady-
ing hand away. She firmly took her accustomed
cookstove stance. "The one at the juncture next to
the dark rider's, the one I couldn't interpret! Red,
don't you see? Scarlet! Scarlett O'Hara! She's the one
you're tangled through!"

Bobbi didn't really see. But Witchie didn't have a

chance to explain, because from somewhere down the mountain floated the sound of sirens, drawing closer. Witchie jerked her cornstarched chins in annoyance.

"Either the law tracked us here by that simple-minded gypsy, or somebody saw the fireworks and called in an alarm."

"Well, let's get moving!" Bobbi exclaimed.

"You get moving. Take Shane to your mother." Witchie gave Bobbi a shove to emphasize the order. "Go! Ride!" The girl looked at her wildly, then scrambled onto the black horse.

"Wait," commanded Witchie. "Take Kabilde." She scuttled to Shane's side and held the pow-wow staff up to Bobbi.

"No!" In sheerest fear. But then Bobbi tried to make it sound as if she had other reasons. "I—I couldn't take your staff. You'll need it! What if Bissel—"

"Bullshit, girl! You want the cops to get hold of it? Take it!"

Crunch of gravel, along with sirens and roaring engines, sounded down the lane. On Shane's back, Bobbi sat frozen. She would sooner have lifted a live rattlesnake than touch Kabilde, after what she had recently seen.

Witchie reached up, grabbed Bobbi's slack hand and put the walking stick into it, hard. "Git!" she decreed fiercely. "Run!"

It was Shane who ran, and Bobbi was on him, with a hand tangled in his mane and the pow-wow stick hanging heavy in the other.

He carried her away. Through the gone-to-scrub pasture he thundered, dodging young hickories and maples under the light of a horseshoe moon, and he

plunged into the truer, darker forest just as headlights were brightening the sky.

The fire trucks roared into the clearing and stopped
near the parked buggy, but found nothing except an
unconscious Amishman and a muttering old woman
searching for her purse. They could get no sense out
of her. She seemed witless. There were scorch marks
all around the Amishman, but no fire. It was anyone's
guess what had happened to him. His horse seemed
to be gone, they noticed that, but they didn't notice
the black-handled hammer lying at some distance in
the darkness.

PART 3

The Old Man of the Mountain

Grant Yandro looked out of his cabin at the rain. He should have been out and doing, rain or no rain, but he seemed to have no gumption since Bobbi had gone off. It was a week to the day since the girl had run away, and even to Grant, who prided himself on being a strong thinker, the rain seemed not just rain at all but a weeping of the world. Sky, doing what he couldn't let himself do. Old fool that he was.

On the bare, wooden table stood the coffinlike wooden box he had given the girl, and after a moment he turned slowly back to it. For the past few days, feeling that he had to do something, Grant had been looking at random through the clippings and photos and notes inside it, Wright's things, as if the remnants left by the son might somehow tell him something about the daughter, something he needed to know in his heart to get her back. . . .

Between two fingers, not for the first time, Grant Yandro lifted the yellowed newspaper clipping, Wright's only published poem.

"The old gods live in hidden forms.
In the autumn night the wild geese fly,
A cat roams under the bloated moon,
The gypsies ride the highways still,
Somewhere the horses run wild.
The cunning mustangs defy you on the mountains.
You have heard the dragon roar in the dark . . ."

"What nonsense," the old man muttered, dropping the clipping to the top of an untidy pile, though he had in fact sometimes heard strange noises in the dark. He did not like the night, and he regarded sleeping as an unpleasant necessity. He had uneasy dreams whenever he slept. They troubled and annoyed him, and he took care not to remember them. The way people sometimes told tales of ghosts and supernatural things annoyed him as well. Simple-minded Dutchmen and their talk of hex . . . He let no thoughts of such nonsense enter his head. Never had. Never would.

A knock sounded at the door, and without waiting for an answer the Dodd boy came in out of the rain. Travis had been spending a good deal of his time at the Yandro cabin since Bobbi had disappeared. The boy seemed to feel somehow to blame because he had been the last one to see her.

"Morning, Mr. Yandro," he said awkwardly.

Grant nodded. Travis sat down across the table from him, knowing without asking, by the set of the old man's face, that there had been no further news of Bobbi, not since the police had picked her up at Veto and lost her. Travis looked over Grant Yandro's head out the window, and the old man knew without saying anything that Travis was thinking the same thing he had been thinking a few minutes earlier. And hating to think it, the same way. That Bobbi was out in the chill rain somewhere.

"She'll be fine," Travis said, meaning, I hope she's OK.

"Hell, yes," Grant Yandro grumbled, promptly and with more conviction than Travis had been able to muster. "She's a Yandro. Wherever she is, she's damn well fine."

Silence, except for the patter and trickle of the rain.

Grant Yandro added quietly, "I just hope she forgives me and gets her butt back here sometime before she's old and gray."

Travis got up to go out. "Time for school, boy?" the old man asked him.

"Huh? Oh. Yeah, sure." Travis lifted a hand in a hesitant goodbye and let himself out. A moment later Grant Yandro saw him walking down the lane toward the bus stop, disappearing behind trees. The boy carried no books. But then, it was not unusual for a boy to bring no books home.

The last thing Grant Yandro would have thought was that he was watching the departure of another runaway.

Chapter Fifteen

Bobbi laid her head against Shane's neck and felt her heart go hot.

To keep her head from being hit by branches in the dark, her eyes from being injured by twigs, that was why she rested her head on the horse's neck. Stallion who was Paladin, Zorro, Dark Rider. But feeling the pull and surge of the hard muscles as Shane galloped, the rhythmic rocking of the body between her knees, she thought briefly of the arms of Shane, the man, around her, and her thighs seemed to turn to water, and she pushed the thought away.

Shane slowed to a walk even before the sirens were out of earshot. Bobbi knew then how bone-tired he was. Cautiously she sat upright on his back, her left hand shielding her face.

"I can walk," she said to the black, pricked ears

showing in front of her, blacker and more shining than the night.

Faintly the globe of the staff in her right hand began to glow, and in it Bobbi could see Shane's face. Shane the man, dimmed as if he stood in twilight. His forehead, deeply shadowed beneath the brim of his black hat. The straight lines of his face, weary. But his fire-blue eyes blazed as bright as ever, seeming as always to consume her, to take her in, so that she could see nothing but Shane. And all the while the horse between her knees walked on.

"A man's got to carry his burdens," Shane the man said to her, "and pay his debts."

"Bullshit," Bobbi said promptly, though her heart had started pounding like a hundred hooves at the sight of him and she would not have thought she could reply. "I don't plan to be anybody's burden, and you don't owe me a thing."

Shane said, very low, "I owe you plenty. What you done back there—"

"It doesn't matter. You're tired. I've been sitting in a car. Let me walk."

"Proud as a stud with seven mares," said Shane wryly. The low, tight tone had left his voice. He spoke easily, friend to friend, and Bobbi retorted in the same way.

"You should talk!"

"Have some sense, Bobbi! What if the posse comes? You got to be on me and ready to go."

He was right, and she knew it, and she sighed. "All right," she said reluctantly. "But as soon as it's daylight, we start looking for a place to hole up so you can get some rest."

Without speaking to that Shane asked, "Where is this place we're going?"

As best she could, Bobbi told him. She knew that she and Grandpap drove through Crown Stone when they went to see her mother, and she estimated the distance after that to be maybe two days' ride on horseback. She knew which mountains to cross: Bupp's Knob, where she and Witchie had found Shane, then Eagle, Blue Baldie and Witherow's Ridge. She knew the way by car. But following hard roads and following ridgetop trails are two far different undertakings, as she found when she tried to tell the way to Shane. The institution was isolated far out in the country, because peaceful, scenic surroundings were good for the mentally disturbed, the administrators said. Because towns and the people in them don't want the crazies too close at hand, Bobbi knew from hearing her elders talk. Whatever the reasons, the place was put so far from anywhere that she couldn't explain to Shane how to get there.

Finally, in brilliance or exasperation, she said to the walking stick, "Kabilde, can you show him?"

The surface of the globe swirled as if gray mist or smoke moved there. Shane's face vanished, and instead Bobbi saw the so-called cottage where her mother lived. Since Chantilly Yandro was not dangerous, she had been placed in a small "group arrangement" at the edge of the campus. The image began dwindling, as if a camera was drawing back to show the larger scale, and hastily Bobbi thrust the cane forward, holding it by the tip, so that Shane could see.

After a moment its light dimmed, and she drew it back. The globe had gone dark and blank. She could not talk with Shane any longer.

The mustang walked on. It started to rain.

A steady, chilly, soaking springtime rain worked its way through her windbreaker, soaking her to the skin even through her boots. Hunched over in mute protest, Bobbi rode. Shane speeded from his walk to a trot only when he reached the base of Bupp's Knob, where woods turned to small, ragged fields and where a few houses stood, a few small roads ran. He trotted and cantered across the benighted valley to the base of Eagle, where woods began again, before dawn. Then he slowed to a walk again and began toiling his way upslope. The rain went on. Big, secondhand drops of water plopped down from the trees, somehow even colder than proper raindrops. Bobbi set her lips hard. There would be no use complaining.

She could not tell when sunrise was. Black night turned to gray, rainy day, was all. Sometime still in morning, Shane crested Eagle. Then he stopped. Woods stretched for miles all around. Few people came to the top of Eagle except in hunting season. Bobbi got down, and Shane did something she had never seen him do: lay down flat on his side and fell at once into a deep sleep, the sort of sleep a stallion in the wild seldom allows himself. Or a gunslinger.

In the pouring rain. Bobbi wished she had something to cover him with, but there was nothing. No shelter for her, either.

She sat down on the soaking pine needles near him, stuck the end of her braid in her mouth and sucked it. She felt hazy and stupid with fatigue of body and mind. Mostly of mind. Too much had happened, too fast, and she could not focus on any of it, and it took her a while to realize that she was thirsty. There had been no stops to drink at streams during the night, and the rainwater that had dribbled into her mouth was not enough. Nor was sucking at her braid enough.

She looked at the walking stick lying on the ground. The carved snake looked back.

"Sorry," she said, remembering that the staff did not like to be laid flat. She leaned it up against a tree, wondering why Kabilde was so reticent it hardly ever spoke aloud. She positioned it gingerly, then pulled her hands away and wanted not to touch it again, for she could not gauge the staff's mood, and still felt half afraid of it, though she had been carrying it most of the night. But her throat ached with thirst. After a moment she reached for the crystal handle, unscrewing it. Kabilde, as she had thought it would, knew she was thirsty. The stick presented her with a flask full of clear, cold beverage, and she drank it all. "Thanks," she said humbly as she replaced the stopper and returned the flask to the staff.

Her body was confused by nighttime travel and the strain of being a runaway. She felt very tired yet not at all sleepy. Now that there was a chance to sleep, her eyes opened so wide they burned. Her hands fiddled with twigs, and the loud chirp of a bird made her jump. She sat in the rain, uselessly wondering where her bag of spare clothing had been left in all the confusion, whether at the gypsy camp or in the trunk of a gypsy's car or behind a rock in the abandoned pasture near the buggy. After a while it occurred to her that she was hungry. Her body was not sending her clear signals, but she had to be hungry. Not expecting much, she took the handle off the walking stick again. There was a spiral-striped plastic cannister full of M&M's in there. She giggled and ate almost all of them, stopping only when she began to feel sick.

The day felt very long already, and it couldn't yet be noon. Bobbi sat with the calf muscles of her legs twitching, restless and shivering with cold and bored and feeling very much alone. She wanted something, but she wasn't sure what. And the walking stick was the only waking person—or at least, companion—on the mountaintop with her.

"Kabilde," she requested timidly, "can you show me my father? I mean, when he was alive. What he was really like."

Because she had been mostly talking to herself, it startled her badly when the passionless voice of the staff answered her. "What is gone is gone," Kabilde said.

"You can't show the past, then," Bobbi managed to reply.

"Only what is."

The staff's white light faintly glowed, the mist swirled in the crystal, then cleared into—mountain mist, rising beneath the rain. Posts of a pipe corral showed faintly through it. The lean, tough, clean-shaven old man stood by the fence, idle, as he ought not to have been idle, and leaning, as he never leaned, as if something hurt him. Staring into the mist, a ravaged look on his face. Her grandfather.

"No!" Bobbi shouted at her first glimpse of him. She shut her eyes and covered them with her hands. Her shout roused Shane. She heard the black horse stirring, and then she heard the dark rider's voice speak to her from the walking stick's globe. "Bobbi."

"What," she muttered. Shane's voice was low, intense, vibrant. The sound of it always thrilled her. But this time she would not look at him.

There was silence for a while. Then Shane said simply, "Go to sleep."

She did what he said, slumped sideward without opening her eyes, lay in the rain and slept.

When she awoke at dusk, the walking stick stood looking ordinary, or as ordinary as any carved cane with silver ferrule and crystal handle. The rain had stopped. Shane was on his feet, eating the new leaves, mouthing the twigs for the moisture on them.

"Shane," Bobbi said, and she reached for Kabilde. She meant to bring out the flask for the mustang-man. But Kabilde spoke.

"Strike my tip to the ground," said the staff, its glassy voice seeming to float through the air like ice on water.

"Huh?" said Bobbi, though the words had been perfectly clear.

"Strike my steel tip to the ground." A trace of bite in the words. Kabilde did not like to speak twice.

She took the staff by its handle and gave the ground at her feet a hesitant tap. Nothing happened except that water started to seep muddily out of the loam. From all the rain, she supposed.

"Harder," Kabilde ordered. "I said strike."

Irritated, Bobbi lifted Kabilde and gave the mountaintop a hard whack, then stood aghast. The ground seemed to tremble under her feet. There was a splitting sound, as if bedrock had broken. And water burst out of the top of Eagle mountain, a strong spring where no spring ought to be, forming a clear pool before it ran away downslope.

Shane came over, lowered his head in a matter-of-fact way and drank.

"You are strong enough in power, you can do that," Kabilde said with no passion of any sort in its voice. If Bobbi had hurt the staff, it was not telling. "Mrs. Fenstermacher cannot."

"Huh," Bobbi muttered, feeling not very fond of Kabilde. And afraid, though not very afraid; she seemed too tired all the time to be very afraid. And if she had thought about it, she would have known her fear was not really of the walking stick.

That night she and Shane traveled at speed when the forest allowed it; Shane had rested, and his cracked hoof no longer troubled him. Sometime around midnight Bobbi ate the licorice Kabilde gave her, and for the first time in her life she thought with longing of proper cooked food, of hot carrots and potatoes and pot roast. She shivered in her damp clothes. Her arm ached from carrying the staff. Whenever she tried to hold it across Shane's withers, or against her chest, or any other way than straight down at her side, it caught in the ever-present trees and bushes, and more than once she thought of ditching it, except that she knew Witchie would never forgive her.

Witchie. How was Witchie doing, she wondered, and where was the old hag? Not in jail, she hoped. Bobbi knew she had to get the pow-wow staff back to Witchie first chance she got, and not just to be nice, either. The thing was weird. Bobbi didn't want to carry it around for long.

By dawn, the character of the land had changed. No longer was Bobbi riding a black mustang through miles and miles of mountaintop forest. It went on, sweeping north and eastward, without them, but they had come down into cleared foothills, a maze of farm lanes, cornfield, pasture, and barbed-wire fences. Shane snorted and leaped the first fence from a stand-still, dodged the woodchuck holes crowding at the woods line, then struck out with a long, reaching lope across the open expanse beyond, where trees no longer hindered him. Wyoming, Bobbi thought. He's thinking of running the rangelands of Wyoming. With relief that equalled his, she laid the walking stick across his withers, shook the ache out of her arm, then hung onto the stick with one hand and the black mustang's mane with the other as Shane jumped fence after fence. Bobbi winced at each fence. Around horses, barbed wire could be trusted only to lay open ugly gashes, bring the animal crashing down in a bloody tangle. She knew Shane was no horse, what-ever his form, but still she flinched each time he bunched his haunches to leap.

He felt her stiffening. At the first farm lane, he changed course to canter along the grassy ruts, fol-lowing the crazy zigs and zags as the lane followed field lines, cornered around field ends. Down a long hill the lane led to a farmyard, and Bobbi winced again as Shane carried her at a gallop past three barking farm dogs chained to their shelters against the barn. She did not turn her head to watch the lights go on in the house. Shane had struck a dirt road at the head of the driveway, and he galloped along its meandering course, letting it take him, like a stream, in its own winding time down the hillsides.

As the sun came up, Shane slowed to a walk, then stood still on a rise for a moment, breathing. In the distance, far down the valley, Bobbi could see the blunt redstone towers of the asylum where her mother was kept. "That's it," she said to Shane. "How did you know?" Not expecting an answer.

He went on at the walk.

It felt odd to Bobbi, a mountain girl, to be able to look around the open farmland and see where she was going and where she had been. Ahead, no bigger than her thumbnail, stood the redstone towers in their fenced park, their haze of greening maple. And glancing behind her, seeing the fields and fences, the fallow, veering course of the farm lane and the house where the three dogs had barked—seeing the soft brown bit of fluff that was one of the dogs—seeing the fencelines (though not the barbed wire fences themselves, at the distance) and the tan sweep of the dirt road into folds and over hilltops, Bobbi seemed to see the tiny figure of a girl on a black mustang, the girl's head up and facing the wind, the horse's legs no bigger than eyelashes, seemed to see it clear and wee as if in Kabilde's globe, the girl and the horse galloping, always galloping. Ghost of her own past, behind her.

But Kabilde could not have showed it to her. What was gone was gone.

"Bobbi."

The voice sounded inside her head. "Speak of angels," she said sourly, though she had not in fact spoken of ghosts. The white haze of her father's presence hovered in air ahead. Shane walked steadily toward it, and it kept an even distance ahead of him.

"Bobbi, what do you want with your mother?"

She did not in fact know what she wanted her mother to do about Shane. But the question went deeper, touched a sore spot. There was something she wanted of her mother, a need felt more than thought about. And trying to think about it, to put it in words, tangled her up and threw her and made her mad, just as thinking about her grandfather did. An angry answer jumped out of her.

"What's it to you? Why are you always meddling?"

Shane walked steadily on, ignoring her shout, either ignoring or not seeing the white blur in the air ahead.

"You may recall that your mother and I were related by marriage," Wright Yandro said mildly inside Bobbi's head. "I take an interest in what affects her."

Her anger gone, Bobbi looked up curiously, staring at the cloudy whiteness in the air.

"What were you and Mom like?" she asked. "I mean, really?"

All at once, though nothing had swirled or shifted in the white blur, she could see her father's face, as if a puzzle-picture had just come into focus for her. Or as if she had just allowed herself to see him. He looked not much older than she was herself. Of course not; he had been just past his teens when he died. And the look on his face, as if . . . Bobbi felt an odd tug at her heart, seeing him so young, so—so feeling, as if he could have been—something to her.

She said, "I mean, did you—love each other?"

"Nah. People just get married because they detest each other. Judas Priest, girl!"

The tart reply sounded so much like something her Grandpap might have said that it made her angry again. Her jaw clamped tight, and her father's face was gone; only a cloudy whiteness remained.

She said, "Go away. Quit bothering me. You're dead."

"Bobbi, if you'd just give it a chance I wouldn't have to be dead to you!"

"You're messing around in my life. Pretty soon you'll make me as crazy as my mother. Are you the one who drove her crazy?"

She said that just to hurt him. But he answered her with a trembling voice. "Bobbi, you know she—she lost it after I died. The war—the war did it to her. It was a dirty, stinking little war, and she had ideas—of what a war should be—and when they sent me home in pieces—"

"Go away!" she shouted at him. "What's gone is gone." She shut her eyes and willed him away. When she opened her eyes again, the white haze of Wright Yandro's presence had disappeared.

Swiveling on Shane's back, she scanned the land behind her. A shadow lay over it. A cloud was passing.

She turned to face forward, looking out over Shane's fox-pricked ears. What lay ahead, lay ahead.

Chapter Sixteen

By midmorning she and Shane had reached the Safe Haven Home for the Chronically Disturbed.

A gaunt, gargoyled structure, massively built of brick-colored Pennsylvania redstone on a foundation of gray granite, it loomed four stories high, plus towers. The small, iron-barred windows and the dark weather stains on the stones made it look like some glowering, weeping house out of a Gothic horror story. Not a place Bobbi had ever very much liked, but the fence around it was only the usual wrought-iron manifestation of wealth, dating back to the time when the mansion had been built by some rich steel magnate from Pittsburgh as a summer home. The ostentatious gates stood wide open in expectation of deliveries. Shane trotted in and up the paved, curving drive. A man in coveralls stared at him and Bobbi. Neither of them stared back.

"Over there," Bobbi said, pointing with the walking stick. But Shane had already recognized the cottage and was heading that way.

Built of the same redstone as the rest of the place, it might once have been the caretaker's home. Now it housed six of the less violent, though not necessarily housebroken women. Shane stopped close by the door, and Bobbi slid off him and ran in, taking Kabilde with her. Wobbling, because she had not even waited to get her land legs back, she ran. The coveralled fellow would be talking with his boss by now. And a black horse standing at the cottage doorstep was hard to miss noticing. There would not be much time.

A middle-aged patient shuffled past her like an old woman, muttering to herself and rolling a sizable ball of lint and carpet fuzz and hair combings between her forefinger and thumb. Her hand was misshapen from a lifetime of constantly gathering and holding such balls. She had been at the home for as long as Bobbi could remember, but neither of them looked at or greeted the other. Somewhere in one of the rooms the screamer was screaming. Bobbi knew better than to pay any attention. There was always a screamer in residence, and there always would be. A chunky nurse in white pantsuit and thick-soled white shoes came out of a room, saw Bobbi and nearly dropped the tray she was carrying. Bobbi ran past her to find her mother.

Chantilly Lou Yandro was in her room, playing with makeup while her roommate crooned and rocked, mostly naked, in the middle of a rumpled bed. Chantilly Lou at least was fully clothed, Bobbi noted thankfully. She had on a silk-look emerald-green evening gown, Cinderella style, as if she were going to the

prince's ball. Her slightly pouting lips were perfectly
outlined in vivid scarlet, but she had other colors of
makeup clownishly smeared all over her face. Her
mane of brunette hair hung wildly tangled, full as a
horse's tail before a lightning storm, above her slender, narrow shoulders. She regarded her daughter
reproachfully. "Melly," she drawled, "why have you
taken Ashley away from me?" She fluttered her
eyelashes, black and thick, courtesy of Cover Girl.
One thin hand languidly moved an invisible fan.

Invisible except to Bobbi. She saw the form behind
the form—

No time for that. "I'm not Melly," Bobbi told her
impatiently. "I'm Bobbi. Your daughter, Bobbi."

"Of course you'd say that, Melanie Hamilton. You
always were a fool. A simpering, mousy little fool."

Somewhere in the building Bobbi heard the thump
of running footsteps. She grabbed her mother by the
wrist. "Come on," she ordered, and she half-led,
half-dragged Chantilly out of the room. Bobbi was
taller and stronger, but the woman who thought she
was Scarlett O'Hara fought, of course. "Melly! You
turn loose of me! What's got into you?"

"The Yankees are coming," Bobbi told her between clenched teeth.

"Oh!"

Chantilly gasped once in excitement or terror, then
silently hurried along at Bobbi's side, down the corri-
dor to the front door of the cottage. Bobbi could only
hope there would be time for whatever was supposed
to happen when she met Shane.

It didn't, or there wasn't.

It surprised Chantilly not at all to find a horse
waiting at the doorstep. She scarcely glanced at Shane,

but looked around anxiously for the Yankees. And there wasn't time for Bobbi to do or say anything, even if she had known what to do or say, for with a whooping siren and a scream of tires a police car pulled in at the gate. Bobbi was more or less expecting that, but she was not expecting Samuel Bissel to get out of it.

"Yonder's my horse," he told the township sheriff lumbering out from behind the steering wheel.

"It's the Yankees, Mom! On the horse, quick!" Bobbi gave her mother a boost. Chantilly went up with a coquettish little scream and a flutter of her full skirt. With an odd, slow-motion clarity, as if she would remember them forever, Bobbi noted her mother's bare feet nudging out from underneath her emerald-green hem, small and soft as a child's.

"Stop where you are!" the officer ordered.

"Go, Shane!" Bobbi yelled. The pow-wow staff in her hand blazed with white light, and under her hand the wood writhed; Kabilde was rousing. The sheriff stood frozen and staring at it; Shane could have walked right past him and he would not have moved. But Bissel moved. Bobbi saw the Amishman reach with a callused hand, pull his hammer out from under his black, buttonless coat, and she braced herself. Probably he would knock her out. But by then Shane and Chantilly could be long gone—

Shane was standing right by her.

"Shane! Get a move on! Kabilde can hold them a few minutes."

Bissel swung his hammer, and darts of fire flew up from it. Bobbi felt the blow, but something powerful in her hand, and something hot and fierce in her heart, kept her from being too much staggered by it.

For a second her vision went black, but then she could see again. Kabilde's white-hot fire did not blind her. She could see the sheriff's head turn on his beard. She could see the sheriff's head turn on his short neck as he looked at the Amishman, aghast. She could see Chantilly sitting rapt on the black horse's back, something wild and yearning showing in her dark eyes as she watched the flare of cannon and mortar. She could see the blue blaze of Shane's eyes turn nearly as white as the flame of her staff.

And in the strobe-white light of those eyes she saw the face of Shane, the man, as she had seen it once before at a desperately hard time. Shane could speak to her without Kabilde's aid at these times of worst need. . . . Something in the set of his mouth like anger, but not anger, exactly. Through a sort of drumbeat noise in her ears she heard him say, "I'm not the sort of man who leaves my friends in a fight. Get on me."

"You can't carry us both!" she protested. She saw only Shane, not Samuel Bissel, but red fire must have flown again. She felt the hammer strike. It hurt. She thought she would fall.

"I'm the one to say what I can't do. Get on!"

The fierceness of the dark rider's voice gave her strength. She stumbled up the cottage steps and vaulted onto him, behind her mother. Then Shane galloped, with Bobbi bouncing on his rump and Chantilly swaying like a willow in front of her—sometime, somehow, Bobbi noted with surprise, Chantilly had learned how to ride. And the snake, bigger than a cobra, rearing over them both and hissing and spitting wildfire at Bissel as they galloped past. And the white fire blazing and clashing with the red. And all the orderlies at the doors, and all the crazies looking out of windows, laughing or shouting or screaming. And the cop staring as if he was going to faint, never even reaching for his gun.

Shane galloped out the gate and down the paved road. When he found a narrower, dirt road he turned onto it. The white fire of the walking stick dimmed and went dark, but Shane kept galloping. Bobbi felt his ribs straining, heard his breath coming hard. There was nowhere to go but the dirt roads, where police cars could still follow. She knew he couldn't take to the farm lanes and jump the fences, not with her sitting on his hindquarters.

"Shane," she said, "stop."

He kept going at a stubborn, plunging gallop.

"You hot dog," she complained, "stop a minute, would you? I want to see something."

He slowed to a jarring trot, then stopped, his sides heaving. Bobbi slipped down and walked around in front of him, where she stood with the walking stick.

"I am not getting on you again," she told him. "Take my mother and go. I'll take care of myself. Kabilde will help me find you once the cops give up."

Shane gave her a glare, tossed his head and pawed. Even the carved snake on the staff, which had settled back to its usual size and place, moved to look at her. Feeling the movement, she looked down at it.

"Kabilde," she appealed, "would you tell him he can't get anywhere, carrying all of us?"

The snake did not speak. But the globe of the handle glowed smoke white, and a face appeared in it. Bobbi blinked, then smiled. It was Witchie.

"So there you are," she grumped. "About time you

thought of me." Though in fact Kabilde had thought of her, not Bobbi or Shane.

Bobbi couldn't tell where Witchie was, but she could see the old woman hadn't rested much. Her triple chin showed red creases instead of cornstarch. Her braids looked frazzled.

"You've got Scarlett? Then head for the Hub," she told them. "We'll settle Bissel's hash once and for all."

"We got cops after us," Bobbi said. For the past few moments she had been aware of sirens in the distance.

Witchie seemed not to hear either Bobbi or the sirens. "Head for the Hub," she repeated. "Shane knows where it is."

"But Shane can't carry double! And don't let him tell you he can," Bobbi added as the black mustang started to toss his head and paw again.

Siren whoopings suddenly grew louder. The police had turned onto the dirt road. This time Witchie heard them. "Holy gee, girl!" she snapped. "I want my staff back. Get a move on!"

"But *how?*"

Shane had his own ideas. He butted Bobbi hard with his head, sending her staggering forward. From the walking stick's globe, Witchie glared at her.

"Don't you have the brains you were born with? Use Kabilde." The old woman turned her back and stumped off into the mist. Bobbi was left staring at the dimming staff in her hand.

"Melly," her mother inquired blandly from Shane's back, "who was that?"

A white haze had appeared in the air off to the left. "Bobbi," it importuned her mind.

The flashing lights had come in sight down the dirt road. Shane's blue eyes were blazing.

With an effort Bobbi ignored all of them. "Kabilde," she demanded of the walking stick, "What the hell was she talking about? Can I ride you?"

And in its glassy-smooth voice, without hurry, the walking stick began to chant.

"With a heart of furious fancies
Whereof I am commander,
With a burning spear
And a horse of air,
To the wilderness I wander."

The sheriff's car was pulling to a stop a few paces away. But Bobbi scarcely noticed, her attention entirely taken up by the strangeness happening under her. With a thunder sound, air was moving, it was solid, she was straddling it as if riding a wild stallion, and it was carrying her—up, away, onward, at speed— and in her hand Kabilde flamed, a leaf-shaped flare of fire at its head, a burning spear—and she knew then that thunder was the galloping hooves of the storm horse of heaven, and lightning a blazing spear, and she was riding a horse of air, and she knew she was as crazy as her mother.

Beneath her she saw Chantilly riding a black mustang at a dead run across the fields, saw Shane leaping the barbed-wire fences as if they were cobwebs, saw her mother's slim body whipping with the rhythm of the gallop, the long, dark tangle of hair snaking on air, sensed rather than heard Chantilly's soprano laugh. She did not bother to look back for the cops. They would be staring the way she was, and very nearly as scared. Shane and the ground were—below her, entirely too far below—

She grabbed at a mane of air, felt it under her hand even though she could not see it, clutched it. "Down!" she pleaded to whatever was listening. "The cops will see me up here," she added. "Spot me from all over the county." Her voice was shaking.

Low-pitched laughter answered her, and in the confusion of her mind she did not know whose laughter, her father's, Kabilde's, thunder laughter . . . Nor did she much care. "Worried about the police, Bobbi?" a voice mocked, and she did not know whose voice, or from where, or care. All the strange things that had been happening to her, all the business of the Hidden Circle, all the ways of magic and of form beyond form had spun into a muddle for her, and she felt far too tired of it all to sort it out. All she wanted was solid footing again. But—

The weird steed carrying her, whatever it was, started swooping downward at a terrifying pitch and speed, as if it would crash into the ground.

"Not so fast!" she yelled.

"Never satisfied." The cool, taunting voice, she suddenly knew, was Kabilde's, and in that moment she no longer felt afraid, but profoundly angry. She glared at the pow-wow staff in her hand, focusing her anger at it as she had once focused her whole attention on Witchie's back door. "Ow," said Kabilde. Its voice revealed no more feeling than it ever showed, but Bobbi felt her insubstantial mount slow and upright and steady itself, so that she drifted down by easy stages until her mount of air was galloping nearly on ground, beside Shane. And Kabilde's blaze of white fire quieted.

"We do, after all, want to hide from the police now that we're out of their sight," it said, its voice slick as melting ice.

"Huh," Bobbi said. "You never used to talk so much."

Kabilde said, "I'm tired, too."

She thought about that, and her anger at the pow-wow stick vanished. "Yes," she admitted, "I guess you would be."

Silence for a short while. The field they were crossing was hummocky and riddled with woodchuck holes, not the best place for a gallop. Bobbi hoped Shane was watching his footing. She knew he was, but glanced over anyway. Chantilly met the glance, riding happily, seeming not at all perturbed that Bobbi's horse was invisible to the naked eye. "Watch me take this one, Melly!" she cried as they came up on the next barbed-wire fence. "Tally ho!" as if she were following the hounds instead of being hounded. Her emerald-green skirt billowed out behind her. Chantilly rode astride, her bare feet hugging the horse's barrel, but the form behind the form . . . For a moment Bobbi watched the young belle with the flat-brimmed riding hat tilted over her green eyes, the fashionable riding habit showing off her seventeen-inch waist, the tiny, polished boots glinting under her skirts as she rode sidesaddle, taking the fence expertly, reins held firmly in soft, gloved hands. . . .

Shane leaped the fence in a graceful arc. Bobbi's horse went through it. No harm, she reminded herself, but her stomach seemed to have gotten stuck up her throat somewhere, and she could not help imagining she had felt a rusty barb graze her backside.

"Kabilde," she said wearily when she could speak, "I know you're tired, but you've got to stop that sort of thing."

The pow-wow staff answered with no change of tone, "I can't keep this up much longer."

She looked at it curiously. Its globe had gone dull and dark. She said, "You miss Witchie."

Kabilde did not answer.

Bobbi called, "Shane."

The mustang-man slowed to a canter, turning his proud, black head to look at her. Then he turned entirely and came to a stop, seeing her pitch off her steed of air and land on her back on the ground. Bobbi rolled with the force of the fall and came to her feet under Shane's nose, holding Kabilde in her hand. Big-eyed, her mother looked down at her. Her mother who was Scarlett O'Hara, riding a horse who was no horse . . . In that moment Bobbi decided that her life had gotten entirely too complicated. Her father's cloudy presence, at least, she seemed to have left behind. Thank God, or the three highest names, or whatever.

"Why, Melly!" Chantilly exclaimed. "You've lost your horse! Now how are we ever going to run that bad old fox to his den?"

Bobbi said, "Shank's mare."

Chapter Seventeen

"To the wilderness I wander," Bobbi muttered.
"Huh. Don't I wish."

In the woods she had felt safe from all the people
who were after her, but this farmland was entirely
too open. During the past few hours, on their way to
the Hub, she and Chantilly and Shane had hidden
from the passing police in a huge, old rust-red barn
with twelve-pointed hex signs on its peaks and white
outlines, devil's doors, witches' windows, painted on
its sides. They had followed the course of streambeds,
shielded by the brushy banks, wading in the water.
They had kept behind the straggles of trees along
fencerows. There was nowhere else to hide. Bobbi
walked or jogged at Shane's side, carrying Kabilde.
Because of her bare feet, Chantilly mostly rode. Chantilly had proved to be remarkably skillful at spotting

and evading the "Yankees," and after a while Bobbi's fear of being captured had settled into a quick-breathing patience. At least in the open farmland she could see where she had come from, where she was going. She didn't feel lost, in the open. A person could feel lost, bewildered, wandering in the wilderness.

Though, in fact, she didn't know where she was going. She was following a black mustang with a gunslinger's soul. She might as well have been in a forest full of ghosts and shadows. An old witch laughing amid the trees. Dragon's roar in the night. White haze in the moonlight. Dancing gypsies. A body, buried deep. Howl of wolves.

The wilderness was in her mind.

"Melly," her mother complained from Shane's back, "I'm hungry."

Bobbi was hungry too. "I'm your daughter," she said.

"Melly, don't we have a bit of pone, or—"

Bobbi turned fiercely on her, speaking out of the hunger within. "Look at me," she demanded. "I'm your daughter. I'm Bobbi! Look at me! See me the way I really am!"

Her mother answered this outburst with a blank stare. "Well, fiddle-dee-dee!" Chantilly declared. "Don't be in a pet, Melly. I was just asking."

Shane had come to a standstill, swinging his head to look at her. But instead of meeting his gaze Bobbi strode up to her mother's knee. "Bend down," she ordered.

Chantilly tossed her head and did not obey. For the moment, clenching her teeth, Bobbi played her assigned part.

"Bend down here, silly. Your hat ribbon's coming undone."

"Oh!" Pleased, as Scarlett O'Hara was always pleased by attention of any sort, Chantilly leaned over to be ministered to. Bobbi grabbed her mother's head between her hands, glared into the dark eyes so much like her own, pressed her forehead hard against her mother's forehead, so petal-soft of skin, so white. Her mother's startled hands came up and gripped her wrists as if to tear her hands away. Bobbi spoke quickly.

"You are Chantilly Lou Buige Yandro," she commanded. "I am Bobbi Lee Yandro. I am your daughter. See me!" And with all her strength she willed it.

And beating down her strength, battering it and cutting through it, she felt—a will far stronger than her own. A madwoman's single-minded, steely resolve to make the world what she wanted it to be. Bobbi felt—felt—

She pulled away, broke free of Chantilly's grip on her wrists, ran a few steps in her heavy, soaking boots before she slowed down and trudged on again. Shane walked at her side. She felt his glance but would not look at him.

"She's twice as strong as me," she said, very low. "She almost—she almost turned me into Melanie."

Shane's head swung toward her. She looked away, as if looking around her for danger, though she could see nothing. Tears blurred her eyes, stupid, stinging tears. And in her heart burned the angry, hurting, hungry feeling, the same as—what she couldn't get past, what was keeping her away from her grandpap—

"Yankees!" Chantilly exclaimed as they approached the crest of a hill.

"Ask me if I care," Bobbi muttered. Nevertheless, her head came up to see the police cruiser.

Then it was hide again, duck behind the rise of land, head toward the corncrib standing at the field's corner. All afternoon it was duck, dodge, hide. The "Yankee" sightings grew fewer and farther away; Bobbi began to hope that she and Chantilly and Shane had left the focus of the search behind. But still, the day was nothing but stalk, skulk, hide. The land had softened from corn stubble into pasture growing rank with spring grass; her mother, without preamble, had slipped down off Shane's back to patter along at Bobbi's side. Bobbi felt hunger knotting her insides so that she could scarcely lift her heavy feet. The sun was sinking low. No rest, had to press on, but soon darkness would help them hide—

Shane cantered up the next hill and stood at the very top of it, head flung high, looking all around him defiantly, like a stallion surveying his domain. Bobbi gawked. Craziness in the air, she thought. Shane had lost his mind.

Chantilly scampered up the slope and perched on a single boulder there, a rock as big as a mill wheel and nearly as circular. She arranged her full skirt, soaked in streams, draggled with cow dung, to half cover it with mud-splattered green folds. Scarlett O'Hara had settled on the ottoman at Twelve Oaks. Green was Scarlett O'Hara's favorite color. It brought out the green of her sly, jealous eyes. "Well," said Chantilly brightly, "here we are."

Bobbi came trudging up at the best speed she could manage. "Is that true?" she demanded of Shane. "Is this really it?" A sweep of pasture, a rounded hill with a rock on top—

Shane turned his intense gaze on her, but a smoky-thin voice from the vicinity of her right hand answered, startling her. Kabilde.

"This is the Hub," the walking stick said in its dispassionate way. "No one else has eyes to notice, but we of the Circle know. The mound was shaped by ancient people, the yellow-skinned people who came even before the red men. They raised the earthwork over their honored dead; the dust of their bones lies underneath. Millennia have passed, and the mound has weathered away to the shape of a breast, but we of the circle remember. The rock is even older than the bones, older than the shape of this continent. The people who made the mound have carved their runes on it. No muck-minded farmer would ever know, but we know. Under moonlight, they still show."

Come here who will, Shane's stance atop the hill seemed to say. This is the Hub, the ancient, sacred place, and I will defend it.

Bobbi said to her mother, "Would you get up, please? I want to look."

With a flounce and a swirl of polyester, Chantilly flitted away, and Bobbi looked at the stone. She could see no runes, no carving of any sort, but through her planted feet she began to sense a feeling, an understanding, wordless and bone deep. This was an old place. The Hidden Circle haunted the old places. The stone topped the mound like the nipple on a pap, breast of earth; and earth was the oldest thing of all.

Shane stood deeply breathing through widened nostrils. Bobbi stood beside him and looked around at farmland, distant wooded mountains, sky. White clouds were beginning to glow saffron, lavender, rose. Bobbi stood by the black horse and watched the sunset. There would be time enough to eat, afterward. . . .

The sun blazed in chariot spokes through shifting clouds, then sank lower, spun free, the solo dancer in a kaleidoscope sky, turning into a circle of scarlet.

Chantilly Lou Yandro walked lightly up the hill, out of the dance in the west.

The madwoman had been playing around the base of the mound, sometimes sitting like a lark in the tall grass, sometimes busy with her hands, sometimes jumping up to swirl off to another place. Because she wanted something from her mother that she was not getting and never would, Bobbi had not paid much attention until Chantilly came up the hill wearing the sun like a broad-brimmed hat. Chantilly had made herself a garland of violets to wear against the whiteness of her neck. In the wild curls of her dark hair she had placed the white blossoms of phlox, and she carried sprays and clusters of it in her arms, white and purple and wine red, and for the first time Bobbi noticed how weirdly beautiful she was in her long dress, her waist small, her breasts half-bared above the flowers. Chantilly's face, rapt in madness, was as soft and unlined as that of a child. She had washed it in the dew on the lush pasture grass, and it rose white and innocent above the flowers, her lips lustrous red, her eyes dark and shining. She swayed as she walked, and Bobbi saw hoops swaying, silk flounces edged in velvet, green morocco slippers.

Scarlett O'Hara came, red lips pouting and slightly parted as if waiting for a kiss, long eyelashes wisping down and then up again so that glowing, liquid eyes could gaze. Straight at the black horse she gazed. Straight into eyes of wild-larkspur blue.

Scarlett said, "Rhett."

Like black silk Shane's hide lustered. Sweat of fear made it shine.

Bobbi saw the fear-sweat slick his neck and chest and shoulders all in a moment, saw him stiffen and start to tremble as she had seen him tremble once before, when he was trapped in a dark stall, terrified of castration—terrified. Shane was as deeply afraid of this woman as he had been of the scalpel. The dark rider, panicked by a slender girl-woman . . . "No," Bobbi whispered, seeing the form behind the form, seeing too late what she had done. This was the one who had so often betrayed him. This was the woman who had tamed and befooled and betrayed him, all his lives. It was she who had sent him away to the wastelands, a wild horse. It was she who could coax and cajole a wild horse to her and lay her hands on its forelock.

One hand outstretched, Kabilde in the other, Bobbi started toward Shane to lend him her strength. She would place her hand on his neck to comfort him. She would drive her mother away with the staff—

Kabilde writhed and twisted in her grip. The snake's head darted up at her face, its small eyes hard and glittering. Bobbi jumped back, nearly dropping the pow-wow staff. The snake faced her steadily, its small tongue flickering, wordlessly warning her away from Shane. What was to be, was to be. The cards had told it on Witchie's table. Witchie had battled Bissel so that it could happen.

"Rhett," Scarlett O'Hara breathed, "you have come back to me."

Shane stood quivering, his eyes wild with terror. Why did he not run, if he was so terribly afraid? But he was the dark rider. Honor held him where he stood. He would not run.

Aglow in the scarlet sunset light, with white flowers caught like souls in the tangle of her hair, Bobbi's mother faced Shane on the hilltop. Blossoms drifted down from her breast, her arms. She lifted her hands to either side of Shane's black head, pressed them there, gazed into his staring eyes and kissed him.

There was a harsh, clanging sound, like the clash of some brutal gong. The sky darkened, for all in a moment the sun had sunk. And the dark rider changed under the madwoman's hands. No horse stood there. Shane stood there, Shane the man, or the man Bobbi called Shane, shaken and trembling. In black silk shirt and black breeches he stood there—the clothes were as much a part of him, of what he was, as a black stallion's black hide was of it. But four moon-crescents of iron had fallen clanging to the ground. On his neck, at the open collar of the shirt, showed odd white markings, a brand or scar. His face—the look on his face tugged at Bobbi's heart. A man doomed to love . . . He stepped back from the full-skirted woman standing before him, but swept off his broad-brimmed black hat in the presence of a lady.

"You are mistaken, ma'am," he said. His deep voice shook only slightly.

Scarlett O'Hara did not step toward him, for in her way she was as proud as a Yandro. White blossoms stirred around her head as she lifted it. "Why, Rhett Butler," she declared, "don't be a fool. I know you."

Seeing him standing there, bareheaded, with his blue eyes shadowed, his face pale and his dark hair lifting like a mustang's mane in the evening breeze, with his proud chest heaving beneath the black silk and the new moon rising over his left shoulder, Bobbi felt a sudden hot, dark surge. She wanted him. He was so wild, so beautiful; she wanted to possess him, to own him, to keep him always. He was hers; she had known him first! The weird wooden snake swaying in front of her face could no longer stop her. She cast Kabilde aside, hearing the sharp hiss as the staff struck the ground, ignoring the sound—let the staff do what it wanted. She doubted it would hurt her. In three quick strides she was at the dark rider's side.

"His name is Shane!" she challenged her mother, challenged Chantilly who was prettier than Bobbi would ever be, who looked younger than her own daughter, Chantilly standing there so willowy with white blossoms in her hair while Bobbi clumped about in mud-caked boots and jeans. Chantilly who would never give her daughter what a mother should, what Bobbi needed and craved.

"Shane!" Bobbi repeated. Her mother had flowers in her hair, but she could not have him.

"Melly," Chantilly snapped, "you keep out of it!"

A white form flitted near her in the dusk, frantic, shouting her name. Her father wanted to speak with her. She ignored him. She heard nothing he said. He might have been hammering at the doors of her mind and she would not have heard, for a low, intense voice, the voice which had always thrilled her, was speaking to her.

Shane said, "Bobbi, she's right. You'd best stay clear of it."

Bobbi turned and looked at the dark rider in the dusk, and for all his toughness she knew. Something in her knew his soul. And though his gaze on her did not waver, she saw the shadow that moved near his mouth, and she knew he was wishing himself dead. The woman who had brought him back from mustang form was worse, more fearsome, more devastating

than the castrating scalpel to him. The knife would
have taken his manhood, but she would take his soul,
and his life, and his mind.

"I'm not going to let it happen," Bobbi said to him,
knowing that he knew what she meant. With all his
lifetimes he knew.

"There's no help for it."

Bobbi's mother stood by silently, smiling to herself, dimpling like a courting girl with a secret.

But there was help; it was so simple! Bobbi said,
"But I can offer you loyalty. I would keep faith with
you until I die. I would never toy with you and tame
you and betray you. I would love you."

She felt an odd stillness for a moment, as if the
entire world had stopped in its circling. And she saw
the sudden flickering of something heartbroken in his
eyes, and saw that maybe she had not done good
after all. The hope hurt him worse than the despair.

He said, "You deserve better."

Would love him? What had she meant, saying she
would love him? She loved him then, there, at that
moment. Her heart turned to water, just looking at
him. And whatever he had said about deserving made
no sense. She drew a breath to tell him—

He took one quick step and touched her mouth to
stop her. It was the first time she had ever felt his
touch, Shane, the man. Fingers on her lips like a
kiss, then gone.

"Bobbi. No. Please. If I let myself love you—" His
voice trembled so badly that he stopped and sucked
breath, trying to steady himself. His chest sobbed as
if he were weeping.

Standing by, watching, listening, the madwoman
softly laughed.

Bobbi felt the sound chill her, then shut it out of her mind, left it on the air somewhere along with the voice of her father's importuning ghost. She did not look at her mother. Nor did Shane. But his voice, when he spoke again, was calm. Worse than calm. Dull, dead, like the voice of a doomed man.

"If I let myself love you, it would destroy—what you are. It would make you—just like the others."

How could that be? He was the one who would give her what her mother could not, what no one else would, what she had always wanted, what would still her yearnings and make her always happy: love forever, love immortal and eternal. And what she could give him in return . . . She looked at him, seeing his shadowed face strong-lined and pale in the light of a horseshoe moon. Knowing with all her heart that she was the one who could put the blue fire back in his eyes.

He said, "Go away from me, Bobbi. Please."

Instead, she tilted her head toward him, lifting her chin, parting her lips to kiss him. "Shane," she whispered, her eyes half lidded, and he did not pull away from her. He was tame. He was hers. His strength was gone.

"Rhett Butler," called Chantilly Lou Yandro sharply out of the nightfall, "don't you dare kiss that tart." And by her side a white form bobbed in air, frantic. Faintly within her mind she heard its voice shouting at her, "Bobbi, no!"

And then she felt the touch of those immortal lips on hers, and she heard nothing but the pounding of her own heart. And she was hot, and full, and strong, strong with a woman's witchery, strong as any twelve virgins, strong as Chantilly because Shane was hers.

She felt the hot rush in her breasts move down. She felt her lips move, her body move, felt Shane's mouth and body answer, and she knew that soon, as soon as she could lead him away to a private place, he would be all hers, heart and body and soul.

"Rhett!" Chantilly shrilled, aghast, and Bobbi broke the kiss and turned on her.

"He is Shane," she averred to her mother, "and he is mine."

"Call him what you like," said another voice harshly out of the darkness, "he will not be yours." A deep, iron-hard voice. A black form, soot-black, shadow-black, standing in the night. Sweep of black robes. "He is Shane," the necromancer said, Samuel Bissel said, "and he is Rhett Butler, and Paladin, the wandering black knight, and he is the tavern prince, and the Scarlet Pimpernel, and many others. And he is mine."

Chapter Eighteen

As if he had flown down out of the dark heart of the moon, the trickster stood tall on the stone atop the hill. In his primal form he stood, robed in darkness, tall and looming on that high, holy place.

Frightened, Bobbi looked to the beautiful man standing at her side. But he seemed somehow weakened, shaken, unable to move, as if some invincible power held him prisoner. Feeling her glance, he said to her in an unsteady whisper, "The trickster holds the rock."

Bobbi looked at Bissel. Power even greater than his own flowed into the smith like suckle from the pap of earth, faintly haloing his head, his beard, his glinting eyes with a milky white glow. Bobbi could sense it more than see it, but she never doubted power was there. Under Bissel's feet the spirals and circles and meandering lines of ancient petroglyphs showed on the rock, glowing the same milky star-faint white in the moonlight, their meaning as inscrutable as that of the cuneiform scar on Shane's neck.

Shane whispered, "He—he has put his grip on me. Steel, plus—stone. . . ."

Kabilde lay at a small distance. Bobbi ran, three hasty strides, crouched and grasped it. But the staff lay inert, nothing but wood, in her hand.

"You've broken it, youngster!" And Bissel laughed loudly, laughter that pealed steel-hard, like hammer on anvil.

"Kabilde," Bobbi whispered urgently to the staff, "wake up!"

No rousing of the carved serpent answered her, no blaze of white light. Bobbi felt remorse squeeze her heart, aching worse than fear. Kabilde had spent itself and spent itself to aid her, feeding her, defending her, giving her a horse of air to ride—and she had flung it aside. She had hurt Kabilde, maybe even—maybe even killed it. . . . Crouching on the damp ground with the staff in her hands, she let her stare flicker away from Bissel a moment; she looked down at Kabilde, checking with eyes and hands—no, the carved snake was intact, the wood not split anywhere, the small head not broken away.

"Kabilde," she begged the staff, "I know you don't think much of me right now, but I'm not asking you to help me. Shane's in danger!"

Kabilde did not stir. Bissel laughed again.

"The dark rider is mine!" His triumphant voice echoed like clanging metal in the night. "You can do nothing to prevent it, young sorceress."

The words brought Bobbi to her feet. "No," she

said fiercely, "He is mine! Go away, sooty old man."
And to the world at large and in particular to the
inert staff on the ground she declared, "Very well, I'll
fight him myself."

She saw the glint of the necromancer's grin; it
enraged her. But before he could laugh at her again,
Shane's quiet, vibrant voice took hold of the night.
"You are both wrong," said the dark rider. "I do not
belong to you or anyone. I am my own. I am—a free
thing, a roaming thing. . . ."

Bissel shifted his glance to Shane, and Shane's
voice started to struggle, and then words came out of
him as if against his own will.

"I was—I was a free thing, running, wandering.
Then they trapped me, and roped me, and threw me
down, and burned the brand on my neck . . ." His
voice faltered and faded away.

"I claim you by that brand," said Bissel.

Only Grandpap could truly claim him by that brand,
Bobbi thought hazily, and he would geld him. But
no, Shane was a man now, and they didn't castrate
men . . . or did they? What did Bissel want to do
with Shane?

"Why?" she demanded of the Amishman, aloud
and strongly. "What do you want him for?" But even
as she spoke the words, she knew the answer.

"Power," said the smith simply. "The dark rider
will give me power as of wild horses. He will add his
magic to mine."

Even though they came from the trickster, the
words were true, stone true, and to the marrow of
her bones Bobbi knew it. And the truth, the truth
she knew in her heart, enraged her more than any lie

would have. "In a pig's eye!" she shouted, with more force than eloquence, and she charged.

His gaze, still on Shane, jerked around to her. He stood, looming and still—for a moment she thought that her sudden attack had startled him so badly she would reach him. Then she saw his naked upper lip twitch over his glinting teeth, and she knew that, contemptuously, he was waiting for her.

Her hands clawed toward him, darting at his hateful face—and he twitched his hand a little, one finger, and as if she had hit a giant fist of air Bobbi fell back onto the ground.

Her own anger pulled her back to her feet—her fury, rather, and she focused all the force of it on Bissel through her mind, her glare, as she had focused her stare on an unlocked door and on a powwow staff—doorknob and staff had knuckled under, but Bissel seemed not to care. Perhaps only goodhearted things cared. The black-hearted trickster grinned, lifted his finger, and knocked her down again, harder.

And again, and again, each time she struggled up, and she was no longer a fury, but a dogged fighter, punch-drunk, reeling, and a small voice inside her mind, perhaps her own, certainly a Yandro voice, said to her, "Even a mule don't need to be run over by a truck before it takes a think, Bobbi." And Bissel, growing bored and annoyed, knocked her down with the whole force of his sorcerous hand, so hard that Bobbi lay on her back with the breath knocked out of her and her hands clawing at the air in front of her face.

A red glow of his own fury had started around

Samuel Bissel's head. "Begone, girl-child!" he commanded.

Bobbi scarcely heard him, for her entire groggy-minded attention was taken up by the sight of her own hands in front of her. They were bent, and crooked, the hands of an old woman, and against the trickster's dull red nimbus they were the same sooty-dark color as his robes. A trick of the nighttime light, perhaps . . . But no, it was the cloth of her gloves, the fleece and fine calfskin of her cuffs, charcoal black. . . .

Bobbi had seen such moon-curved hands and fur cuffs before. White, she thought hazily, they are supposed to be white. And too beaten to fear the utter strangeness of what was happening, she knew she was seeing herself, the form behind her own form, and it was that of the sorceress. But how had she gone dark?

She had gone—the same shade as the necromancer, just the same.

"Begone!" Bissel roared. "The black rider is mine, youngster!"

"No," she muttered, but a squeezing feeling around her heart kept her from shouting it aloud. She and Bissel, both dark in sorcery? Bissel wanted to possess Shane—just as she, Bobbi, wanted to possess him. Bissel craved something and thought the dark rider could give it to him—just as she wanted something from him. Even the things they wanted were much the same, if she let her mind think truth. . . .

She sat up. It was a struggle even to sit up. She hoped that if she did not stand up, Bissel would not strike her down again until he had heard her words.

And she told the trickster fiercely, "Shane will be

free. The dark rider, by whatever name you call him, will be free. I vow it."

And not far from her side, as if waking from sleep, the sensate staff Kabilde flared into white light.

Bobbi smiled. "Kabilde and I vow it," she amended. And she stretched out her hand for the pow-wow cane, and her gloved hand, the sorceress hand hers and not hers, was white, the fleece and leather of her sleeve white as moonlight. And she stood on her feet again, the hazelwood staff in her grip, and she felt strong again, all her aches gone, her mind clear and fierce.

Still standing in his place, Shane turned his head with an effort and looked at her. She could feel more than see the blue fire in him, smothered, struggling, but still there, like embers under ashes.

"Bobbi," said Shane. He was not the sort of man to say much, but that one word told most of it. And she did not mind that he could not help her. It was her fight.

The necromancer Samuel Bissel stroked his dark death wand with one hand, and it changed into a hammer with a head that glowed red. He raised it.

It was showdown time.

Kabilde's white fire clashed with the death-wand's red glow, and black night pressed down all around, and there would be a combat, a duel, between staff and staff, between the trickster and whatever power she, Bobbi, could call to her aid. No more trifling now from her enemy. No more finger-taps. And in a way Bobbi was terrified, but in another, bone-deep, rock-deep way she was oddly calm. Black-hearted greed's name was Bissel, for the time, and greed was

her enemy. How well she knew it now. . . . This
battle had to be.

"Aaaaaaah!" she yelled, a soldier's yell, and with
staff upraised she charged as her father had once
charged death in Nam.

She had to reach Bissel, had to knock him off the
puissant rock . . . But he flicked his wrist, moving his
hammer a little. Fiery spicules flew, and Bobbi stumbled back, batted away like a mosquito, a fly, the
merest annoyance. Bissel twitched his hammer, tap-
ping at air, and Bobbi felt a blow as if a club had hit
her. Hammer taps now instead of finger taps, she
thought with bitter amusement. I have come up a
notch. Tap, tap. Rocks the size of cannonballs raining
down. Tap. A tree falling on her. She kept her feet,
but she staggered so that she could not set one foot
ahead of the other, she could not move from her
place.

In front of her, facing Bissel, Kabilde loomed up,
huge, white-shining with his own wrath, terrible.
Kabilde would help her—

Then the smith lifted his hammer and struck in
earnest, and Bobbi fell, whacked down like a gnat,
and beside her on the ground Kabilde coiled, writhing in an agony like her own. And everything went
black—she could not see for pain. Or, no, the staff's
white light had—gone out. . . .

"Bobbi." The voice of the serpent came to her,
taut and faint but still dry as smoke, smooth as glass,
through the blackness. "I—can't do—any more. The
sword. Draw the sword."

"Kabilde," she whispered, wanting to say, I am
sorry, wanting to say, Don't hold it against me, what
I did—though she knew by then that the staff had not

held it against her, had not sulked, had helped her for all it was worth—and there was not time to say anything. The whispered word had to say it all.

"I am—spent. I can't fight. Take the sword."

Her hand felt the crystal globe in the night, still warm from combat. She had not reached for it; it seemed to have presented itself to her grip. She pulled out the sword with a long, smoky sound, smooth and dry as Kabilde's voice. The blade, long and narrow and mirror-bright, glinting in the moonlight. She could see it, she could feel the globe in her hand, she felt new strength. Sword lifted skyward, she struggled up from the ground, stood spraddle-legged, like a gunfighter, weaving only a little.

A sound loud as clashing iron rang out in the night. Bissel was laughing at her, shouting with laughter.

Let him laugh, she thought, resting the bright blade of the sword lightly against her left hand, holding the warm grip, warm as a friend's glance, in her right. Let him laugh. It gives me time to catch my breath.

The trickster himself could scarcely breathe for laughing. She could see him dimly by moonlight and the light of the stone. Bissel, a dark form bent over by his own glee, straightening himself with an effort. "You foolish upstart!" he exclaimed when he could speak. "I was with Laertes, wielding the poisoned rapier against Hamlet. I have known swordsmen! I have fought D'Artagnan, Sir Percy Blakeney, Zorro; and you think that you, a mucking farm girl, can come against me with a sword? A pitchfork would make you a worthier weapon!"

"I hacked a copperhead apart with a hoe, once," she retorted grimly, and she attacked him.

She caught him off guard. If it hadn't been that she did, indeed, swing the sword like a hoe, she might have drawn his blood. As it was, the shining sword blade caught the light of the new moon and sent it scudding across his startled face, wide-eyed above his beard; then the hammer head shone just as mirror-bright, then flamed. Bobbi felt the blast lift her and fling her down, and the world was black as old blood.

Through her red-dark pain she heard a frightened voice. "Oh, my," it drawled. "Was that Yankee fire?"

Her mother.

Anger blazed up in Bobbi and sent her staggering to her feet. She hardened the muscles of her face, narrowing her eyes, and then she could see Chantilly standing nearby, her face flower-pale in the moonlight. Her mother, her own beautiful, loony, useless mother, who would probably watch her die and say, "Oh!" Her mother who did not know her, who called her Melly. Her mother who had never—

The hurting, craving something she could not or would not name. That she had wanted, always wanted, long before Shane had walked into her life.

Bobbi still held the long, slender sword in her hand, the shining blade that craved Bissel's blood . . . but Bobbi stood as motionless as Shane, trammeled like the dark rider, caught up in a trap made of her own rage. Her mother in front of her—Bobbi wanted to send the sword darting at Chantilly, but she could not do it. Why? Why not? Bissel standing atop the rock behind her—she no longer cared what he did to her. Why was he her enemy? She remembered; he threatened Shane. And there stood Shane, like a dream under a horseshoe moon, and he had been her friend for a while but even if Bissel did not

take him he would leave her. Go away to wander. He
would never give her—

The something she could not seem to get past. The
hurting, wanted thing Grandpap had taken away.

It all whirled through her, a chaos made of hoop
skirts and stormwinds and gypsy dancers, Witchie
and circling hex-sign cards, Bissel the trickster,
Chantilly-Scarlett, Rhett-Shane-dark rider and Grandpap Grant Yandro, which was her enemy? The thought
of Grandpap burned in her heart. She saw Chantilly
standing stupidly, and Shane, white-faced, struggling
to take even one stumbling step—and with a yell
made half of despair that she could not attack any of
the others, Bobbi turned and lunged at Bissel.

He raised his fiery hammer and struck.

Her own burning anger made Bobbi strong and
savage. She felt the blow, but it did not knock her
down; it merely kept her from getting as close to
Bissel as she wanted, close enough to topple him off
the hilltop rock, close enough to try out her sword on
his body. She feinted with her bright blade, and
Bissel countered with his hammer—she thrust, but
could not reach her enemy; the warlock smith shud-
dered as if something chill had touched him but did
not give way; he struck again. Bobbi felt herself
staggering. Even rage could not hold her up much
longer under such magical battering.

"Bobbi," she heard Shane's labored voice, close at
hand but not close enough, "I can't—help."

"You damn Yankee, let Melly alone!" Chantilly
shrilled. Bobby saw her heaving bosom, her clawing
hands as she came running. Bissel flicked a scornful
glance at her, motioned with his hammer, and Chan-

tilly seemed to run against an invisible wall. Her emerald-shining skirt swirled, she fell and lay still.

Bissel turned, and his eyes seemed to flame like his weapon, and Bobbi knew that with one more blow she would be downed like her mother. There had to be—some way, some help . . .

"Witchie," she whispered. Witchie had made a sort of daughter of her for a while. But it was not enough. There had to be someone who—who loved her more.

Loved her.

All her anger was gone. Hurting and yearning filled her instead. Love. It was the thing she wanted so badly that she could not name it. It was what—her grandfather—had taken away—

"Grandpap!"

Bobbi no longer felt strong enough to stand. She was falling, and she knew she would not get up to face Bissel again. But as she fell she screamed aloud.

"Pap!"

With a vengeful roar and a clap of huge wings, the dragon came down from the distant mountain, out of the black sky, faster than stormwind, out of the maw of the moon.

Bobbi lay on the ground and looked up as it swept over her. It was the dragon with gray hair, the one she had seen once in Shane's eyes, once on an old woman's fortune-telling cards. Immense, with a hard, lean face and leathery wings it flew. Samuel Bissel threw up both his hands when he saw it, not in attack but in hopeless defense. There was a fiery blossom, like a huge, single full-blooming rose, whether from Bissel or the dragon Bobbi could not tell, but it seemed to fill the night sky, fill the world. The dragon's swooping charge never faltered. Nothing could stop it. Bissel gave a throaty cry and threw himself out of its way, off the rock.

And then Shane was springing forward, the dark rider, grace and strength his once again, leaping like a cat as the dragon wheeled past, and Shane had hold of Bissel by the wrist, trying to wrestle the hammer out of his grasp. The smith was strong; he fought back. Bobbi struggled to get up—not to help Shane, not really. It looked as if he didn't need help any longer. She badly wanted to give Bissel a black eye or two for her own satisfaction. But she felt as if she had been beaten up by experts. Too weak and sick to move.

Then she saw her mother get up off the ground. "Damn Yankee!" Chantilly screamed, and she hefted a sizable stone and conked Bissel with it.

Standing behind Chantilly in the tricky moonlight Bobbi thought she saw Witchie. She blinked, gave up, closed her eyes and let it all go away into blackness.

Chapter Nineteen

Bobbi awoke a few minutes later to find Witchie leaning over her. At some time the old woman had found her way back to a supply of cornstarch; in the moonlight Bobbi could see it shining whitely from the accordion folds of her neck. Her pointed hat shone whitely, also, and her long hair, loosened from its braids, and her white robes, and her silver belt; all shone in the moonlight. She was the sorceress. I thought I was the sorceress, Bobbi thought hazily, but she suspected it didn't matter.

"You're in your work clothes," she mumbled to Witchie.

"And got here with my backside dragging. Too late to do any good." Witchie was just replacing a blister-pack of smelling salts in the capacious depths of a

251

huge white purse. "But you managed wonderful without me," the old woman added.

Bobbi eyed the purse suspiciously, wondering if it
was capable of producing whatever was requested of
it, a magical handbag, like Witchie's attic, or like the
staff—

Kabilde.

"Kabilde," she whispered.

"It's all right." Witchie seemed to mean what she
said, but Bobbi scowled up at her in protest.

"It—it's not all right. I think I—hurt Kabilde, and
then the hammer—"

"I said it's all right," Witchie interrupted, peevish
as ever, though a gentler tone underlay the words.
"Kabilde will be fine. Just needs rest, is all." Witchie
picked up the staff from where it lay propped across
her purse and held it upright, softly stroking its silver
ferrule, its globelike handle.

"Kabilde's one to spend himself when it comes to
the death wand," Witchie added.

Bobbi wanted to say something more to Witchie
and to Kabilde. Something like, Thanks. But Witchie
would have grumbled at her, and there were people
standing near, crowding all around, one of them kneel-
ing and holding Bobbi's head on her lap between
warm hands, people—

Bobbi stared, and blinked, and shifted her glance,
and stared again. No forms behind the forms this
time. These apparitions were as real as Shane. And
she couldn't look at any of them without her heart's
turning to water or freezing into ice. Holding Bobbi's
head in her arms, looking down with soft eyes, the
madonna. The poet, reaching out to her. The golden
hero—Bobbi gazed at him with a twist of her heart

and an odd feeling that she had seen him before. The king, standing on the rock with Bissel's hammer in his hand—she couldn't look long at him. The priest, at the king's right side. Lady Death, at his left. She couldn't look long at them, either.

The old gods had come to the Hub.

Witchie hunkered down by Bobbi's side and ran her gnarled old hands down Bobbi's belly and legs and arms. Feeling for injuries, Bobbi thought hazily at first, but it was more as if Witchie had straightened her, smoothed her as she would a rumpled bedspread. Then she placed one hollow palm on Bobbi's forehead. With an intent look in her hazel-yellow eyes she muttered a few words Bobbi could not understand—in German, perhaps. Then she said, "There."

Then she grumped, "Land's sakes, girl, get up! The Twelve have gathered."

Bobbi struggled and sat up, feeling with a thrill the touch of the madonna's gentle hands helping her. She hurt all over, every bone aching from the combat with Bissel, but she felt strong enough now to stand. "Is—was—was Pap here?" she asked Witchie or the night. "I—hollered for him."

The poet reached down and gave Bobbi his hand, helping her to her feet. Once up, she could see the dragon crouching behind the king, and she was glad the strange, pale-faced man who had helped her up had not taken his hand away from hers too soon. She wobbled with a shock that was not fear. The dragon was—Pap. Yet it was not Pap.

From behind her she heard Witchie say, "You are virgin and innocent and hero, Bobbi. And a touch of villain, like everyone. And you have it in you to be

madonna and sorceress and poet. Nearly all of the
Twelve are in you. Some of us are in everyone. And
you are in us."

Bobbi stared at the dragon and began to understand. Pap was in it. But it was more than Pap.

Witchie stumped to her side and said, "It's your
mother's madness in you that makes you see us so
clearly. And your father's poetry. And it's the inborn
gift that lets you wield the staff."

She heard Witchie without really listening, for at a
small distance from her stood Shane, beautiful in
darkness, with his black hat in his hand and the wild
forelock of his black hair shadowing his blue eyes. He
stood back from her, gazing at her but keeping that
distance, like a wary wild stallion. "Bobbi?" he said
in his low-voiced, quiet way, asking if she was all
right.

It was not going to be easy to set Shane free.

Her mind labored and ached like her body and her
heart, trying to sort out shadows from truth. Where
was there a home for her, really? The dragon was Pap
and yet not Pap, and the poet her father, yet not her
father, and the madonna was her mother, but her
real mother stood nearby in bare feet and a muddy
dress, green polyester silk shining in the moonlight,
and her mother had—had plundered Shane's soul
from its hiding place, and she, Bobbi, had made
Shane a promise. . . .

Light flooded the pasture, and not from moon or
magic, though Bobbi thought at first it might be from
magic. There seemed to be many huge stars sending
out singular beams. It took her a moment to recog-
nize flashlights, and to blink and squint into the

darkness behind them, seeing the silhouetted forms of police.

"Crap," she muttered, standing still and looking at the cops with eyes prickling with tears, too tired and hurting to run away from them, almost wanting to go with them—but she couldn't go home, not yet, maybe not ever, since she had laid her touch on Shane. . . .

Gnarled old hands grabbed her—Witchie's. An eyeblink later Bobbi was twenty feet up in the air, tangled in the boughs of a—tree?

There had been no tree on the hilltop before. But there it stood, solid as the mountains, drinking deep at the breast of earth, as if it had been there for many lifetimes of a muck-slinging farmer; there it stood with Bobbi sprawled uncomfortably in its clutches while the officers of the law walked beneath her. Large, oval leaves shielded her from their view. She knew those leaves, though it was maybe a bit too early in the season for them to be so far unfurled, and certainly the tree was too large and sturdy for a—witch Hazel. . . .

She clutched at Witchie's branches, her mind in a swirling, kaleidoscopic confusion. Looking down as she was on a man who had been a mustang and a dragon who was the old man of the mountain, it should not have surprised Bobbi that Witchie could change shape, but it did. She would have yelped out loud if it were not for the burly cops directly below.

"That's her!" she heard one of the police officers say, and for a moment she cringed. "That's the one run off from the asylum," the man amplified. "The one in the long dress."

"You see the girl?" another officer asked.

"Nah. The girl ain't here."

"Could she've run off when she seen us?"

"We would've seed her. She's probably with the old woman somewheres. The old woman ain't here either." To Chantilly the cop said, "Come on, ma'am." He reached out a burly hand to take her in.

Chantilly snatched her arm away from his grip and drew back her hand as if to slap. "Cuff her," the man said to his partner.

"Wait a minute," the other replied, and his voice turned courtly as he spoke to the madwoman. "Little lady, you come with us, please."

Chantilly blinked, then adjusted the world to suit her. "Why, Ashley!" she crooned. "I declare, you do look so handsome in your uniform!" She laid her slender fingers in the crook of the softspoken cop's elbow. His partner offered her his arm on the other side, and the two of them escorted her downhill toward where the car with a star on the door waited.

White petals drifted down from her hair as she walked. On the stone-tipped mound, the dark rider stood and watched her go. And from her hiding place Bobbi also watched.

The remaining officers looked around at the people on the hilltop. "All youse," one of the cops said heavily at last, "are trespassing. Youse clear out of here, now, or we'll have youse for vagrancy."

Bobbi could not believe it. Couldn't they see the dragon holding Bissel between its clawed hands? Couldn't they see the mystic symbols glowing on the rock? The rich robes and glinting crown of the king? Couldn't they see by Shane's blue-blazing eyes that he was not just a man? But come to think of it, they had not seen a hazel tree appear in front of all their flashlight beams where no tree had been before.

They had not expected to see anything but countryside and runaways and vagrants, and that was what
they saw.

The men of the law stood watching for a while as
the immortal members of the Hidden Circle moved
down the hillside to the pasture bottom. Vagrants
shuffling away into the night, that was what the cops
saw. They would return to the hilltop as soon as the
police went away, and both "trespassers" and cops
knew it. After a few minutes the cops turned and left,
conversing sardonically between themselves. As their
flashlight beams dwindled down the hill, Witchie
pulled in her leaves and limbs, pulling herself back
into form of an old woman again, shrinking down to
her normal stumpy size, and Bobbi found herself
standing on the ground again, and the gnarled, crooked
old hands released their grip on her.

"You been eating too much, girl," Witchie grum
bled. "You weigh like a hod of bricks."

Bobbi didn't answer, for Shane was walking toward
her.

Shane, coming up the hillside to stand before her,
and the mist was rising from the pasture grass, smoke
white in the moonlight, half hiding him, and she felt
as if she were seeing him in a swirling crystal and
could see only him. She looked into his shadowed
eyes, and they were his soul's haunted dwelling. The
madwoman had gone away, Scarlett O'Hara had gone
away without even looking back, but the dark rider
stood in as much danger as before. Being human
made him vulnerable not only to Chantilly Lou Yandro.
He was vulnerable to her daughter. He was vulnerable to love.

He met her eyes without speaking, awaiting his doom.

And even then, knowing what she knew, she wanted to lift her hand and touch his wild, black hair; she wanted to smooth the forelock above his blue eyes. He thrilled her. She wanted to tame him, to possess him, to hold his soul, fluttering like a fledgling bird, in her soft-fingered grasp.

She said to him, "You were right. I would be as bad as the others. I thought it was your love I wanted from you. It is love I want, and you would give it to me. But somehow, even just thinking about you, it all turns—dark."

He said, "It's not you, Bobbi. You offered goodness, and you meant it. It's me, something about me. I'm poison."

"No," she said simply, "you're power."

"You've got power of your own, Bobbi."

"So did Bissel."

He quirked one shadowy corner of his mouth, acknowledging. "You've got honor," he said.

The integrity her grandfather, Grant Yandro, had taught her. She nodded and said, "I have to set you free."

He said, a small tremor in his voice, "It's not easy. You've got hold of me by the heart. Standing here, looking at you, I keep thinking you might be the one who has strength not to betray me, you might—you might really be the one to deal straight with me."

Her heart fluttered like a dove, but somehow her voice held steady as she said, "That's exactly what I'm trying to do."

And gazing at him she felt her heart calm, then swell with an aching happiness. Somehow it had

happened; somehow it had all come clear for him.
The straight lines of his face showed sweet, still and
clean; the trembling shadow was gone from near his
mouth. The doomed look had left his eyes. He stepped
back from her, and he was Shane again, the dangerous stranger, the wandering man in black.

"I thank you," he said to her. His gaze was alert, as
if always expecting trouble; yet, when he turned to
her, intent on her alone.

"For what?" she whispered. For in that moment
she had forgotten all that had just happened, and it
seemed to her that she had done nothing for him,
and never could do anything. Wanting him to be
with her was like wanting to keep the wind in a
birdcage. He was not hers to hold.

"For getting me out of that stall. Out of that pre-
dicament and a couple others." Shane almost smiled.
The slight crinkling at the corners of his eyes, she
guessed, might pass as a smile in his case. "Who
would have thought these little hills could be so risky
to horses."

She saw something stir his calm face, and she said,
"You'll miss running on the rangelands."

"Yes . . ." He turned his intense blue gaze away
from her, and for a moment she thought it misted
like a river valley in the night. But then she saw that
he was appraising this new pasturage like a stallion,
watching for the predators, waiting for sunrise. "But
there are other lands to range," he said.

With an easy sweep of his arm he put on his hat,
then touched the brim with his fingers, preparing to
leave her. She wanted to cry out and keep him a
while longer, but instead she stood with her head up,
watching him. "I thank you," Shane said again. It was

not an easy thing for him to say, or one he was accustomed to saying, and she knew it.

She nodded, and he turned and was gone in the night within a heartbeat.

And for the first time she grew aware that the madonna and the poet and Witchie and all the Twelve stood not far away, watching as well, as if what was happening was of importance to them. And as she blinked—water in her eyes; I must be tired, she thought vaguely, it must be very late—the king turned in a swirl of shining robes and stepped upon the rock. "Young sorceress," he said.

It was not a summons Bobbi could ignore. She moved her weary feet and went and stood before him, though she could not make her blinking, smarting eyes withstand the sight of his face. The others had gathered around; she could feel their presence at her back.

"Magic is a shining blade of double edge, power and peril in one," the king said to her, "and you wield it well."

She remembered the choice of the sword as her father had written it: Take up the sword, and venture into beauty and danger. Or sheathe it, and take a chance on mortal happiness. Within a heartbeat, without hesitation, she said, "I sheathe the blade."

"Bobbi!" exclaimed a throaty old voice. Witchie sounded aghast. Bobbi turned to her and impulsively took hold of both her clawlike hands.

"Aunt Witchie, all I want is to go home. Really." Tears tingled in her eyes; she knew them for tears now.

"Huh," said Witchie more calmly. "Well, of course you do. Just come see me when you're ready, Bobbi

Lee Hepzibah Snort Yandro. Don't you know I've made you my heir?" Witchie embraced her, arms reaching not much higher than Bobbi's waist, elbows-out and tough as iron. It was like being hugged by a cookstove.

Over Witchie's shoulder Bobbi asked the king, "Can I go home?"

"Of course." His voice was neither kind nor unkind, merely stark. His authority was based not on power, but only on this: that he spoke truth. "You are very tired, youngster. Lie down and go to sleep while we tend to our prisoner. You will go home tomorrow."

Bobbi lay down at once, where she was, amid grass and wildflowers, with her head on a cushion of heart-shaped violet leaves. From somewhere coverings appeared; the madonna came and loaned her cloak, the poet laid his tabard on her feet, the king gave his mantle. Wrapped in the things so that they cushioned her from the damp ground and warmed her, Bobbi curled up and went to sleep.

Chapter Twenty

When Bobbi awoke, the sky was brightening with
sunrise. Against the wild-rose sky the Hub, the mystic hill, swelled round and empty. Bobbi sat up and
saw Witchie sitting nearby like an old snapping turtle
resting amid the phlox and plantain, in her soft and
faded housedress again, with Kabilde in her hands.
There was no one else in sight.

Witchie straightened, swiveled her thick body as
much as her short neck and nodded at Bobbi. "Feel
better?" she asked.

Bobbi did, indeed, feel much better, but in a
nearly indescribable way, as if she had undergone an
epiphany. The earth felt very solid under her resting
hands. Looking at earth and sky, she saw them clearly,
in every detail, with no mists in her mind to obscure

them. Looking at Witchie, she saw the blunt, earthy goodness in her, as if seeing the bedrock of her soul.

"Did you pow-wow me?" she asked Witchie.

"You know I did. But that was for your body. The king put his hand on you, for your heart. You're highly honored, girl."

Bobbi nodded, understanding why everything seemed different. "I feel—connected, somehow," she said to the old woman. "I feel like—like I know what is real."

The swirling, circling chaos in her mind, gone. She knew Witchie, knew the pow-wow woman to her heart, but the form behind the form no longer blurred her sight. She carried the knowledge of it inside her. And Shane—she remembered Shane clearly and with bittersweet pleasure but no pain, as if it had been years since she had seen him. And she carried the knowledge in her heart of all that he was.

Witchie told her, "When you said you sheathed the blade, you know you got to abide by that till the Twelve says otherwise. You got to come before the king before you can use your powers again."

"Ask me if I care," Bobbi shot back, her eyes sparkling. Joy seemed to be creeping into her from the hill beneath her hands.

"Wiseacre," Witchie grumbled. She creaked up and beckoned Bobbi to get up also. "Come on. We're invited to breakfast over at Eve's."

Getting to her feet, Bobbi knew she had not eaten in entirely too long. She wobbled where she stood. "Eve?" she inquired, lightheaded and a little silly. "What's she having? Apples?"

"Respect, girl! Show some respect! She's a powerful member of the Circle." Witchie stumped over,

scooped up Bobbi's bedding, then led off at her customary scuttle across the pasture. Bobbi followed
more slowly, swaying dangerously with each step.

"How far?" she called.

Witchie pointed. It was a white farmhouse, not far.
"Lots of us live right around here," Witchie said.
"Your mother populates this whole countryside with
her dreams."

"Oh." Bobbi followed as best she could, and came
to the kitchen door only a little bit behind Witchie.

Eve turned out to be the madonna Bobbi remembered from the night before. She met them at the
door, and Bobbi knew her even though she wore a
sweat suit and jogging shoes, even though her hair
was permed and her face different from the Pieta face
Bobbi had seen under the moonlight. Bobbi knew
her from the tender weariness of her eyes, the rondure of her belly, the curve of her arms, as if she had
carried many babies and embraced many children.
This woman was Adam's bride and Mother Mary,
Ellen O'Hara and Penelope and a hundred more.
Bobbi saw no form behind the form, but knew the
Madonna in her heart.

She made herself be sober, and showed no disre-
spect when Eve served apple fritters and toast with
apple butter for breakfast.

An hour later Witchie led her out to the barn,
where the Kaiser lurked like a behemoth in its den.
"You got it back!" Bobbi exclaimed.

"Sakes, girl, how'd you think I got here? I don't
fly." Witchie laid Kabilde on the back seat of the
Kaiser carefully, as if on a cot. "Cops had it," she
added gruffly, "and I had to wear them down before I
could have it back and go my ways, or I would have

been back to you sooner. But you might have done better on your own."

"Huh," said Bobbi.

"I think you did," said another voice, a voice within Bobbi's head. Within the shadowy belly of the barn, a white form drifted.

"Hello!" Suddenly Bobbi realized she would have felt sorry not to see her father's ghost again. She was glad that sheathing the bright blade of magic had not taken him away from her. But she did not want to talk to him in front of Witchie without explaining herself. "Aunt Witchie, my father's here. Can you see him?"

"Course I see him," she grumbled. "I'm the one who woke him up and wished him on you in the first place."

Bobbi stared. "I thought you said you didn't know my father!" she shouted.

"I didn't. I just roused this here ghost. It's not the same." Lifting her three chins, Witchie settled herself and her massive purse in the front seat of the Kaiser. Then, "I didn't know he'd make such a meddler," she added with a touch of contrition.

"I didn't meddle at all last night," the spirit protested.

"That's true," said Bobbi. Except perhaps for telling her to use her brain, she thought, and she had badly needed that bit of help.

"I wasn't used to having a daughter," said Wright Yandro in a softened tone. "I never had a chance to know you till Mrs. Fenstermacher turned me loose, Bobbi. Then it seemed like everything I did made you mad."

"It wasn't you, so much," Bobbi said quietly. "It was just—I had to find some things out."

"I'd forgot what it was like, being young. Now I know I got to let you grow, can we start over?"

"As—friends? You know the past, when you were alive, that's—past."

"Yes. Friends and kinsmen."

Father and little girl were gone forever. But it would be nice to have a Yandro at her side. Bobbi swallowed, smiled and nodded. "I'd like that," she said. "I'm going back to Pap," she added.

"I know. See you sometime soon, then." Wright Yandro faded as he spoke.

"See you," Bobbi murmured.

She took her place on the passenger's side of the Kaiser, and Witchie prodded the starter with her toe.

It was maybe a three-hour drive back to Canadawa Mountain, or four, the way the Kaiser bumbled along. All that had happened, all the long and hidden way Bobbi had come, and she would be home in a few hours.

Hills and valleys, hills and valleys, the huge old car dwarfed by them, sailing them like a tiny boat, up a crest and down into a trough and up again. Witchie took the old Lincoln highway instead of the turnpike, making the way leisurely, and Bobbi didn't mind. She and the old woman talked a little. The walking stick did not speak; resting, it had gone into a sort of trance. Witchie and Bobbi stopped for lunch at a diner; meat loaf special, small jukeboxes sitting with the catsup on each table, homemade apple pie. Before midafternoon Bobbi stood at the bottom of her Grandpap's gravel lane, saying goodbye to Witchie.

"I made you my daughter when I gave you that

name, you know that," Witchie said to her out of the Kaiser's window, keeping her throaty old voice tough. "So you come see me."

"I will," said Bobbi. "Only—Aunt Witchie, how do I get to Seldom? Where is it? I've never seen it on the map." She remembered the tram line, but the mountain trails that had taken her there were a tangle to her.

"My golly days, girl!" exclaimed Witchie. "You mean you ain't figured out that yet? Seldom is wherever you are."

Bobbi gawked at her.

"There's seldom been such a nuisance of a youngster as you," Witchie declared with equal affection and annoyance, "and seldom one with as much gift and grit, and seldom a young woman with as much sense and heart. Seldom is where you live. You'll be the next hex witch of Seldom some day."

"Aunt Witchie," Bobbi burst out, "I don't care about all that! How am I going to find my way back to you, is what I want to know!"

"The same way the dark rider did. You just think about me when you're ready, and I'll feel you coming. You'll see." Witchie harrumphed, trying to keep her voice under control. "You be good till then," she said sternly, and her sharp, yellow-eyed glance slid away.

"Wait," Bobbi said. She bent and kissed the old woman on her soft cheek, and Witchie's knobby hand came up a moment to squeeze hers, but Witchie would not look at her. "Goodbye," Bobbi said. "Goodbye, Kabilde," she added to the staff on the back seat, though she knew it could not hear her.

She waved goodbye as the Kaiser rolled away,

stood watching until the old woman was out of sight. Then she stood a moment longer, drawing breath. The leaves were coming out on the locusts and hickories. The place felt and looked strange in the way of a familiar place after an absence. Strange, though it had not changed, because Bobbi had changed.

In new clothes that looked old before their time, Bobbi started walking up the lane.

Just out of sight of the road, someone was standing and waiting for her. Someone young, slim, blond.

She stopped when she caught sight of him. Travis came up to her quietly and did not try to grin. All his nervousness seemed to be gone, and Bobbi stared at him, surprised because he was there, surprised because she knew she had seen him before in an utterly different place and in a form not quite his own. Travis, but not entirely Travis. He had been at the Hub, too.

"I'm glad you're back," he said to her.

He was not at all surprised to see her. He had been waiting in the lane as if he expected her. "How did you know I was coming?" she demanded.

"I didn't until late last night. I was real worried." His eyes, oak-brown and serious, never looked away from hers. "I felt like it was my fault, somehow, for letting you go—"

"Bull," Bobbi interrupted.

"I guess." Travis smiled slightly, a shy smile that lighted up his thin face. Someday, when he was not so thin, he would be handsome. "But I was worried anyway. A few days ago I run off myself to go find you."

Bobbi's lips parted, but she felt so astounded she couldn't speak. There was something standing in front

of her that she hadn't seen . . . not only the form
behind the form, but something more, and it had
been there for the seeing all the time.

"I went down to the tracks and hopped a train,"
Travis said, "and I hung around the hobo camps and
the freight yards—"

Bobbi got her voice back. "You out of your head?"
she demanded. Hopping trains was dangerous. Men
got beaten up, killed, on the freights and in the
freightyards. People whispered that things happened
to boys in the boxcars, things worse than killing.

Travis said, "It was the only thing I could think
of."

"Are you all right!"

"Fine. I was scared a few times, but I'm fine.
Anyway, I heard some talk. About a bad dude going
after a girl and getting killed by a black horse. And
about the gypsies hiding a girl and an old woman
from the police. I was just about to go off and try to
find the gypsies, when this—man came. And he sent
me home."

A hush in Travis's voice made Bobbi look hard at
him. "What man?" she asked.

"Just a, like, a vagrant. But not a bum, exactly. He
didn't walk like a bum, and he had this black leather
jacket that must have been good once, and black
jeans, and they fitted him slick. He came and found
me before daybreak, woke me up. And when he
looked at me . . ." Travis's voice trailed away, and for
the first time his eyes turned away from Bobbi's eyes.
They looked over her shoulder and far away; they
became distant, unfocused.

"What!" Bobbi demanded.

"I—I don't know. He was different. He had this

THE HEX WITCH OF SELDOM

really strange sort of a scar on his neck, like he had been in a prison camp or something. Anyway, he sort of hit me on the shoulder and told me to go on home." Travis's eyes came back to Bobbi's. "He seemed to know all about me and what was bothering me. Told me you'd be along soon. There was a gypsy in a Cadillac waiting for me, brought me here, and I been watching."

Bobbi walked up the lane. Fir trees stood tall above her. Travis walked beside her, silent.

"The stranger who woke you up," Bobbi said finally. "Black hat."

"Yeah," said Travis. He looked straight ahead and kicked at a stone with his booted foot. "Took me a while," he said, "to think where I seen anything like that scar of his before." He looked over at Bobbi and asked in the same quiet tone, "You in love with him?"

The question didn't startle Bobbi, nor did she mind Travis's asking. It was almost as if he had a right to ask. "Yes," she answered, "sort of," and then she shrugged and gave Travis a smiling glance. "He's too old for me," she said. "About a thousand lifetimes too old."

Silence for a while as they walked. Then Bobbi asked, "You said anything to Pap about all this?"

Travis shook his head. "He'd think I was crazy." He looked over at Bobbi. "He's been about half crazy himself since you been gone. Why'd you go off that way? I mean, I know why, but why?"

"Long story," said Bobbi.

"Tell me sometime?"

"Sure."

"OK." The Yandro place was coming in sight. Travis

stood still and let her go on alone. She walked slowly, trying to think of what she was going to say to her grandfather. "Get a move on," Travis called softly after her. "The old man's up in the orchard, last I knew."

He wasn't. He was in the house, sitting idle in the middle of the afternoon, staring at nothing. But when she opened the door he jumped up, his head thrust toward her.

"Pap," she said, and that was all. Everything else she had thought to say to him vanished from her mind because of what she was seeing: tears coursing down Grant Yandro's weather-toughened cheeks. Three strong strides, and he had her in his wiry arms.

"You crazy young'un," he said when he could speak. "Where the hun you been?"

She could barely speak. "I been OK," she managed.

"I knowed that. Mostly. I was scared—listen, you mulebrained kid." He held her at arm's length so he could look at her, but his big hands stayed tight on her shoulders, as if he was still afraid of losing her. "Don't you ever believe me when I say such a thing. I was scared you wasn't coming bàck."

"I didn't believe you," Bobbi said. "Not really. I was just mad."

"Huh," he said. "God help me." Then he did something he had never done since she could remember. He kissed her, awkwardly, on the side of her head. "Too damn Yandro," he muttered, and he let go of her.

"That black horse," Bobbi said. "He's gone."

"You think I care? Having you back is the only thing I care about."

He had nearly said it, nearly said what she had always wanted to hear from him—

"I love you," Grandpap told her. "I know I don't show it the way I should, so I guess I'd better say it once."

"You didn't need to," Bobbi told him, and she was telling the truth.

"After them mean things I said, felt like I better set the record straight."

"You didn't need to, though. I knew, once I thought about it. Came to me last night."

Grandpap said slowly, "I dreamed about you last night. Scared me. You was in some sort of trouble. I wanted so bad to help you. But when I woke up I didn't know where you was. It about drove me nuts."

"I'm back now," said Bobbi.

Epilogue

The old woman sat in the ladder-backed, cane-seated parlor rocker, admiring the room. She had just found runners in her attic, and she had put them down to protect her carpet. Between them and the braided rugs, the carpet itself hardly showed. It would last almost forever, like the seldom-used Kaiser, now back in its snug garage. The old witch at the wood's edge had also placed slightly-used candles on the coffee table in pink ceramic holders shaped like flowers. The pink of the holders matched the faded pink of the swagged lampshades. The parlor looked nice, she decided, and she would have to invite Ethel over to admire it. She was glad to have the hay, the oats, the water buckets and the horse out of there.

"It's good he's back," she remarked to Kabilde.

The staff stirred slightly in its urn but did not answer.

"The dark rider, I mean," Witchie went on. "Riding the rails, now. This worn-out world needs him. He will catch some people by their hearts. The stranger, walking into their jaded lives. Widening their eyes. Making them remember the old words: pride, courage, honor. When he goes, they will say to each other, Who was he? Where did he come from? How did he get the scar on his neck? And they will make legends about him. But it is not the scar they will mostly remember."

Witchie paused, and the walking stick said rather coldly, "What, then?"

"His eyes," Witchie said. "No one can ever forget his eyes."

The staff said even more coldly, "What of the girl?"

"Bobbi?" Witchie looked hard at Kabilde, then smiled, a gentle smile, for her. "She is all right. When you are feeling better, you will be able to see for yourself."

Kabilde demanded, "How can you say she is all right?"

"It stands to reason. Her grandfather is ready to give her what she needs for the time."

"Is she dreaming of a perfect lover, as her mother does? Is she expecting the man she calls Shane to come back to her?"

Witchie said, "She will have a lover. The dark rider made sure of that. She is all right, I tell you."

"She had better be," the stick said.

"Bobbi would land on her feet in any event," Witchie added. "She is a scrapper, and she is a Yandro. And she will find us if she wants us, old friend."

The staff stood in its holder, silent and dreaming.